flatscreen

flatscreen

a novel

adam wilson

HARPER  PERENNIAL

NEW YORK • LONDON • TORONTO • SYDNEY • NEW DELHI • AUCKLAND

HARPER ● PERENNIAL

HarperCollins books may be purchased for educational, business, or
sales promotional use. For information please write: Special Markets
Department, HarperCollins Publishers, 10 East 53rd Street, New
York, NY 10022.

FIRST EDITION

Designed by Michael P. Correy

Library of Congress Cataloging-in-Publication Data is available upon
request.

ISBN 978-0-06-209033-1

12 13 14 15 16   OV/RRD   10 9 8 7 6 5 4 3

for my brother

An object at rest tends to stay at rest
unless acted upon by an unbalanced force.

—*Sir Isaac Newton*

Hold steady.

—*The Hold Steady*

Part I

one

But maybe Mom's not the place to start, though she's where I began (in her I took shape, grew limbs, prepared to breathe oxygen, albeit with a slight asthmatic wheeze that has not been helped by cigarettes), and where all this coming-of-age stuff inevitably buds then barely blooms, like the pale azaleas Mrs. Todd put on her porch every spring but never watered, letting the rain try to raise them up, make them stand and receive sunlight, just as the constant dull glow of the television tried with me, equally failed.

No, this is not about Mom, Dad, or anything Freud said—books I haven't read, though I've seen *Siggy's Sexy Secrets* (Cinemax, 2005), get the general gist. It's about a house, should begin there, just as it will end there, not before guns, drugs, strippers, and other tenets of contemporary suburban life enter the mix like Kool-Aid, leaving the water blood-red, sickly sweet.

If it is about Mom, I don't want to know. We've all sucked a nipple or two, trolled MILFSandtheirILKS.com, seen a late-forties peroxide blonde bent over at Whole Foods, imagined licking between her legs, then being sucked in like a vacuum, condensed, resting in her expanded torso, suspended in fluid like floating gizzards in a jar of chicken fat.

I'm getting off track.

Mom got the house in the divorce but it belonged to Dad. His hands had placed the I beams; his sweat had dripped into the foundation, manifested itself in the basement's musty stink. Dad was there in the contours: tall-man toilets, sleek jut of post-deco faucets, abundant closet space. Still, we stayed for four years post-divorce. Then Benjy left for college. She and I: separate solitudes, separate floors.

I also finished high school. Instead of college, sank deep into my basement abyss. Watched TV for months, barely attentive, broadening my knowledge of subjects I'd missed in school: politics and current events (MSNBC), contemporary culture (E!), home economics (Food Network), geography (Travel), the secret life of fauna (Discovery), the last days of Eva Braun (History), Beavis and Butthead as cultural barometers for the Clinton years (MTV2), Jon Stewart skewering the world with Sunday crossword witticisms (Comedy Central), Humphrey Bogart's slow-cool-sad-but-fuck-me eyes that I wanted to steal, to wear through the streets beneath my thickening, Dad-inherited black brows (AMC). I kept the lights off, rarely went upstairs.

The physical isolation was too much for Mom, who understood that cramped-ness equals intimacy. She put the house on the market.

No offers. It's a McLovely McMansion Jr., well structured, formally fine-tuned. But it's also a ranch-style split-level (hence the Jr.), doesn't give the appearance of affluence homeowners in the neighborhood wish to radiate. School district is the nation's finest, location prime, but the price was too high for most, not show-offy enough for those who could afford it.

When the Kahns showed up, I wasn't expecting much. Actually, I wasn't expecting anything, because Mom hadn't told me they were coming. We weren't communicating. She was mostly couch-anchored, sipping chardonnay, knitting an endless scarf, sobbing gumdrop tears into her pink fleece Slanket. I wasn't capable of dealing with her pain, of being the man who makes everything okay. I wanted to be that man—to hold her defeated body while we shared in the promise of televised sunrise—but I didn't know how to approach her. Everything scared the shit out of me.

So: I was surprised to be interrupted from sleep by a man in a wheelchair pushed by a brunette in a V-neck blouse—the V weighed down by a pair of large sunglasses to reveal a freckled valley of cleavage.

I said, "What the fuck?" as the lights went on, and Mom said, "This is Eli's room," without mentioning the fact that I, Eli, was lying pantsless in said room, drooling.

First reaction was to cover my erection. The brunette smiled. Mom rolled her eyes. Mr. Kahn didn't seem to notice.

"Erin, my love, I think this space will suit your erotic needs charmingly," he said.

"Dad," Erin said. "Please . . . we're in . . . besides . . . maybe we should come back when . . . um . . . maybe when . . . Eli, is it? . . . has had a chance to . . . wake up a bit."

Kahn eyeballed the room: dusty collection of kid soccer trophies, old prom pic.

"Should we see the rest of the basement?" Mom said.

"Yes," Mr. Kahn said. "It's as if you've read my mind."

Benjy was in the kitchen, effortfully ensembled in ironed jeans and starch-stiff white tee, tucked. Hair had been trimmed, slicked. Each time I saw him he looked distinctly older, like Dad's absence had sped the aging process. Ate standing up, checked his watch like he was late for something, which he wasn't.

"Shouldn't you be at college?" I said.

"High Holidays. You forget?"

"Didn't know you came for round two."

"Yom Kip's the important one. Day of Atonement."

"When is that, tomorrow?"

He looked me over. Open bathrobe revealed a defeated-by-gravity stomach. Hair was a bird's nest. I was a wounded, well-fed bird.

"You got a suit?" he said.

"I don't know, dude. Who are those people downstairs?"

Benjy took a bite from his sandwich, looked at his watch again, plucked a nose hair—unmirrored—with impressive accuracy.

"Don't think you'll fit into your old suit."

"Downstairs," I said. "People? Wheelchair guy? Brunette?"

"They're the Kahns. Buying the house. Good wheelchair access because there's only two floors and the garage opens into the basement."

"Serious?"

"Yes, I am. Daughter's quite attractive."

"Quite," I said in a tone that accused him of douchebaggery. "Any coffee?"

Benjy nodded at the empty maker.

"It's three in the afternoon."

"Who tucks a tee shirt?" I said, went out to my smoking chair.

A rusted deck chair next to a soda bottle filled with ciggie butts. Lit up, looked at the trees, imagined they didn't lead to the Mitchells' landscaped lawn, but to a deep forest filled with soul-singing, silicone-enhanced Amazon women.

Screen door opened. Mr. Kahn wheeled himself out.

"Nice boner in there."

Dark eyes, almost black. Waves of lightly salted ginger hair hung feral from his head like the abused dome-bristles on an expensive, over-loved doll. Slim-cut burgundy suit; gold-stitched lapels accented by matching, pointed pocket square. Bow tie dramatically untied. The man was anywhere between forty and eighty. A squint accompanied his smile. Face was familiar.

"Thanks," I said.

Kahn didn't look at me. Instead scanned the backyard, not with a prospective buyer's assessing gaze but with a ferocious stare, as if, not bound by the wheelchair, he might dive onto our lawn, attack weeds with his dirty fingernails.

"It's good to be young," he said. "Isn't it?"

"I guess."

"Time is a harsh mistress. Not as harsh as my actual mistress. She's a real nut job. My first wife was the craziest, but that's neither here nor there."

"Oh."

"I noticed a distinct odor in your bedroom. *Cannabis sativa*, if I'm not mistaken. Sweet leaf. Panama Red. Mexican dirt. Rub it on me belly like guava jelly. I don't have connections like I used to. Think you could help an old man score?"

"Probably."

"I can offer you money and goods. I get a world of prescriptions these days. There's nothing they won't give an ex–movie star in a wheelchair."

"You were a movie star?"

"TV. It's the new film. Or the old Internet. The small

screen keeps getting bigger. Soon they'll be downloading my dick into outer space."

Pictured Day-Glo laptops floating through atmosphere, forming cock-shaped constellations.

"What does that even mean?" I said.

"It means posterity is bullshit, and pussy is gold. It means nighttime is the right time. You get my drift? It means the world turns, my friend, no matter if your blood runs red or blue. But I see that you're a philosopher. That's a good place to start. You remind me of someone, an old friend."

It's a thing women say when they don't want to fuck you—notification upon entering the friend zone. This was different. Kahn made eye contact. Face on pause, unsure whether to balloon into giggly animation or fall frownward: the look of remembering something funny about someone dead.

I'd seen it on my mother on a number of occasions, when she'd caught me red-handed in petty insubordination—stealing wine or loose dollars—and remembered her brother Ned, the way his guilty pink cheeks were a splash of expressionist sunlight.

The look passed. Kahn opened his hands, palms up, as if awaiting an offering, or checking for rain, or else hinting that I too must outstretch, place my paws on his. He'd had his share of lotions and treatments, that much was clear, but the papery remains of wheelchair calluses still speckled his hand skin, and new blisters were already forming on the tips of his fingers and lower halves of his palms.

"I'm a philosopher?" I said.

"A seeker of truth. Like scholars and nymphomaniacs."

Considered myself neither, with the potential to be both.

"You really want to buy this place?"

"I want to live forever, but I'll settle for suburbia."

"Meaning death don't have no mercy?"

"Meaning tits are built for milking."

In the kitchen, my brother had Erin's rapt attention. We could see them through the screen door. Her face was chubbily attractive: dimpled, blushing. Northeast sensitive skin, light makeup. Eyes: hazel. Build: athletic. Strong shoulders. Standard-issue outfit: black blouse, blue jeans, brown giddyup boots.

Benjy tucked a fugitive flyaway behind her ear, said, "Applying to law school."

"She's a sucker for men who are the opposite of me," Kahn said. "In that I taught her well."

"My brother's no prize. Trust me."

"Who said anything about prizes? What I'm talking about is pain, and the ability to avoid it. She has an ear for the silence of easy money. Got that from her mother. Guys like you and me prefer bang-bang, shoot a can."

"You and me?"

"I recognize my own kind. Don't deny it. You've never worked a day in your life and don't plan to. It's a noble pursuit, but it's also supremely selfish. We're carried by our daughters and brothers, wives, mothers, lovers. We're pathetic wards. We're anchors and they're beautiful ships stuck in dock until we unhook ourselves. I'm trying but it's hard. I cling to those highs and lows, those legs wrapped in fishnet hose. Those legs just walk on past. I'm dragging behind, holding on for dear life. I can see from the look in your eyes that you too are a failure in that regard."

"I'm a failure in many regards."

Kahn removed a business card. "Call me when you can help me out."

"Will do," I said.

He turned his chair, wheeled back toward the kitchen. Erin opened the screen, lifted him inside. Her biceps bulged from a lifetime of lifting. The card said: *Seymour J. Kahn: actor, cripple*. Cell and e-mail listed below.

two

Establishing Shot:

V.O.:

> *My mother was born for the grainy light of classic American cinema. With her tennis whites and platinum highlights she might look beautiful in that forgiving light, the testaments of age, white wine, and heartbreak erased by the camera's flattering eye. But this is the high-def era. Every blemish is mercilessly illuminated.*

Cut to: Through the window she's graceful in the kitchen, flickering like lightning in the streetlamp shadows. Zoom in and we see that her motions are jagged, her fingers shake. Face is creased, cavernous. Natural gray of her hair shows in the roots.

three

Bird's-eye view: Congregation Beth Shalom might appear to be part of the Pine Hill Mall, which is sometimes referred to as the Mall at Pine Hill. If the mall is Quinosset's Mighty Mississippi, then Beth Shalom is a tributary akin to the Yazoo River (*Fire on the Yazoo!*, Left Hat Pictures, 1987).

Large building with a larger parking lot. High Holidays: front lot like a rap video removed of black people. Mercedes, Lexus, Beamers. This is where we used to park until Dad left. Then we drove a Camry, and they stuck us out back.

Jennifer Estes waved us in. Her orange mesh vest was the kind crossing guards and trash-spear parolees wear—a servitude marker, sun-bright. Visible from fifty yards: her bounce and hip shimmy, wind-borne hair.

Jeremy Shaw used to be the parking attendant. A Head-First kid—from an alternative school within my high school—a good guy. His dad was janitor at the synagogue. They lived in the Beth Shalom basement. We weren't friends but shared nods and thin joints by the old bomb shelter, not saying much, passing it back and forth.

Last year Jeremy hung himself in his bedroom while Henry Villeva and Jamal Green played *Grand Theft Auto III* in the living room. I heard Alison Ghee—his ultra-skinny, no-less-sexy-for-it girlfriend—had cheated on him. People said she gave him herpes. I never believed it. Thought he was just a sad guy living in a basement. Once dreamed I was sitting shotgun in his pickup doing 120 on the Zakim Bridge when Jeremy turned, drove us over the rail. A peaceful moment. We spun like a failing propeller. Watched the bridge lights recede. Sank to the pavement, fell on the sleeping city as if it were a mattress, as if death itself were a soft mattress.

Jennifer smiled at me. Couldn't tell if it was the type of smile that said, "Do me!" or "Time for a new suit. You've had that one since you were fifteen, and you've put on a few pounds."

Gave a half-wave that I thought looked cool, disaffected. As we walked past, my mother tried to fix my tie.

We had the good seats, up front, won from Dad in the divorce. If there was a single person making peace with God as the Schwartz family strutted up the aisle, she was doing so while mentally commenting on the fact that my pants only came down to my shins. Not that we were special. Whole show was a social affair. Women showed off new outfits, men showed off new wives.

Like Dad. Pam wore a leather miniskirt, applied lip gloss, added a seven to her Sudoku panel. The twins passed a pack of Lifesavers. I patted Dad on the shoulder. He looked up, nodded, offered a handshake, but I was already halfway up the aisle. His hand dangled, retracted.

Walk to our seats took fifteen minutes. Mom had to stop-and-chat with six groups of people. I flanked her dutifully. Avoided eye contact with my former classmates. They went to liberal arts schools in Maine or Connecticut, majored in IR, econ, etc., returned to proud parents, maple-glazed brisket, younger girls—QHS seniors—sweating in halogen classroom deserts, waiting for Prince Cohen to arrive via Amtrak.

Older siblings were I-bankers, traders, account managers, other things I only understood in theory. No clue what they did, but the result was money, piles of it, stored in steel vaults, spent on tools of entertainment pricier than the super high-def 120-inch plasmas now on sale for a low, low price at Robot World in the Pine Hill Mall.

Not that I hated them so much as hated myself for not being one of them. I was a glorified townie without the glory. No rugged good looks or blue-collar gas-station-employee pride. No fading memory of a football career. No greaser girlfriend, legs thick and strong like the twin pistons on my (nonexistent) restored Camaro.

The girls here—slender, over-eyelined, snuggly shawled in black cashmere—went to BU, Northeastern, prepped for careers in PR, HR, other initials. Mean-sexy with salon-styled hair, slipping shoulder straps. Eyes peeled, panning for potential husbands. Gave me a look that said, "Yes, we cum-guzzle weekends and some Wednesday nights, post–*Sex and the City*, bewitched by Samantha's skanky spirit. But never for fat boys in ill-fitting suits still living with Mom, hardly shaken by un-stoned 'I'm a fuckup' revelations, no job, no portfolio, no property, no chance for a seven-figure bonus come Christmastime." Daughters looked just like their mothers.

Knew I didn't look like Dad, but wondered if people thought I looked like Mom. Mascara had already smudged. Women whispered as she moved past. Felt the urge to stand in front of her like Secret Service, block the eye-bullets with my blubbery bod. Maybe if I held her arm and corrected my posture she would see that we were in this together: this town, these stale, life-lorn lives. But she would have shoved me off. I was her shame in my too-short pants. Fair enough. This was her world, not mine. She tried to follow its rules, she failed; my existence underscored her failure.

Picked up my prayer book, thumbed the pages, braided the fringes of my tallis. No one paid attention. Maybe some oldies whose faith had come and gone, but now, with the end drawing near, it was God or zilch. The cantor's voice trickled with vibrato, rose up to the high ceiling where it was contained in the building (no musical bird soaring to heaven), accepted reverb from the stained glass, bounced down into our ears and his. A hundred syncopated pacemakers kicked garage backbeat while Cantor Branson hymned.

There was beauty in the music itself, ethereal organ in perfect counterpoint to Branson's earthy tenor. You could get lost in it, space out, stare at the stained glass, or retreat into your own head, where the sounds drowned out the other sounds, annoying and imagined, like my brother gleefully whispering, "Tough shit. I go to college where co-eds swill keg beer, while you stay with Mom in this purgatory of postadolescent angst."

Left for the bathroom before the start of the sermon, because you're not allowed to move once the sermon starts. If I timed things right, I'd be locked out, wouldn't have to sit through Rabbi Zarkoff's talk. Zarkoff stood on his tiptoes when the pitch of his voice rose, camp-lisping like an alum of the Richard Simmons Rabbinical School: "Joseph was a special boy with a special coat."

Strangely, the "yes-on-eight, yes on the word *feygele*" contingent had no complaints about Zarkoff, who was a private bachelor, Harvard-educated, acceptably conservative in regards to Israel. I liked him too: his unself-conscious style; his interest in the Old Testament's moral ambiguities; his way of smuggling queer theory into Talmudic analysis, same way Mom mixed ground turkey in the burger meat— our best interests at heart. But I was restless, wanted to get high.

On my way out, I found Seymour Kahn sitting by the exit, staring at a high-school-aged blonde a few aisles over. Erin sat next to Kahn. Next to her was a pretty black girl of about thirteen. I tapped Kahn on the shoulder, flashed the universal "Smoke a joint?" hand gesture.

Pushed Kahn past the back lot into the edge of the woods. Small clearing I'd been going to for years. When I was in high school, I thought getting high at temple made it more spiritual. Then realized it didn't.

Lit the joint, passed it.

"Take a few."

Kahn closed his eyes, inhaled. I leaned on his wheel-chair, delicately, to see if it would support my weight. Chair began to roll. Grabbed the handles, reeled him in. Took all my strength. Thought I might have pulled a muscle.

"Trying to kill me?"

"Sorry."

Kahn coughed, spit in the dirt, grinned. Smile showed yellow-tipped teeth, a menacing overbite.

"You need to get laid. Your pores leak sexual frustration. I can smell it on you."

"What does it smell like?"

"I'll tell you what it doesn't smell like."

"Roses?"

"You laugh. But when I was your age, I fucked every-thing that moved. It wasn't a good weekend if I didn't wake up with puss dripping out of my dick. It's the whole problem these days: AIDS, Christians, Islam, condoms, well-made vibrators. No one fucks anymore. Maybe the French, but fuck the French."

"What's wrong with the French?"

"The French are good for two things: filming and fucking. Godard knew how to rouse a cock. So did Brigitte Bardot. But they eat too much duck. It makes them soft. The duck is a weak animal."

Kahn was the only person I'd met other than Uncle Ned who'd even heard of Godard or Bardot. QHS wasn't known for cultivating high culture. More emphasis was placed on standardized test prep and Web 2.0 acumen. The post-lib-arts era: all tech training and multiple choice. They fed us game-show-style shots of noncontextual knowledge, taught us to tick the right boxes with our number-two pencils. No passionate and unhinged English teacher with a soft spot for slacker budding intellectuals (*Dead Poets Society*, Touchstone, 1989). It's true there were theater kids who called their hats *chapeaux*, duck-walked the halls reading aloud from the Romance poets, but they had nothing to do with me. We called them Shakespeares. Pure AP, with big egos and their own set of thrift-store-clad wood-nymph-wannabe women. Just another clique among the envied cliques. My own friends—John Sammel, Matt Lappin, Sammel's older bro—were unaffiliated free agents, not a true clique. We were bound by pot-smoking prowess and the delusion that listening to loud music could replace regular sex as an outlet for hormonal energy. No shared sensibility among the group, no deep sense of outcast brotherhood. Our lack of female friends created an undercurrent of unspoken animosity; we each blamed the others for this glaring, unforgivable oversight.

I'd personally come across the cinema classics at the side of Uncle Ned's sick bed, watching rom-coms from the forties filled with witty repartee, and coiffed and healthy heroes like Cary Grant, whose sturdy screen presence nearly negated the foreboding sense of death in Ned's apartment. Later found the A/V room at the Quinosset Library, where I mourned my uncle's death by suffering through the rapturous cinema of postwar Eastern Europe. There was comfort in the corners, under A/V room dark. Each lone cinephile partitioned off by cubicle walls. Take off headphones and you could hear halogen buzz, A/C hum, nothing more. Always slightly too chilly for tee shirts, slightly hairraising. Something electric in the quasi-silence, and the way we all stared. This was pre-Netflix, pre-Hulu, pre-pirateddownloading, pre-Mom-bought-premium-cable. Back then my isolated screen viewing involved the silent companionship of other library loners, mostly Asian twentysomethings consumed by the eros of anime. Now I watched alone on laptop, desktop, flatscreen. I communed with the world from the comfort of my couch, denying real time, like an anthropologist attempting to study a distant, extinct species, wondering what went wrong.

Kahn knew what went wrong.

"No one fucks, no one fucks, no one fucks. Can it be that no one fucks? What, then, pray tell, were the sixties even for?"

"Some people must fuck," I said. By some people, I didn't mean me.

"Your mother looks like she hasn't had a decent dick in her since they killed Kennedy."

Was it true? No boyfriends. Had she tried JDate? Speed dating? Struck out? Sadness too embedded to be hidden behind mascara? Hoped I was wrong, that there were Craigslist encounters or married tennis doubles partners entering via the porch for late-night hookups. She deserved a man with silver hair-wings, silver pockets, a summer house. Someone she could go jogging with, hold beneath the covers, be reassured by when she asks, "Am I the mother I . . ."

"You can get more of this?" Kahn asked.

"Usually it's even better."

He nodded. "Good boy."

"I can probably hook you up tomorrow."

"And we'll see about finding you a slot for your man part."

"Man part?"

"Your schwartz, Schwartz."

"You have a vested interest?"

"Don't flatter yourself."

But I was flattered.

People were already coming out. Dad fondled his tie, yukked it up with his poker buds, ran a thumb through his comb-over. They saw me pushing Kahn.

"He even helps the handicapped in his spare time," Dad said.

Kahn gave them the finger.

"I was worried sick," Erin said.

Kahn ignored her, addressed the black girl.

"And how's my Nubian princess this morning?"

The black girl gave Kahn the finger.

"Like father, like daughter," Kahn said.

"This is my sister Natasha," Erin said.

Natasha waved. Benjy was giving Erin that puppy-dog bullshit I'm-in-love face.

"Let's trade," I said to Erin. "I'll give you Benjy for these two."

Erin laughed. She liked my brother's candied whisper and ironed collars, I could tell.

Walking to the car, thought I might come back later, burn the building to ashes, blaze of fall glory, flame and amber leaves in high relief against the Quinosset dark. Burnt down to the hallowed ground like the First Temple.

But no murder in my heart, or political outrage. My imagined arson was purely aesthetic, ecstatic. More like that movie with the freeze-frame ending, actor entombed in midair, in fist-pump approval of his own bravura before the credits roll, movie ends, crowd goes home, real-life copycat gets seven to ten upstate, so much for romance.

four

Facts About My Father:

- From November 1975 until March 1976, Dad disappeared. Not literally—he claims no alien abduction or celestial sabbatical—but not figuratively, either, in the took-too-much-acid-spent-a-year-licking-childhood-toys-in-a-closet sense. Nor did he go to Vietnam, disappear emotionally upon his return. According to my uncle Sal, he went somewhere—another state, country, or maybe just down the street—no one knew where. Not so weird in and of itself. The seventies, etc. What's strange is it wasn't one of those "When he came back he was a totally different person" things. My research (uncle, grandma) shows he was exactly the same as he was before. He never mentioned it.

- Played baseball in college. He was good. Not good enough for TV, but good enough to regret his decision not to sweat out a few seasons in Single A (Peoria, Beloit, South Bend, some beautifully named mid-American dust-burg), exalt in the occasional starlit base-trot, bleacher-drunks screaming, "Hail! Savior! Sultan of mosquito nights, bring back my boyhood!"

five

On the drive home Mom asked if we were fasting. We said no. She said she was fasting to make us feel guilty for not saying we were fasting. When we got back to the house we ate leftover Chinese food.

After lunch, Benjy wanted to go for a walk, to give me brotherly advice and have me reassure him I wasn't fucking up. He'd been doing this a few times a year since Dad left. He was the adult now: condescendingly arrogant, clean-shaven. Moved through the world like a marathon runner, deliberate and mid-speed. He paced himself. Kept one eye on those who fell behind. And perhaps deep down I wanted him over my shoulder, observing my blunders with frater-nal felicity, figuring himself the safety net I so desperately needed. But less deep down I thought he was an asshole.

Street was quiet. No fighting neighbors, crying babies. Suburbs in autumn: eerily serene. Houses tried in all their pallid glory to convey immortality with high windows, four-car garages, but the overall effect was sterility. No yards on these new houses. All the green was gone. Square footage val-ued over outdoor acreage.

Walked through the Orchard, a gated community/golf course at the end of our block. Last time I'd been was for Quinosset High's Annual (Unofficial) Senior Scavenger Hunt, where (among other things) underage girls gave BJs to the underage judges while the rest of the twelfth grade watched and videotaped for posterity. I was no Ron Jeremy, but I was there, by the sixteenth hole, as Nina Janovy licked her own nipple in the late May predawn.

Didn't mention the scavenger hunt as we walked through the empty course. Too obvious a memory, an implied discussion that was, therefore, moot. At the twelfth hole, Benjy faked a golf swing, which was actually an imitation of the way our father faked golf swings, which we thought made him look like an asshole.

Past the course, through rows of condos where we'd been to parties when parents were in Bermuda and girls with open houses behaved decadently—learned from summer teen blockbusters—allowing semi-strangers to trash their homes, jump in their pools fully clothed, lick the flesh of pierced, pulpy earlobes in upstairs maid's quarters, or toggle at belt buckles atop white felt pool tables.

Benjy said, "So."

"So?"

"I talked to Dad today. He's . . ."

"An asshole?"

"He's your father."

Benjy hesitated. Knew we sounded like an after-school special, still couldn't deviate from the script.

"He's worried about you."

I wanted us to laugh. Two brothers on a crisp fall day, walking through a golf course, one confronting the other about bad choices, the dead-end course his life has taken.

But it wasn't funny because it was true, it was about me, and Benjy was serious.

"*You're* worried about me."

"I am, " he said and tried to put a hand on my shoulder.

I was walking too fast. His hand grazed my upper back like he was brushing lint from my coat.

"I'm fine."

"What are you . . ."

"I'm fine."

Before, we'd been allies. He was the good son; I was the bad son. Recent confrontations broke an unwritten code that said: "Never speak of the fact that one is the good son and one the bad son."

"You know you have to get a job?"

"Why?"

"What do you mean, why? Don't you want to get out of the house, get some money, get your own place?"

"I have money. Dad subsidizes my lifestyle."

At least he had been. Last two checks had mysteriously never arrived. Was trying not to think about it.

"Isn't that embarrassing, Eli?"

"Whatever."

"I don't mean to be a dick."

"Whatever," I said again. The cry of my generation, or maybe the one previous to mine. Meant what you wanted it to mean but also the opposite.

Almost home.

"What's with you and Erin Kahn?"

"I don't know," Benjy said, and I knew he liked her because he didn't mention her tits.

six

Re: Dad's Baseball Regret:

- Seen him watch the game on TV in August, one of those never-ending West Coast slugfests that lasts until the a.m. hours. Color commentators—jet-lagged, feeling the freedom provided by waning late-night viewership—make half-veiled innuendos to the scantily skirted, naturally flirty anchorwoman checking in for the late-night traffic report.

- He's still awake. Watches even though the game's boring, because for him each at-bat is a unique, intricate equation. Remembers his own equations, physical equations solved by the fit/faithful body that's no longer his.

- When he watched these games, I sat tuned to his sad-Dad frequency.

- Wanted to say, "It's okay, those dumb jocks don't understand the universe."

- Wanted to say, "Why is life bullshit?"

- Wanted to say, "Father, have you ever licked butt cheeks in moonlight or sucked fat clit while Otis Redding comes crinkled with static over the radio in your 1968 Ford sedan?"

- Wanted to say, "Tell me how to feel the way you once felt."

seven

Googled Kahn. Benjy in his room. Mom on the treadmill, working off guilt, Chinese food. Dad outside city limits staring at a 58-inch plasma, loving wife nestled to his chest while the twins played pinball in the east wing. Where was Kahn? He was, for me at that moment, suspended in the immortal ether of cyberspace, twenty years younger, winking at the world through a series of black-and-white headshots.

Kahn's IMDB was like the back of a baseball card of a player at the end of a long, middling career. Stats indecipherable and unremarkable in all manners other than quantity. He'd been a regular cast member on seven different shows, none of which I'd heard of. Made one- to five-episode guest appearances on forty-seven other programs. Sixteen made-for-TV movies, four after-school specials, and a Skinemax flick from the early eighties. One legit film, *Wood and Nail*, critically acclaimed at Cannes for its portrayal of an artiste carpenter's descent into madness.

Bio appeared to have been written by Kahn himself. Section marked trivia read:

- Seymour Kahn has made a career doing crappy shows viewed by idiots.

- The self-proclaimed "King of the Crossover," Kahn holds the record for appearances on the most shows while playing the same character: the brash yet lovable Albert Stamn, who first appeared as a police captain on the short-lived NBC series *Guns and Tarts*.

- In the seventies, Kahn slept with many of Hollywood's leading ladies, and a few of its leading men.

- His first wife, actress Sheila Glent-Kahn, left him shortly after adopting their second child, Natasha, in a desperate attempt to save their marriage.

- Unfortunately, the marriage was unsalvageable, because it turned out Glent-Kahn was a lesbian.

- Kahn did not believe this was an irreconcilable difference. After all, he was part gay himself.

- These days Kahn relies on Viagra to maintain erections.

One reader comment, headed "Is this real?!?" No responses, possibly because no one knew, more likely because no one ever looked up Kahn.

IMDB aside, the web was filled with info on Kahn. Google gave me gold: a *WoMAN MaGAzine* piece about Sheila Glent-Kahn's relationship with costume designer

Mary Aldridge, a *Variety* interview with Kahn from '87, an entire page dedicated to *Wood and Nail* (which had earned a cult following among craftsmen), a series of profiles and interviews with both Kahn and Glent-Kahn ranging from late seventies to present day.

Spent the afternoon reading about Kahn, not sure why. But I soaked it in, felt ensconced by the details of his life as if they were my own, as if it were my story, humble beginnings, child of immigrants, celebrity—American dream and nightmare because it all gets tangled in broken car parts, legs that don't work anymore, wives that don't love anymore, children who couldn't give a shit. Felt like crying at the screen and its whiteness, a background that loomed large beneath the tiny letters that were the words of Kahn's life. Couldn't cry. Tear ducts stuck, dry.

Mom walked in, picked dirty clothes off my floor, put them in a laundry basket.

"Where are all your socks?"

A question so abstract I wasn't sure what it meant. Seemed important, though, like a man without socks could never get by, not in New England with winter coming strong.

"What's happening to me?" I said.

"You like clean clothes, don't you?"

Took a shower with the lights off. Didn't want to see my out-of-shape body, or anything at all. Imagined Jennifer Estes in nothing but orange mesh, whispering in Spanish, cradling me beneath the flowing stream of water.

eight

Jenny(s) from the Block:

- My fascination with Latina women runs deep, but is uncomplicated. To summarize: a succession of busty, bootied nannies rocked me gently, tamed my tangled mane of curls, let me eat all the beans I wanted, flatulence be damned.

- Maria, Mom's former helper, brought me pickled cactus from the homeland, starched my rumpled shirts into submission.

- Seventh through eleventh grade, rocks or not, heart hemorrhaged fountains for Jenny from the block. She stayed taped to the inside of my locker until the Affleck fiasco of '02, when I saw her for the masochistic traitor who allowed the star of *Pearl Harbor* free reign over her divinely molded etc.

- Latin culture—or what little I know about it

(thank you Mr. Gill and the USA-all-the-way public school curriculum)—seems like a nice one for
obvious psychological reasons. Family, food, and
girth are celebrated; TV soaps spin narrative quilts
for daytime junkies; plus: warm weather, good
dancing, pig meat. Qualities worth fighting for,
hence all those revolutions.

- I needed something worth fighting for.

nine

Jennifer's Facebook was without posture. Like she'd answered the questions rapidly, no consideration of real-world consequence. She liked eighties movies, still mourned Bradley Nowell. Occupation: EMT. Relationship Status: Single.

Mom reappeared, racket in hand.

"I'm going to the club if you want me to drop you at Whole Foods. Benjy said he'd pick you up in an hour."

I was twenty, didn't have a license. Benjy had been old for his grade. When he turned sixteen Dad had bought him a Range Rover to make up for marital misconduct. Car was yellow, colossal, called the Short Bus by the clever kids. For a while Benjy was popular, until Sam Arnold got his mom's old minivan, let people ha

ve sex in it for ten bucks.

When I turned sixteen Dad had run out of guilt or money, because I got nosebleed Celtics tickets, no car. Not that I minded. Happy to be chauffeured. Downside was when Benjy went to college, I was left with the infantilizing prospect of being driven around by Mom. Fortunately, she was up to the task. Maybe it was her way of staying connected; inches from each other with arms crossing as we reached for the heater knobs or the radio; chance for a unifying song, something Jewy, familiar, Billy Joel, Neil Diamond; shared memory of an idiotic relative dancing drunkenly at a cousin's bar mitzvah.

Her car was a white Camry. She'd bought a Mercedes SUV after the divorce, but sold it later to pay medical bills when her brother got prostate cancer. Now Ned was dead and I bet she wished she'd kept the car, as the money she'd spent on health care didn't help in the end, and the medical costs had sealed her fate as a social pariah among the wallet-conscious women of Quinosset.

Turned on the radio; Mom turned it off.

"Gives me a headache."

Skirt hiked up. Blue veins, thick as guitar strings. Closed my eyes. Mom called Grandma in Florida, wished her a happy holiday. I was put on the line.

"Hi, Grandma."

"You never call," she said. "Your brother calls."

Mom forked over her Amex, dropped me on the corner. She didn't want to deal with the parking lot even though it was half-empty. Most people were home preparing to break their fasts. Lox and bagels laid across tables, champagne uncorked, cashmere adorned. But Dad's family was going to Pam's sister's place. Benjy and I weren't invited. Fine with me. I liked grocery shopping. I was an excellent chef, a lover of the culinary arts. Had spent hundreds of hours in the thrall of the Food Network watching Giada's pot of puttanesca bubble seductively with anchovy guts; Rachael Ray babble on in kiddie-speak, slobbering over her own mute creations, erotically licking egg-E.-colied chocolate from a wooden spoon; iron chefs, dressed as kings in their bleached cotton kitchen wears; modern cowboys—tanned, mustache-trimmed, cured of Marlboros—stirring five-alarm 80-percent-lean all-meat chili beneath Texas skies.

My palate was unparalleled. Could catch a hint of freshly cut Brie from three houses away, smell the pizza boy before he'd turned onto our street. Knew the tannins in my tea by name, gagged at an extra teaspoon of cinnamon, understood the subtle benefits of star anise.

Started in the veggie aisle, testing the ripeness of avocados, comparing California-grown peppers to Mexican ones, debating pros and cons of fresh lettuce vs. prewashed. Whole Foods was also stomping ground for the idle wives, empty nesters—mothers of my former classmates. As I held a bunch of fresh basil to my nose, thinking, Naples, gardens, stone courtyards, one of these women tapped my shoulder.

"Eli Schwartz. Look at you."

Burgundy velour tracksuit, baby-blue trim. Quinosset colors. Top zipped down to reveal a peeling swath of cleavage. Big fake smile, the kind Mom couldn't manage.

"Well, don't you look just like your handsome father?"

"Hi, Mrs. Sacks," I said. "How are you?"

Knew how she was. Last summer she'd been caught hum-jobbing Eddie Barash, local kosher caterer. Everyone felt bad for her husband Mark until their daughter Sherri explained that her mom's transgression was a perfectly understandable reaction. Apparently Mark had an "addiction to prostitutes" and "needed help." He'd spent the summer at sex addicts camp in Palm Springs, having sex with other sex addicts. Sherri had shipped off to a camp friend's place in Westchester, leaving Mrs. Sacks alone to ponder her fractured fam, play hide the Hungarian pastrami with Eddie.

"I'm fine. Just picking up some extras for the breakfast. We just got back from the island. Sher is in town, does she know you're home?"

"No. I haven't spoken to Sherri in a while."

Not a lie. Hadn't spoken to her since eighth grade when she'd told Emily Dollinger I had only one ball. (I have two.) Childhood friends, nothing more, though I clung to the fringes of her social circle. Once she threw a party and I stole her dad's baseball card collection because he didn't appreciate it. Cards weren't even in plastic cases.

"Sher is at GW. She loves it. Loves it."

"Loves it?"

"L-O-V-E-S. Loves it."

"You sure she doesn't just *like* it?"

"Hahaha. Oh, Eli, you're a joker too, just like your dad."

"My dad?"

"So where are you at school?"

"I'm taking time off. Figuring things out."

Mrs. Sacks eyed my groceries. "You're the cook, or your mother?"

"I like to cook."

"Maybe you'll come make me dinner one day."

"Sure," I said, unsure if she was joking, just conversing, or serious.

"And how's your father? Seriously. You look just like him. Blow him a kiss for me, okay?"

Next stop: ethnic food aisle, where I browsed the Thai marinades, tried to figure out whether wasabi paste was better than the powder kind. As I turned the corner into coffee/tea/condiments, I noticed a familiar face—a middle-aged brunette bent over reading the label on a box of tea. Red thong peeking out of her jeans. She was beautiful.

Before I was caught staring, another woman approached.

"Sheila," she said, softly touching the woman's neck with her fingernails. "I got the Chapstick."

Kahn's ex-wife.

Followed the couple from a distance, watched as they filled their cart with replenishing vitamins, organic vegetables, upscale design mags. Something organic about the two of them too, the way they held hands, held up each item to obtain the other's approval, strolled slowly, didn't avoid eye contact with strangers.

Even pushing the cart, Sheila Glent-Kahn had the posture of an actress, star quality presence. One of those women who didn't wear makeup, didn't need to. Lashes were long and real, and the way her head wove into her neck, which in turn wove into her sunken neckline, made it seem as if her insides weren't made of separate bones and organs, just one center bone, a thin tree trunk sprouting appendages like genetically perfect branches.

Mary was beautiful too, broad, but not overweight. Blond curls bounced like a little girl's and provided her face with a youthful glow you might not expect from a woman whose tailored men's clothing and well-toned triceps implied an all-work, no play, strap-it-on attitude. Both dressed immaculately—Sheila in fake-ripped designer jeans; Mary in a vest, pressed slacks, ruffled button-down. Felt like we were in the country, small town off the coast of Maine; one of the hidden crevices of America where people hide, where they all have stories (according to TV), where everyone knows you, no one knows who you are (*Cheers*, NBC, 1982–1993). As I wound through the aisles behind them, filling my own cart without paying much attention to what went in, I had the urge to go with them, let them nurse me back to health, mother me.

Benjy called. Parked outside. Hurry up. Followed Sheila and Mary to checkout. They went to twelve items or less. Watched from my own lane, hiding behind a food mag as they made small talk with Nikki, my favorite cashier and unknowing object of my romantic observations.

Outside, got in Benjy's car, watched Sheila and Mary get in a Porsche station wagon. Wanted to say, "Follow those lesbos." Didn't because Benjy already thought I was an idiot.

ten

Facts About My Mother:

- Not that she can't cook. Stove-slaved for hours in evenings before Dad returned, quiet set in, sound replaced by smell, tired man too tired to acknowledge the falling sun that lit the sky and illuminated his family as they gathered, rejoined to suck the sweet flesh (chicken) Mom had so diligently prepared.

- He preferred to read the paper. Benjy brought his laptop to the table. I ate with ugly manners. Mom couldn't see me. Tilting stacks of magazines and mail obscured her view.

- When Dad left, the cooking turned to cleaning. Energy was there, but her focus was gone; no attention for recipes or timed flips or fileting the salted, freezer-stiff whole kosher fish she insisted on buying.

- I took over. Been watching her for years. She'd let me hold the knife when it was time to carve the turkey.

- Dad bought an electric knife, though this is not a thing about my mother, or maybe it is.

eleven

Cooked with the screen door open, baseball on the little TV. Season was ending. Air from outside felt like winter. At peace in the kitchen, my Zen space, like others have baths, beds. Made Moroccan chicken in a tagine Uncle Ned had brought back. He'd bought the tagine from a gypsy in Tangiers for five bucks and a box of cigars. People said I was like him because he was a fuckup. Then he died. They stopped saying it.

Meal was a masterpiece: tender chicken in light stew with green and black olives, raisins, chickpeas, garnished with pomegranate seeds; salad with candied walnuts, pear, fresh blackberries; warm pita for dipping. No one ate with me. Benjy was out to dinner with Erin Kahn. Mom drank Slim Fast in front of the tube, watching Jack Bauer save us all, again.

Sat alone in the kitchen, table set for one, trying to eat slowly, savor. Tough without conversation. On the screen, Wakefield floated that knuckleball, dizzied batters. But there was futility in his toss, windup lazier than usual, body understanding the end of a long season. We'd won in '04, and it was supposed to be gravy from here on out, but adam wilson

didn't feel that way. Just a season among seasons, peanut shells to be swept, fresh grass awaiting snow.

Mom was asleep on the couch, toes dangling from under the Slanket, glasses on. The weatherman chuckled, proclaimed rain, wore an ugly tie. I'd seen him once at Whole Foods—Mitch Lieberman—fawned over by eager women, each with a nice Jewish niece who stayed up nights awaiting the slow suffocation of ring on finger.

She snored lightly, like a woman who can't whistle trying to whistle. I removed her glasses, placed them carefully on the coffee table. Long time since I'd touched another body. Hers was cold, curled—a private space. Part of me hoped she'd half-wake at my touch, reach for my hanging hand like a nightmare-ridden newborn seeking sleepy solace. I stroked her hair, pulled the blanket to her shoulder.

In bed, watched an indie flick about some sad sack writer, failed in New York, returning to his childhood home. He had a successful brother who encouraged him to pack it in, join the family business. Scene played out like the one I'd had with Benjy earlier. "I talked to Dad today," the older brother said.

Couldn't sleep. Figured Benjy had one hand on Erin Kahn's stomach, his fingers inching their way under her shirt as he nibbled the skin behind her ear. Got out of bed, went online. Jennifer Estes smiled seductively, like she didn't know we were separated by glass, and she was made purely of pixels.

"Dear Jennifer," I wrote, "I saw you at temple, glowing in neon like a false god. Coffee?"

Erased it just as quickly, navigated to a site where Latina women said naughty things with accents.

42

twelve

Imagined Dialogue:

Jennifer: When I saw you, you looked pure as a newborn with your dangling, post-fashion curls and those big brown eyes. The rain fell like waterfalls, and you bathed. I knew I had to hold your naked-ness against my own.

Eli: Oh, my darling. I saw you too, rain-slickened and shining, sharing your soul with me. Let us undress and intertwine.

Jennifer: I have always wanted to date a man who knows his way around the kitchen. I especially love tender, braised meat in heavy, red-wine-based sauce, falling off the bone. I like lemon meringue pie for dessert.

Eli: Funny, I have just spent the day braising Asian-style beef short ribs, and there's a lemon meringue cooling in my freezer. Here, have a taste.

Jennifer: This is the best food I have ever tasted. I have an uncle who works for the Food Network, and he will give you your own show.

Eli: Will you marry me?

Jennifer: Yes, I will even convert to Judaism so your parents approve of me.

Eli: My brother will be so jealous!

Jennifer: But you are so cool and attractive, and he isn't. It is obvious that your parents love you more than they love him.

Eli: I knew it all along!

Jennifer: I love giving blow jobs!

thirteen

Dan was my dealer, lived around the corner. Convenient because of my driving handicap. Inconvenient because he sold overpriced, skimpy bags.

Dan's dad owned a liquid hand soap manufacturing wholesaler; he'd grown up dirt poor in Roxbury, wartime baby, made his first million by twenty-five, never looked back. Dan's mom was Dan's dad's second wife. She lived in a condo on the north side. Wife Three lived in the house with Dad, though neither seemed particularly interested in Dan or the import/export warehouse he operated out of their basement.

Dan's dad was a sleaze, but he must have been smart or smart enough. Pulled up by his bootstraps, this was his reward: succession of wives, each younger, more silicone-cyborg than the last. He'd grown hefty through the years, gut expanding with bank account. Now, on his throne, Soprano-esque—larger than life, king of the castle, comfortably gluttonous. But maybe, like Tony, he too had secrets and guilt, saw a shrink on the sly, complained of fuck-up son, unreliable tumescence.

He opened the door wearing golf pants, cleats. There were both putting green and practice net in the house.

Wanted to ask why he felt the need for proper attire; surely Wife Three didn't enforce a dress code. But I liked the fact that he allowed himself the fantasy. Not embarrassed to play make-believe. Or he understood it was all make-believe: house, silicone wives, Phil Mickelson impersonation.

A red carpet flowed down the stairs. The chandelier—all sparkles and bling—was blinding. Out front were ten-foot bronze lion statues that matched the trim on the windows.

"Dan's downstairs."

"Okay."

Walked through the foyer into the kitchen, where the maid scrubbed an oven pan and Wife Three sat at the table in black silk robe, reading catalogs.

"Hi," she said.

Didn't know each other's names, but we passed by often. Felt a faint air of conspiracy between us; neither of us knew what the fuck we were doing there. I was almost her age, but she looked so much older, the way she dressed, the perm in her hair that reminded me of Mom's. Wondered if she missed being young, fucking guys her own age—she must have had her pick—staying up late drinking cans of Bud Light, waiting for the light in the room to fall soft.

"Hi," I said, walked down to the basement.

Dan's basement bedroom was different from mine. Five times as big, filled with toys: 60-inch Pioneer PureVision HD plasma, surround sound, walls of DVDs, CDs, stereo equipment, old-school arcade games, pinball, Ping-Pong, air hockey; all that shit.

Dan sat on his bed, shirtless in oversized B-ball shorts, bong ripping, relaxed as always. He wasn't tense like other dealers. Born rich, felt untouchable the same way teenagers think they're immortal because they've yet to feel death's first twitches. I'd only begun to feel the twitches myself. Maybe, because of the newness of these sensations—chronic throat-tickle, morning chest-tightness, unmitigated afternoon headaches, occasional numbness in left big toe, rib pressure after walking more than a block, smoker's black mucus, hairy ears, penile post-ejaculation pain, shoulder soreness, bony-butt-despite-chubby-gut-so-sitting-for-long-periods-sucks syndrome, etc.—they felt entirely overwhelming. They say you start dying on the day you're born, but I think it's later than that. I think it happens when all the other kids are at college and the toxins in the air have nowhere to replicate but your body.

Dan was watching *Dazed and Confused*. I sat on the recliner, let the film evoke false nostalgia for a high school experience I hadn't had but pretended to remember having. Dan passed me the bong.

"This is new," I said. "Indoor?"

"Yeah. Captain Crunch. You taste that hint of black-berry?"

Dan was a marijuana connoisseur, like a wine taster, holding the smoke in his mouth, moving it through his teeth to extract the subtle flavorings, finally exhaling through his nose like a cartoon rhino.

"Not bad," I said.

"How much you interested in?"

"Quarter."

Dan tossed me a Ziploc.

"Word."

Handed over two fifties, the remains of my Daddy Guilt Fund stash. I was like the housewives—living off alimony, cooking alone in stainless steel solitude. Not for long. This was my last hundred, though I was planning to sell half to Kahn, earn a little profit. Beyond that, hadn't considered.

"Saw Jennifer Estes at temple."

"She's not Jewish."

"She parks the cars."

"Fuckin' A. That's what I love about these high school girls: I get older, they stay the same age."

He was quoting from the movie we were presently watching.

"She's only a year younger than me."

"Hot?"

"Yeah."

"True."

Dan had no interest in girls—strange for a dealer. Always thought they dealt so they could hook up with stoner chicks.

"Why do you sell weed?"

"Beats working."

"Can't you just get money from your dad? That's what I do."

"There's no dignity there. What I do is important, man. I perform a service. I contribute to society. I'm great for the economy—all I do is spend money."

Walking out I could hear Dan's dad in the golf room, "Mickelson on the tee . . ." Wanted to walk in, politely clap; myself, a willing spectator of imagined reality, binoculars in hand, watching that drive fly.

As I was going up the stairs, someone else was coming down. At first I thought it was Wife Three, but this girl had face-obscuring, slanted bangs, pale/pimpled skin, and a slim frame drowned in wannabe-black-man bagginess. She pushed the hair from her eyes. Alison Ghee. Jeremy Shaw's girlfriend, the one whose infidelity had supposedly led to his suicide. Another of Dan's customers. Must have been legions of us: numb-seekers, still in town.

Alison walked slowly, like it was hard to stay balanced with a body that weighed so little. Thought she hadn't even noticed me, but after I stepped aside so we wouldn't collide, she turned her neck, looked back, pointed her eyes right into mine, smiled, closed-mouthed. Imagined our lives moved in perpendicular lines as we wandered Quinosset, passing just once on these carpeted stairs. By the time I realized I should smile back, she'd made it to the bottom, disappeared into Dan's room.

Top of the stairs: looked out the window at the backyard pool. Black tarp over it was covered in leaves. Easy to spread my arms, fall through the tarp, drop to concrete. Eight feet isn't enough, though.

Wife Three was on the phone.

"I'm sick of it," she said. "It's like I'm married to Tiger fucking Woods."

fourteen

American Dream:

- Seen all my fantasies enacted in movies, brought to their inevitable conclusions, upended by credits.

- Never seen a movie about a fuckup kid becoming a star chef, loved, in love, reuniting his divorced parents. That movie doesn't exist because it's a stupid idea for a movie.

- If it did exist, it would be cheesy, romantic, mostly bullshit with a few good jokes and close-ups of food.

- Or an indie, end all boo-hoo tragic, hero corrupted by wealth and fame, alienating those who supported him, ultimately returned to loneliness.

- Maybe my problem is foresight.

- Then there's the dream where Jennifer is a mer-maid. I'm an eel, the sea our home. Her life-buoy breasts float un-clammed, as yet unclaimed.

- Real dream is everyone's dream, just as unlikely: intact fam, all mushy, love-struck, looking at pho-tos, recalling old warmth, birthing new warmth, fresh bread from the kitchen odorizing everything with promise.

fifteen

Alison Ghee was waiting for me, leaned up against the black gates that separated the Dan Clan from Quinosset's manicured claws. She puffed a cigarette undramatically: deep, quick inhales, incessant ashing. What I mean is she didn't look cool: no knock-kneed sexy feigned innocence, or lips-of-lust cigarette-as-phallus ring-blowing. I looked less cool than Alison. I was wearing sweatpants.

"How'd you beat me out here? Didn't you just go inside?"

"I'm everywhere. I'm a ghost."

"Oh."

"You've been standing there spacing out for like fifteen minutes."

"I have?"

"Let's go," she said.

Walked up Faber Street, then left on Wilson toward the north side. Houses were older, less ugly, equally expensive. Halloween decorations already up: hanging rubber skeletons strung from second-story verandas, crudely carved pumpkins staring through windows like judging shut-ins.

"Where are we going?"

Said it because I was stoned, wanted to make sure I wasn't dreaming. Not because I cared where we were going.

"Not that I care. I just go with the flow . . . that kinda guy. Just a flow-goer. That's me. Eli."

Sensed I was about to start talking stupidly, so I shut up.

A few minutes later, Alison said, "You're funny."

Tried to make a funny face.

"Now you just look retarded."

We arrived.

Door in the ground led directly to the basement. Knew about these doors, the girls who used them. They were the sassy lovers who didn't love me. Snuck out at night, walked alone in lamplight, cut through yards, arrived at entrances, let themselves in, let themselves be entered. Most people called these girls sluts.

Maybe the problem was basements. Me, Dan, Alison, Jeremy, cut off from sunlight, subterranean suffocating. Damp floors when it rains. Ugly boom boom of a broken clothes-dryer. We were humans, not worms. Needed clean air, over-heard birdcalls, windows.

"I live in a basement too," I said. "We're bottom-dwellers, I guess. Maybe that's why we're such losers."

"We're losers?"

"Buried alive."

"Speak for yourself. And who said I live here, anyway?"

"Do you live here?"

"Yeah."

No pics of Jeremy, no shrines. I'd expected a mausoleum: framed diary entries, cut-up yearbook photos collaged on card-board, obituaries, rosary-strung crosses. Wanted the room to feel like mourning, to wear its sadness on its paint-chipped walls.

Clothes on the floor and on the bed. Computer, empty beers, couple old paperbacks. Open guitar case next to the bed.

"You play?"

"It's Jeremy's."

Could picture it: Jeremy: ignored troubadour, gentle songsmith. Quinosset bard unheard beneath the din of SUV engines, MP3s, electric toothbrushes; sensitive Jeremy complete with archived, estate-approved suicide recordings. We could listen, cry, put them on Myspace, make a posthumous documentary, hold candlelight acoustic vigils.

"He couldn't play it. But he wanted to. I think. He bought it."

Something I would do.

"I'm teaching myself," Alison said, picked up the guitar, strummed a chord, a riff, feigned smashing it, put it back in the case, took off her boots, her pants, her striped cotton panties.

Her skin was thin like rice noodle. Didn't know stuff like this happened in real life. She covered her breasts with her arms, said, "I'm shy," called up a playlist.

"Girls who take their pants off aren't usually shy."

Sounded suave. Something I'd say in my head, not out loud.

"Have sex with me?" she said, as if I needed convincing. "It'll feel good."

Music was right, thus wrong. An anthem of our adolescence, slow-building, violin-accompanied, electro-accented. Singer's mumble swelled into full-voice falsetto. It was the song from a movie about lost teenagers doing drugs in basements, fucking (*Starfucked*, Panther Socks Entertainment, 2000). From the scene in which the downward-spiraling heroine, after shooting heroin, asks a creepy random to violate her, to help her escape the pain of grief.

Alison faced the wall on her knees. I was expected to make an entrance. Needn't be a grand entrance. Licked her shoulders, kissed her back. Alison moaned, or fake-moaned, or maybe just coughed. Remembered the herpes rumor. Held her hips, moved in for a closer look. It was dark, and I didn't have much to compare this with.

"Are you sniffing my butt?"

"Isn't that why they call it doggy-style?" I said, though I didn't feel like being funny anymore.

Thinking about Jeremy: blue face, rotting corpse, wood of his coffin eaten by termites, small shards of wood falling into his eye sockets. Wanted something to remind me of life. Wanted to hold Alison's face against my own, bodies musical, melding, warm breath on my neck, soft kisses against my stubbly chin. Something that wouldn't be sad.

Also, didn't want herpes. Or to spend the next month worrying about possibly having herpes.

"I was just wondering, um . . . I know it's a weird thing to ask . . . but . . . um . . . Do you have . . . ?"

"I don't have a condom," she said.

Forgot about herpes. Forgot about sadness. Forgot about pretty much everything, including Alison. Thought about Jennifer Estes. Forgot about her too. Alison kept turning her head to look at me. Unreadable eyes. Expression could have been bliss or boredom, compassion or contrition. She'd look at me then look away.

Stroked her hair with my hand. Hairspray-stiff, smelled like girl. Felt fake, also intentional. Counted the notches on her spine, wondered about untreated scoliosis, measured her width on a single hand.

Moments later I was thinking about baseball. Alison reached back, squeezed my balls, dug a press-on nail into my thigh. Etc.

"Stay in me for a minute."

Her knees buckled. Fell flat on the bed. I lay on top, spread. Her arms were shorter than mine. Held my wrists with her hands.

"It's been a minute," she said.

sixteen

Sexual Experiences:

- Sixth grade, Brandon Langley's basement birthday (another basement!), spin the bottle. Raina Baum (no tongue), Abigail Anslem (tongue), Tova Mc-Carthy (Irish Jew! My tongue, not hers).

- Eighth grade, Matt Lappin's house. First time I touched a vagina. Also first time I got stoned. I was radiating fierce love. Shelly Peters took my hand, guided me into Matt's room, guided me under her cutoff denim skirt.

- Ninth through eleventh grade, celibate (not by choice). J. Lo, AOL chat rooms, etc.

- Between eleventh and twelfth grade, summer camp, boathouse. Hand job. I was a counselor in training. She was a counselor, well trained.

- Twelfth grade, top level of Papa Gino's/Filene's Basement parking garage, Eva White, Sam Arnold's minivan, attempted loss of virginity. Performance anxiety.

- Twelfth grade, April, my bedroom, actual loss of virginity. Eva White again.

- Twelfth grade, April through May. More sex. Eva. Multiple positions (two).

- Present day, Alison Ghee's basement, Alison Ghee. Sex. Doggy-style. (See above.)

seventeen

The 55 bus was like Alison: sad-smelling, spit-shined, a bumpy ride. Took me close to the Glent-Kahn–Aldridge's renovated Victorian. Seymour was temporarily residing in the pool house. "Just until the papers go through," he'd said on the phone. Didn't ring the bell. Instead came through the garden as per Kahn's instructions.

I'd hoped for a chance to see Sheila again. She'd been on my mind since Whole Foods. But better this way. What would I have said? "I've come to sell your ex-husband a small quantity of a Class D substance. Would you be so kind as to hold me against your chest until I can feel the beating of your heart against my own, thus reconfirming my belief in the existence of the human soul"?

Plus, there was the possibility that Erin, not Sheila, would have answered the door. Surely Benjy had spilled the beans, whispered in the soft light of dusk that his brother was a fuckup, killing himself slowly, immobile, moving only in minuscule steps toward eternity. She would have looked at me with an expression that said, "We get to enjoy grown-up things like dry cleaning and group social life, while you, poor boy, are locked away in paralyzed infancy by your drugs, your inadequate hygiene, and your idle, treacherous heart."

Knocked on the door of the pool house as I entered. Kahn reclined in a La-Z-Boy, eyes closed, head bopping to horns and upright bass. Kahn rhythmically tapped the coffee table in response to my arrival, as if we were part of the jam session, riffing off each other.

"Seymour," I said.

"Charlie Mingus," he replied, eyes still closed.

Small room, sparsely decorated. *Wood and Nail* poster hung on the wall. Dinged-up Golden Globe in the corner. Half-drunk bottle of scotch, vase of dead flowers on the coffee table, 40-inch Sony Bravia LCD. Only pieces of furniture were the bed, the La-Z-Boy, and Kahn's wheelchair. Opted for the wheelchair, immediately rolled backward, knocking over the vase, spilling water on the floor. Kahn opened his eyes.

"*Send me dead flowers by the mail*," he half-said, half-sang.

"Mick Jagger."

"Very good. Now clean that fucking water up."

Got a towel from the bathroom. Kahn refilled his giant crystal goblet.

"I see you started the party without me," I said.

"Kid, I started this party before you were born. This is the tail end, my friend. The dawn is coming soon. Twilight is a sad and beautiful time. I once held a woman in my arms the way the moon holds light, refracting her image for the world to enjoy. Now I can't get a job. Now the drugs have no colors, only inertia. The women wear sunglasses to cover their eyes. You see what I'm getting at? The ghost of a party."

Was it true I'd missed the party? I'd heard a professor

on NPR's *On Point* talking decline of the empire. Romans and Greeks had their fun, look what happened. This was it for us: reality TV, virtual reality, planes into buildings.

"So what now?"

"Now you roll us a joint, of course."

Rolled the illest joint I could manage. Kahn handed me my own giant crystal goblet.

"Listen to this," he said, like I had another option.

"Chaos. That's what that sound is. Fire and sandpaper, harsh breath, an old cargo train. Mingus understood. Listen to those notes. We're just toys of the gods. We're all toys."

His speaking voice—like last time—was mannered, modulated, a performed monologue, as if always onstage, his last great act, modern-day King Lear (BBC, 1983) amid his crumbling castle. I was his remaining audience. He wanted to convince me, seduce me the way he knew how to seduce, by projecting his thunder-low baritone over the music; with the inherent jazz in his slow-heavy grin, his incongruously frantic hand gestures, the mock-lyric toughness of his carefully prepared script.

"What now is we sit still and let them have their way with us. What now is enjoying the calm that comes with epistemological impotence. Grabbing each other by the lapels, staring into each other's eyes. You up for it?"

"You're buying my mother's house," I said. "That's not sitting still."

"I couldn't not buy it if I tried."

"Yes, you could. Just don't sign the papers."

"There's more to it than that."

"We're going to have to move to a condo or something."

"If I didn't buy it, someone else would."

"There haven't been any offers."

The music swirled, turned, simmered into piano-only plunking with occasional human groans. Sipped scotch, single malt, not too peaty, notes of clove. I was used to cheap beer, store-brand vodka.

"This is good stuff."

"We're sitting in a pool house."

"I don't think the weather's right for sitting by the pool."

"Don't you understand? My ex-wife is a carpet-muncher. She treats me like an invalid. Always has . . . even before this."

Kahn lifted his left leg with his arms, dropped it like a weight on an unsuspecting ant.

"She seems like a lovely woman," I replied, stoned out of my gourd, dreaming of Sheila's Pilates-hardened abs.

"I used to live in the house. Not this house, but it was still a house."

"My brother's boning your daughter."

"At least someone's fucking someone."

"I just got laid."

"What do you want? A cookie?"

"I do love eating."

"So does Sheila. She loves to eat pussy. That's why I'm in this pool house."

"They say you can't compete with someone who has the same parts."

"Nothing to do with that," Kahn said. "She just likes the smell."

Alison's smell was still on me. Smelled like camping. Kahn pulled out a prescription bottle. OxyContin: hillbilly heroin. People were robbing pharmacies for the stuff. I'd seen a thing on PBS: kids stealing pills from their dying grandmothers, OD'ing, premature aging, death.

Kahn crushed the pill, put half up his nose. I took the straw, did the other half. Moments later, fingers tingly, Mingus pumping that bass like it was inside my heart. Smell in the air: fall: embers and Alison mixed together in olfactory sweetness.

eighteen

Dreamed a Recipe for Love:

- Grainy French mustard with horseradish
- Egg cartons (with eggs in them) stacked to roughly twice your height (more if you're short)
- Flour
- Panko (you'll need a lot—breadcrumbs can be substituted)
- Mountain of salt/MDMA mixture
- Black pepper
- 100 cloves grated garlic
- Fresh parsley
- 1 Moby Dick–style monster fish
- Mexican beer
- Dill
- 1 gallon pig lard
- Swimming goggles
- Cashmere loincloth (terry cloth will suffice)
- Jennifer Estes

Prep:

Gather the mothers, lovers, fathers, brothers of your fantasies. Arm them with Wüsthof knives, freshly sharpened. Mix mustard, eggs (beaten), flour, panko, salt/MDMA, pepper, grated garlic, parsley. Marinate monster fish in this mixture for 6 days. Rest. Fill the belly with Mexican beer, fresh dill, pig lard. Adorn yourself in swim goggles, loincloth. Kiss Jennifer wholly on the lips.

To Cook:

Hoist monster on a giant spit, fashioned from the QHS flagpole. Burn your possessions beneath the meal. Change your name to Jonah.

nineteen

Woken by a familiar hand.

"Benjy? Whatup?"

Saw Dad in Benjy's face; a softer version of Dad, as he was when he was young.

"Want to hug?" I said.

"You look like shit."

"I feel fantastic. Relax, brother. Sit down."

"Oh, fuck."

"What's wrong, Big Ben? Want a back rub?"

"I'm supposed to invite you in for dinner."

"That sounds absolutely lovely."

Floors were varnished parquet. Small trees: ficus, bonsai, etc. Large Oriental tapestries. Beige paper lanterns tagged with black Japanese characters surrounded the table, casting soft light on the diners, who—in my present state—all appeared to be slightly effervescent. Sheila, in her white, Greek-goddess-style summer gown and strappy copper sandals, was especially glowy, serving heaping portions of fried tofu, asparagus, salad. Watched her hands, the way her fingers curled around the wooden spoon as if it were a long phallus and she the gentlest Aphrodite

America ever knew (*Mighty Aphrodite*, Magnolia Pictures, 1995). Felt like the world had shrunk down until entirely contained in this house; that the hallways off-shooting the dining room led to mountains, rivers, live jungles animated by sweet-scented animal sex (*Jumanji*, TriStar, 1995).

"That Feinberg is a butcher," Mary said. "All mouth no hands. He doesn't shut up the whole time, and you can see his hands wobbling."

"Probably a failed surgeon who went to dental school," Sheila said.

"His own teeth look like something out of Dracula. I don't know why we still go there."

This was a family that made regular trips to the dentist. Teeth were all pearl, no stain (no gap).

Benjy held Erin's hand. Sheila and Mary exchanged private approving glances. Norman Rockwell for the new millennium: happy kind lesbians, black adopted daughter, couple cute college kids. Where did I fit in? I sat in the corner with an aquarium in my spine, lightning in my head, smiling giddily, scratching the shit out of my neck, hoping no one would talk to me.

False hope.

"What's with him?" Natasha said, pointed at me with her fork.

Her accusing eyes were a chestnut brown that matched her skin. Hair pulled back tightly into dual Afro puffs. Body petite, but her presence so large, secure, surely prepped to kick white-boy booty if necessary. Pushed the tofu around my plate, waited for Benjy to save me.

"Eli just got up from a nap," Benjy said. "He's still a bit tired."

"Yeah," I managed. "Sorry, I'm out of it."

Raised my eyebrows to appear more alert.

Natasha moved on.

"I'm sick of this vegan shit," she said, stabbed a tofu cube. "My people are carnivores."

"Natasha, honey," Sheila said. "We've been over this many times. Just because you're of African descent does not mean you're not part of this family."

"I'm not talking about the blacks," Natasha said. "I'm talking about the Jews. Fuck this new age bullshit. I want some fucking brisket."

"When you're out with your friends you can eat whatever you want, but this is a non-flesh-eating household," Mary added.

She smiled as she said it. Not condescendingly, more "Kids these days." Sheila caught Mary's eye, nodded. They would recap in bed tonight, laugh together at their daughter's antics, whisper that they were raising strong, independent women. Good mothers, I could tell; they followed your mouth when you spoke.

"Dad lets me eat burgers."

"Well, your father's getting his own place soon, and when he does, you can go eat burgers there. But while you're here, you'll get your protein from peanut butter and tofu."

"I think it's delicious," I said, in defense of what I viewed as a personal attack on Sheila, my angel. A ridiculous comment, considering I hadn't eaten a bite. But I liked how it looked on my plate, how it smelled in the dining room, the way Sheila spooned the tofu with the respect it deserved, careful not to mush the cubes during ladling.

Natasha looked at me dismissively, returned her attention to the destruction of her food.

"You guys just want me to be skinny like a white girl. Don't you know I need some booty if any brothas gonna wanna take me out?"

"Oh, yeah," Erin said. "Like there are 'brothas' at your high school."

"They bus 'em in."

"I'm Benjy's brother," I said, trying to make a joke. "And I'd be happy to take you out."

"Fat boy, I wouldn't let you fuck me with Denzel's dick."

"Natasha!" Sheila said. "Eli is our guest."

"No, he's not. He's Seymour's guest. Besides, he's so whacked out from being in Seymour's pool house, he won't remember half this shit in the morning."

Sheila looked at me with tender eyes, like a caring, disappointed mother on a well-acted serial drama. Benjy's eyes were not so caring, just disappointed.

"I should go," I said.

"You don't have to," Sheila said, though I'd already turned my back to the table. Drifted out the door without noticing if anyone put up more of a protest. Stopped back at Kahn's pool house. He was in the La-Z-Boy watching a midget hum-job a tranny on the flatscreen (*Taint Misbehavin'* 7, Vivid, 2004).

"This is what it's come to," Kahn said. "I take Viagra just to watch porn. It takes a half hour for it to kick in. First time in my life I've made it past the first fifteen minutes of one of these things. You know they have plots and everything?"

"I know," I said.

The tranny was tall, blackly brown, built like a big-titted power forward. A dead man's face inked on her arm. RIP Jon "J. Dooz" Dee, 1982–2003. She cupped her sucker's head with an oversized hand. Gently stroked above the ear. Sucker spit, kept sucking, sank tranny-stiff wang down his regular-sized throat.

Kahn turned toward me, reached up, placed his hand over my heart.

"BPM slightly above average," he said, slipped his hand down my breastplate, over my ribs, all the way to my pudgy left love handle.

I dropped an eighth of weed in Kahn's lap.

"Can I have some more of those pills?"

twenty

Facts About Me:

- Fucked up in school, fell asleep on too-small desks, facedown, nose smudged with wet ink.

- Doodled in margins, outside margins, hid boners in boxer-short waistbands.

- Thought about dry-aged steaks, fresh-mowed grass, hip bones, indoor grown butternut/honeycomb, THC, MDMA, LSD, SATs, SAT IIs, TV, LCD, DVD, *TII*, TI-83, shaved gruyère, shaved bush, hairy bush, Busch Light, Bud Light, heavy metal, hardcore, hip-hop, new wave, no wave, post-punk, postcoital cuddling, J. Lo, JDate, sweet potato fries, Mom's hands, function of the Internet, size of my penis, coffins, O. J. Simpson, body fat percentage, Brando at the end, Biggie, Biggie dead, 2Pac dead, Cobain dead, Courtney Love still alive, Jeremy Shaw hung from his own ceiling fan, falling carpetward, pulling the ceiling fan from its socket, screws loosed, everything angled and odd, slowly smelling;

Uncle Ned in the ground, disintegrating, unthinking, unmoving, hardly remembered by anyone but me and maybe Mom though we didn't keep his picture on the walls, didn't say his name, didn't stand at sunrise, didn't sing the mourner's Kaddish whose meaning was the melody, not the Aramaic words, which even when translated basically amount to nothing more than praising God, asking for his love.

- Which is what all kids say when they fuck up—"I was too smart for my own good!"—so let's try it another way, even if the first way's partly true: sometimes existential despair + laziness brought on by pot smoking + distraction brought on by sexual frustration does = fuckup.

- Once a teacher said, "Don't sweat the small stuff."

- He said it to me, and I wasn't sure if it meant "Don't worry about the small stuff" or "Don't ignore the small stuff."

- I did read the books, Google their authors, Wiki their Pedias.

- F's on unconventional if pseudo-poetic lab reports.

- What I mean is I knew the facts or, at least, figured I *would learn* the facts, if I could only figure out *the point* of learning the facts.

- When it came time to apply to college, Mom said she just didn't want me to be disappointed.

twenty-one

On the way home, shamed, still made of rubber, enjoying the cool air, saw Dan's maid struggle with two large plastic grocery bags, walking toward the bus stop. Something pretty about her face I'd never noticed before. Maybe the too-bright kitchen lights accented the flaws in her complexion, but outside beneath streetlamp there was grace in her slow stride, youth in her wind-kissed cheeks.

"Can I help?" I said, pointed at the bags.

She gave me a look that said, "I'm too tired to be proud."

Took the bags from her arms. They smelled good.

"Food."

"Yeah, food. She was going to throw it away. They waste so much."

I'd never heard her speak before. Assumed an accent, but she spoke like an old Quinossetian.

"I buy into all that green, recycle, reuse, sustainability stuff," she said. "Gotta believe in something."

"I shop at Whole Foods, myself."

"Whole Foods, Schmole Foods, those people charge up the ass."

"It's true."

"What we need are local farms. Co-ops. Make Wife Three pick turnips in the sun."

"Hmm . . ."

Sniffed her bag. Weird, I know, but I was still high, getting hungry.

"Cilantro?"

"Yeah. They want guacamole fresh every day even though they don't eat it. They think it's a good thing to have in the fridge."

"I love cilantro. I've been making a lot of black beans recently."

She nodded.

"Where are you from?"

"Roadway C."

"Before. I mean, originally."

"I grew up outside of Santo Domingo. In the Dominican Republic."

"It must be beautiful there. Baseball in the streets."

"It's very poor. Lots of crime. Mostly the same idiots as you have here."

"I like to make ropa vieja," I said. "But I have trouble getting the meat tender enough. Is that racist of me to mention a Spanish dish just because you're from a Spanish-speaking country?"

"You're funny."

"I've heard."

"Americans always try to rush. Cooking is mostly waiting. Low heat. It will get softer."

"I don't do anything quickly."

"It means old clothes. In Spanish, ropa vieja, old clothes. A man was so poor he couldn't afford food for his family. He took his old clothes and put them in a pot and added all the ingredients: tomatoes, pigeon peas, green olives, potato. He let it simmer for a long time. When it was done, the old clothes had turned to meat."

"I like that."

"It's a dumb story," she said. "But sometimes dumb stories have good advice in them."

Then silence, conversation replaced by growing rapport between the cilantro and the bakery-fresh sourdough. We reached the bus stop.

twenty-two

On Being Funny:

- People told me I was funny in high school. It was good for a while, the attention, until I understood what it meant. It meant I wasn't other things: sexy, interesting, smart, ambitious. It meant I was going to have trouble getting laid. It might have even meant I was fat.

twenty-three

Back home, eighty milligrams up the sniffer, jay-ski to the dome-ski, eyes dancing glassy in computer reflection, I searched the Internet for Alison. She wasn't there, not in the usual places. Google gave me nothing. Facebook gave me five Alisons, from as far away as Western Oregon, none her. As if her actual physical existence (which I'd yet to shower off) nullified the need for a 2-D online surrogate.

Instead I wrote to Jennifer Estes, who still wasn't real. She was a set of identity-markers (hair: black; lips: glossed; favorite music: Beyoncé) I attached to an imagined angel of empathy.

"J," I wrote. "Can I call you J? You know, like J. Lo. J. Est? Does that work? In French est means something. To be. I remember that from French class. I want to be. I don't know what I want to be. Just to be something. Were you in my French class? Do you know who I am? My name is Eli Schwartz, and I am a rich Jewish kid you smoked pot with once who's put on a few pounds in the past couple years, but cleans up nicely. Actually, that's not true. I'm not rich anymore. I used to be basically rich a few years ago before my dad left, but now we're moving out of the house, and though I wouldn't exactly say we're poor (that would be patronizing to real poor people—not that I'm assuming you're poor, or that there's anything wrong with . . . okay, I'll shut up), I would say we're moving down a tax bracket or so, relegated from the grandiose upper upper middle class to the boring lower upper middle class. I'm not sure why I'm telling you this, other than the fact that I saw you at temple when you were parking the cars, and I thought you might have given me a look, though I wasn't sure what it meant, and I wanted to come out, say hi, but then I got high with Kahn. You don't know who Kahn is. He's this handicapped guy who used to be famous. I'll have to introduce you to him sometime. He's really quite a character. But what am I talking about? We haven't even hung out yet. Let's just take things slow here. I just figured since we're both still in town, and there aren't many other people around, that maybe we should hang out or something. What do you think? I know this is out of the blue, but isn't that how this thing's supposed to work, getting in touch with people from the past? I'm pretty bored these days. I could cook you dinner. I'm a good cook. Great, even. I have so much love in me, and nowhere to direct it. If you don't write back just know that I don't mean anything weird by this message. I'm a good soul who's gone a bit off the deep end. My brother is a nerd, my mother is a drunk, my father is an asshole. I'm trying here, I'm really trying. Please write me back?"

twenty-four

To Be Clear:

- I really did have sex with Alison. She is a real person. Not one of those stories where a guy goes crazy and imagines himself having sex with someone who doesn't exist.

twenty-five

Woke to a text from Kahn:
"Brattle Theatre, 2 pm."

Groggy on the Green Line, ducking Fenway-bound Bro Sox and their pink-appareled gal pals. All shades—from Saxonian pale to sunburnt—forced into bodily contact as the D train hopped the suburbs, inbound. Faint smells of lunch meat and feet-stink. Windows oppressively closed. I had a standing spot between two frat rats, each excessively sideburned, each with a goatee full of sausage crumbs, each tribal-tatted in the bulbous triceps region.

"Hey, guy," one said, as if the effort to recall the other's name would be both painful and lame, a waste of Red Bull–enabled energy.

"Ya, dude," his friend replied.

Tried to bend low, limbo-style, hover well under the bridge formed by their hands on the above subway rings. All I got was armpit, nose full of Axe. This was the world, the one I'd been avoiding. The truth of mankind apparent in blinding sun-swell as we climbed the Brookline hills toward the Citgo sign.

"Ate these fuckin' hot wings, dude," Bro A returned. "Like Satan took a shit in ya mouth."

"Ya, dude," said Bro B.

"Dropped a bomb after. Fuckin' neon orange. Just like the wings. Fuckin' beautiful. Went into the other stall to wipe so I wouldn't ruin it. Took a picture on my phone. Sent it to all my buddies."

"Fuckin' sick," Bro B said.

"Hilarious, dude. You eva do that? You eva take a picture and send it to ya buddies?"

Because why not share the ugly inside us? Why not revel in the devil, expelled? Let's be brave, let's be brazen, bare it all in Jpeg form.

They got off in time for opening pitch (1:35 vs. Blue Jays), in time to swill Miller Lite, sing "Sweet Caroline" along with thirty thousand other B-hatted hopefuls as our boys in white stepped from dugout to diamond.

Hadn't been to a game in years, not since the Ned era, when he'd pick me up in his urine-yellow '86 Chevy Love. We'd snake across the Pike (no power steering), honking, singing along to BCN or AAF. Overpay for parking, then park in the bleachers eating relished dogs, admiring Anna the ball girl's bouncing B cups, willing ourselves into collective reverie.

No one to go with now, Ned was dead, Dad out in Sudbury, Benjy not a fan. It's true I'd had friends once, but they were gone too, off to college, G-chatting the days away, waiting for night under campus lights, hair assholically gelled.

Switched at Park to the Red Line, headed for Harvard. Where once sat women—mothers, commuters—now there were coeds, 18 to 25, my demographic. They studied under dark-tunneled duress, textbooks flopped open over hiked skirts, hands frantically highlighting with thick neon Sharpies. Even in public they were in their own worlds—calculus, bio, postfeminist theory—sheltered from subway odor by perfume force fields, sequestered from frat-chat by DJ-sized headphones. Pristine ladies of the Red Line: pedestaled by their own pampered beauty, deaf to my desperation.

At Kendall, a group of black girls got on, all young, all a gaggle with hood slang and unrestrained laughter. Loose-fitting Nikes over tight-fitting jeans. Natasha was among them, just another subway bopper in the USA: sassy and befriended, admired by her peers.

Waved my hand in warm hello, but the girl wasn't actually Natasha, didn't want my tender friendship.

"Whatchou looking at?"

"Yeah," her friend added. "Fuckin' pervert."

Because looking was illegal. Nothing worse than to focus eyes on another, study how she went about the world. We were isolated selves, shoved into solo corners, stabbed by stuck-out umbrella ends and pangs of futile human4human hunger. We publicized it all on the Internet, from inner thoughts to excrement, exhibitionists until someone turned to look. Then suddenly we were shy.

Head down in reply. Floor thick with mud, liquid life. Sunkist can rolled through the aisle. Gum wrappers glued to the floor. Mushed remains of a Snickers bar.

Couldn't remember the last time I'd left Quinosset. Used to come here all the time, peruse record stores, stock up on army surplus attire back when that was hip and maybe so was I. Seventh grade? Tenth grade? Who could remember? Biggie was right: things done changed. But the reliable Pit was still roughly the same.

A dugout redbrick arena surrounding the subway stop.

Clubhouse for castoffs: teen runaways, day-trip skater punks, post-love-dread-hippies smoking mom-filched Salem Lights. Lappin and I used to join in poser repose. Tried to coolly hover on the fringes, sneaking looks at the goth girls, pretending we belonged. We didn't belong.

In a sense the Pit kids were like me, but bolstered by the confidence of their anti-everything convictions. They'd forgone the comforts of bed, bath, etc., for pseudo-socialist camaraderie. Slept over heating vents. Spent days scaring tourists by poking out pierced tongues, wildly ollie-ing, groveling for dollars. Drank beer from paper bags, called cops pigs, hustled out of sight.

Today the Pit was packed. Like a Pit kid convention: dudes with rattails, dudes with hemp tails attached to their pants, dudes tattooed to their bodies' limits with images of dragons, medieval weaponry, evil-looking clowns. They condescended over the interloping others—Harvard kids, adult homeless, street musicians, lunching bank tellers— who shared their brick empire. Played something called the Penis Game. Started with one guy whispering the word "penis." Then the next, singing it a little louder. Taking turns until, eventually, the bravest among them screamed "penis" in full voice, in triumphant glee, as if the word could shatter the world. The Penis Game's subtext was oddly affirming: "The body exists. Don't deny that shit, son!"

Plus something encouraging in the way they all laughed, rubbed shoulders, affectionately called each other "shit stains" and "clit-dicks," head-butted, fake fought, fell off skateboards, fake cried, fake died, faked fuck-sounds, fake mugged freaked tourists only to point and laugh, rejoice in the power of defining an environment. It all seemed choreographed, this Pit-stage scene. Like some avant-garde performance piece, untrained actors just happy to be there, thrilled to know their lines, get them right, watch the audience react accordingly.

Onward.

Brattle Theatre: last of the art houses. Seats still cramped, uncomfortable. Add your own salt to the popcorn. Screening room basically empty. Just me and an elderly couple, wool-cardiganed, sipping Vitamin water. Lights down. Exit signs cruelly lit to distract audience from on-screen immersion, remind us of the outside world's continuing existence. Credit screen: *Wood and Nail*. A film by Dietmar Klee.

Opens wide on some serene wilderness. No animals. Just weak sunlight through leafless trees, ground dotted with snow. Slope of hills, small sound of wind. Close in on a man-made structure, only one for acres around. Entirely built of unprocessed wood, unvarnished, unpainted. Fully tamed, but so expertly as to give the impression that this place has sprung straight from snowy ground, untouched by man, a feat of naturalistic architecture. Like a tree-house cathedral, complete with tresses and turrets, columns and skinny steeples that appear unprepared to withstand nature's wrath. But they stand resiliently still, don't shake or shiver. Hammocks in a courtyard gathering dust. Ground littered with burst balloons that look as if they've been there for years. Camera moves 360 around this mini-kingdom. Out back there's a trash pit on fire, contained flames reaching up to the sky.

Cut to inside. Kahn sits in a wooden wheelchair at a lap-level circular saw. Pulls a clean piece from the contraption. Admires it, first with his eyes, then with his fingers. Minutes pass. Kahn's beard is thick. Carrot-colored curls hang halfway down his back. He's bundled. A chewed cigar sits smoking in an ashtray. Kahn sips straight from a bottle of rye. Puts the bottle back on the dirt floor. Picks up his piece of wood again. Tosses it violently, with more force than you think he can muster. He has thick arms. The wood hits the wall, weakly splinters, that's all. Falls. Kahn picks up the cigar. Spits into his hand. Puts it out on his palm. Camera closes in on Kahn's hand. Cinders stain his skin. Cinders swirl in golden light.

A woman enters, stage left. A beautiful woman: lithe, blond, at least six-two, six-three. Some German giant, genetically blessed, inhumanly symmetrical. She wears a summer dress: gray cotton. You can see that she is frozen. Skin blue. Fingers shaking. No shoes. Dirt between her toes. You can see that she is sad.

Days pass. Kahn sits in silence. He drinks, he smokes, he sleeps. He doesn't leave the studio. The woman brings him sandwiches. She goes back to her room, to her canopy bed that's been physically built into the floor, like a dais covered in cotton pillows. She buries her face. She stares into a mirror. She chillily bathes.

Weeks pass. The woman takes a lover. I'm not being precious. On the DVD liner notes this chapter is titled "Woman Takes a Lover." The lover is the man who delivers the milk. Thick-armed, appropriately flannel-garbed. Good in the sack. They fuck without fuss or conversation. Strip down, insert. Pump away on pillow mountain, slowly sinking to the surface of the bed. They do it loudly, at times angrily, at times ecstatically. All possible positions. It looks like they're actually having sex, the actors. Real penetration. Certain angles make this obvious. The man's uncircumcised penis is the size of a small arm. The woman's blond bush bursts forth like some extinct species of shaggy rodent. In a good way.

This circumstantial shift at first seems to have left no impression on Kahn's character. He knows about the affair, is neither bothered nor excited by it. But then a strange thing happens. He begins building again. His workshop is arranged for easy use by a man in a wheelchair. Everything is lap level. All tools bolted to the wall within arm's reach. The room is arranged precisely for Kahn's use, but still things are hard.

(Through conversation between the woman and her lover we understand that Kahn has lost the use of his legs in a work-related accident that occurred shortly after the completion of this wooden kingdom, and that may, in fact, have been self-inflicted, committed on purpose.)

He still struggles. Scrapes his arms. Scraps whatever project he is working on. But he does not quit. Starts another project. Something is emerging. Some ill-defined wooden object.

Concurrently with Kahn's new wave of inspiration, the weather changes. Snow pours down in clusters. Wind wakes the surrounding trees, tears them from the ground. The earth is unsettled. The woman becomes ill. She develops a fever, probably from all that time spent in unseasonably skimpy outfits. Her lover tends to her, but he too appears to be dying. He too has lost weight. They no longer fuck. They fill the kettle, sip from small cups of tea, lie distant on separate sides of the bed.

As the storm rages on, Kahn becomes further incensed into action. He closes in on completion, staying up past dawn, sanding, shaping, extracting finger splinters. Eventually his project is complete. A wooden flower, four feet high. In full blossom. Wood petals thin as paper. Detailed down to the tiniest bits of sawdust pollen. The film ends as it began. The woman enters the workshop. Her body is blue. She stares at Kahn.

At the exact moment the lights went up I received another text from Kahn: "Do you see?"

twenty-six

The Status Quo:

- So my father never built me a tree house. Big fucking deal.

twenty-seven

Fall came. Landscapers walked the streets, Hispanic mostly: Dominican, Ecuadorian. They drove paint-flecked pickups. Summer I'd see one napping in back, but once it got cold they took breaks on the tailgate, drinking coffee, smoking cigs, laughing laughter that didn't feel universal, but specific to a softer language, free of sharp consonants that leave the tongue curled awkwardly, unprepared to emit low sounds from the gut instead of the throat.

Noises would start early, seven or eight a.m. If the guys lived in Quinosset, they lived in the lettered streets, but they probably didn't live here. Probably woke at sunrise, kissed their sleeping children, piled five into the cab of the truck, headed down Route 9 from Roxbury or Dorchester.

Meanwhile, the women I imagined to be the wives, sisters, cousins of these men poured out of a baby-blue van, unloading yellow buckets, mops, vacuums. They had their own rhythms: sneakers squeaky against soapy floors, Dirt Devils sucking dust from ignored crevices, silverware herded, clinking like cowbells. Giving our house one final going-over before Kahn replaced us. Mom wanted the house to shine, even though it was only Kahn who was moving in. Movers were coming at two. I hadn't finished packing. Still at my computer checking Facebook to see if Jennifer Estes had written me back. She hadn't.

Two minds when it came to packing. First: get rid of everything; let the trash collectors haul it. Could "turn over a new leaf," as Benjy had said the previous fall, out in the backyard. I was smoking a cigarette, watching him rake leaves because the landscapers didn't come to our house anymore; since Dad had left, they only went to the neighbors. Benjy raked like he lived, like a bird eats, little by little, looking anxiously over his shoulder. Thought it was a cheap metaphor, telling me to turn over a new leaf while he was raking leaves. "Did you just come up with that?" I said, flicking my cigarette, half-aiming toward one of the leaf piles, half-fantasizing it would catch hold, burn the house down.

Couldn't burn anything. The house was sturdy, carved in my mind: life I'd lived so far, personal eternity, until death or dementia takes hold, but even then, trapped in my bones, reborn into the earth, the grass, what the hell am I talking about? A pile of old *Rolling Stone*, *Spin*, *Sports Illustrated*, some books from high school, CD jewel cases? That's why my second mind—true mind—was to keep everything, all the evidence I'd been alive, starting in '86, year Buckner let it through his legs (metaphor for my birth?), surviving: one divorce, one brother, one dead uncle, one terrorist attack (three hundred miles south), one hurricane (farther south), pneumonia at age eight, multiple ear infections, one herpes scare (things were looking okay), bad grades, bad haircuts, bad breath, chapped lips, numb toe syndrome (imaginary), headaches, dick aches, farting, insomnia, etc.

Had *Rolling Stone* going back to '99, my bar mitzvah year, world going Y2Krazy, hoarding cans, wishing themselves apocalypse. Year Dad stayed out late, while Mom sat waiting at the kitchen table, leg tapping like a metronome, nails scratching invisible words in the formica counter, eyes shifting between the little TV and faux-retro Coca-Cola clock.

I was a magazine man, liked the feel of paper, its glossy tactility, the space it filled. On one cover, Kurt Cobain is named artist of the decade. A headshot, fierce in detail. All those lines on his face would have been covered by makeup on anyone else, or airbrushed out entirely. But with Kurt they want you to see the pain beneath the surface. The photo must document the authenticity of his angst. We're meant to look at his pale eyes and unwashed hair, know he meant every word, meant that slug.

Wondered if my own face looked the same—sleepless, prematurely aged—but I wasn't pretty. My eyes are brown. Hair curly, unmanageable. Can't brush it from my face, can't sweep it behind my ear with chaos-cool. Didn't have the balls to kill myself. Afraid of death. Wanted rest, not eternal rest. Mainly rest from the interminable noise of vacuums and treadmills, the sounds of my plugged-in mother, who happened to walk in my door at that instant.

"What are you doing?" she said. Her hair shined platinum. She'd had it colored recently, to impress our new neighbors.

"Just packing these magazines."

"You can't take all that stuff. There's no room for it."

"I'll make room."

She picked up an empty soda, eyed it, sank it in the trash with a surprisingly accurate underarm toss.

"Eli," she said, like she was talking to a stubborn child. Mom bent over again, picked up a crumpled newspaper.

"I'm saving that."

"This?" She looked at it. "It's from May. All crumpled up."

"There was something in there I wanted to save."

An article about a Japanese installation artist who takes everything from his apartment, sets it up in a gallery, an exact replication of his own living arrangement. Gallery stays open twenty-four hours. People can use the apartment as they please—sleep, lunch, work, etc. He'd set one up in Boston. I'd considered going, hadn't. Never been to an art gallery before, couldn't see myself among the wine and cheesers. But I'd kept the article. On the floor, but I'd still kept it, read it over a few times. At another installation he'd just cooked pad thai, served it to people all day. That could be me. Ladling food into Styrofoam bowls, nodding. Spreading simple pleasure.

"Keep it if you want it."

"It's about this Japanese artist guy."

"Do you want it or not?"

"Just toss it."

"I don't have time for games. The movers will be here soon. And turn that music down a bit."

"Fine."

"C'mon Eli," she said, left the room.

Took everything off the shelves: sports trophies, which get taller and taller, then end at eighth grade when I started smoking pot, didn't feel like running sprints, not worried I might need better stamina for sex when it actually came; baseball glove, a Wilson, soft black leather, frayed edges, hardly fit over my hand anymore, still smelled like spring somehow; ten-sided dice from my "Maybe I'll fit in with the D&D freaks" phase.

Closet: large box of old baseball cards, including the valuable ones I'd stolen from Mark Sacks. Figured I'd give them to Benjy's kids one day so they'd like me, defend me when Benjy called me a fuckup. Packed my prom pictures, me and Eva White, a sophomore, my girlfriend for a couple months. Dumped her because she was a mathlete, even though she was cute, didn't make me use a condom because her parents were hippies, let her go on the pill starting when she was fourteen. She used to cry after we had sex. Said it was because she was happy, but she didn't seem happy, just young.

More photos: high school, sophomore year. John Sammel had just gotten an eighteen-inch glass bong. The next weekend his parents were away. A whole gang of us christened Billy Bong Thornton, which Sammel had unoriginally named after the bong Dave Chappelle uses in the film *Half Baked*. I'd bought a disposable camera to document the experience. Surprising to see myself among friends. In one shot Danielle Poole has a hand on my shoulder. Year everyone had hemp necklaces. Danielle was the only girl. Hooked up with older guys, like Sammel's brother, but never with us: me, John, and Matt. We all wanted Danielle. She'd sit on our laps to torture us.

Put the pictures back in the box, shut the lid. Hadn't spoken to John, Matt, or Danielle in ages. Danielle's family had moved to Atlanta, so when she went home for the holidays she went there instead of here. John and Matt were roommates at UMass. They used to e-mail, try to get me to visit. Lived in a dorm where no one went to class and everyone smoked pot all day. I'd love it. Kept saying I would go without intending to, not sure why, just not up for it. They stopped inviting me.

Brought the cardboard boxes up to the front hall, dragged the trash to the curb. Two guys stood outside a moving van, big white guys, one with a goatee, the other with a handlebar mustache. Tee shirts even though it was freezing.

"You the movers?"

"Fuck does it look like," Goatee said.

"Good point," I said, led them inside.

"You guys want some coffee, soda?" Mom said.

She'd laid out bagels on the kitchen table, too. We hadn't had guests in a while.

"We're on the clock."

"We taking all this stuff?" Mustache said.

"Everything goes," I said. "Fire sale."

"What's for sale?" Mustache said. "That end table?"

"What are you, a homo?" Goatee said, then, catching himself, turning to my mom, "'Scuse me, ma'am," then back to Mustache, "What are you, a queer?"

"Nothing's for sale," Mom said.

They had dollies, didn't actually need our help. We sat on the steps, watched the men with our possessions. Every few minutes Mom would stand, pace across the front lawn, say, "Careful with that," or "That's an antique."

At one point she sat down next to me, leg against mine. Looked straight at me. Thought she was going to say something reassuring, like "Everything will be okay," but she didn't. Don't know if it was because she couldn't get the words out or because she needed me to say them to her instead. We sat like that, my bare left foot grazing her sneaker, a fake fingernail pressed into the excess fabric of my jeans. She said, softly, almost inaudibly, "Your father should be here," immediately turned in the opposite direction.

Walked behind the van to smoke a cigarette. Heard Goatee say to Mustache, "How much you think a place like this goes for?" and Mustache say, "'Bout a mill," and Goatee say, "Fuckin' A."

Took a few hours. We put the remains in my mother's car. Should have been a sunset to drive into, mumbling "Never look back" beneath our collective breath. There wasn't. Already dark. No stars, either, only Mom's headlights. Headlights don't illuminate much—fifty feet at most, small stretch of road—enough to keep us moving safely forward.

Part II

one

Old Old House:

- Don't remember the old old house in Salem on the North Shore. Dad preferred it there, near the water, so I've heard. Small house. Toolshed out back. He used to build chairs, coffee tables.

- I look at pics sometimes, at my small face and Benjy's, at Dad's large hands I'd always wanted to match, finally accepted I wouldn't. Mom could be a young starlet, true blond. Could be photos from a flashback sequence, a flashback to better times. In the same way—filmic—they seem overly posed, poorly performed. We knew what faces to make when the bulb flashed.

- No idea if I'm right—if our smiles were bullshit, if my parents' clasped fingers were dutiful, cold.

- Dad thought men should work with their hands. Didn't like being a businessman, but he liked money.

When we moved, he threw himself into home building. He had control over the designs, would show up on site, hammer nails. Doubt he does much carpentry these days.

- Once I asked Mom why we moved out of Salem in the first place. She said there weren't enough Jews.

two

When I finally heard from Jennifer Estes, two months had passed. Mom and I lived in a heavily carpeted condo overlooking Route 9. Nights we faced the tube, semi-silent, semi-sleeping through cop shows, serial hospital dramas, syndicated sitcoms, anything laugh-tracked or techno-scored, loud enough to distract from the fact of our shared, superfluous existence. Like before, only in the same room.

The 42-inch LG LCD flat was comically oversized in the new living room. We'd brought the decorations from our old walls, still hadn't unpacked them. They sat in boxes in her closet beneath a pile of shoes and the clothes she hadn't brought enough hangers for.

Mom never asked about my life, what I intended to do with it. Would have been angry if she had, said leave me alone, live and let nap, like she could talk, etc. But part of me wishes that she'd prodded, told me to get a job, get off my ass; that she'd whispered in a half-awake hush that love exists and, as a young man, it was my duty to find it, tether it, rub my eyes as it disappeared in the wind, restart the cycle.

Instead we ate takeout on ottomans, staining ottomans, staring at anything but each other, occasionally mentioning Benjy, my grandparents, Thanksgiving.

Thanksgiving was approaching. All my high school friends would be home, i.e., Matt and John. I was supposed to spend it at Dad's, theoretically hit the homecoming football game, and go to a party where I'd drink cheap beer, find an ugly-duckling-turned-sorority-confident swan, shoulder-chipped, something to prove. Mom was heading to Florida to see her parents.

Meantime we were stuck in the condo. I wasn't cooking. New kitchen had an electric stove. No reception on the little TV. The kitchen was depressing. Depression succeeded by guilt about the fact that I'd been a spoiled rich boy in a heaven of culinary modernity complete with six-burnered gas grill, wall-mounted magnetic knife rack. Now, in a normal kitchen, I moped instead of cooking and making do. Still watched the Food Network, internalizing sous-vide techniques, knife maintenance tips, recipes involving rare fruit and twelve hours of your life. Saw myself on *Iron Chef*, taking down Batali in Kitchen Stadium, world looking on, impressed at my knife skills, blown away by the sensibility of my palate, finesse of my presentation, unusual combos I could fuse into forkfuls of ecstasy. Imagined the judges saying words like "delicate," "nuanced," "subtle and beautiful," that these words applied not only to my culinary creations, but to me as a human being.

This fantasy—which bore no relation to reality—was depressing.

Had trouble sleeping. Six a.m. I'd be up, watching recycled news on loop: same story, different channels, few facts, endless speculation. All these self-appointed pundits, smile-stiff anchors, desexed morning hosts in holiday-themed skirt suits, talking endlessly, as if with all this talk we might arrive at resolution. But we didn't arrive, just fell farther into abstraction, away from meaning, toward a mangled language. Is it romantic bullshit to say I felt the same—myself an endless abstraction shrinking from the tangible world into an internal brain bubble, filled with words, feelings, nothing to tie them together, no understanding of how to use them to formulate a plan for future action?

Mom would materialize, drag her sleep-frizzed self toward the ever-floor-wet bathroom, eyes closed, navigating by sense of smell (*Tommy*, RSO, 1975).

Then stay for an hour before making her exit, transformed. Makeup covered the sadness, exhaustion, other more complicated feelings. Hair had been wound, tugged, brushed into submission. Cracks in her skin had been filled with creams that, despite packages promising eternal youth, gave the impression of someone who's been in the sun too long.

For some reason, the sight of my mother helped me fall back to sleep. Maybe it's an animal thing, pheromones like a lullaby. Wake up later to an empty apartment.

Days didn't consist of much. Usual shit: TV, Internet. Wasn't smoking pot, and not by choice. Quinosset was going through a drought. Every time I called Dan he gave me the bad news. Not that it mattered. Dad still hadn't sent a new check.

No Oxy either. Wanted more but couldn't bring myself to go over there. Did wonder what Kahn was up to, what the house looked like with Mingus blasting, Kahn screaming backyard soliloquies. But something had happened when Kahn had bought the house; some unspoken line had been drawn between us. I stayed away.

Not going to be one of those guys who gets on a high horse, says quitting drugs changed his life for the better.

Sobriety didn't suit me. No possibility of oblivion, endless neutrality.

Afternoons Mom would come home, run the treadmill, which was now in the living room. Between the white walls, few windows, and buzz of the treadmill, the apartment gave the impression of being some odd asylum for the calorie-conscious insane. All we needed were other patients.

So, I'd escape to my room, turn up the tunes, scour the net for reassurance that a world existed outside my walls. I liked celeb gossip. The characters were familiar; I'd grown up with them, watched them ascend like bats at sunrise. Comforting to know they were human, had nipples, cellulite, sweatpants.

On Facebook I found Beth Cahill, a girl I'd hardly noticed in high school: plain, unperfumed, not accentuated with pricey X-carat accessories or XL breasts. Now she was some kind of hooker. FB page linked to a sexual services ad from the *Boston Phoenix* featuring Beth bedecked only in panties and jeweled tiara, offering erotic massage for the moneyed lonely.

Found Alison too (I'd been spelling her name with two L's instead of one), though, like Alison herself, there wasn't much to find. No info other than essentials: age, hometown, graduation year. A single picture: she sits upright in the QHS courtyard, framed by trees, staring past the camera, unaware she's being photographed. Mouth open, gap-teeth too big for her face; she's joyously unself-conscious. Hair short, highlighted blue, no bangs. Blue on the tips of her hair matches her eyes. Sometimes I'd stare at the picture for minutes, wondering where she was now.

Thought of Alison often, but she'd left me little to think about. Her eyes, smell of her hair, sea-salt feel of her fuck-thrust. Preferred to think of Jennifer, whose imagined perfection beat Alison's too-human condition.

Read blogs by young American soldiers, stranded in Iraq, covered in sand and sweat, longing for Big Macs, blond pussy. Searched their monologues for profundity, explanation for bloodlust, what it felt like to watch the life float from a man like fast-escaping gas from a broken propane grill; what it was like to know your body had produced death the way it produces urine or semen; to know your actions had caused reactions. Figured I'd be okay in the army, no choices, following orders, wearing a uniform. Maybe I'd die. Body carried in a plane, flag-draped, celebrated. Mom cries. Benjy touches her hair as the sun sets, pulls it from her eyes. Audience claps, weeps (*American Grunt*, Sony, 2005).

Mostly I looked at Jennifer's profile, waited for a reply that didn't seem to be coming. By the time Benjy came home from college for break, I'd given up. I hid in front of my computer, stared hard at the screen in the unrealistic hope that if I stared hard enough Benjy wouldn't notice me. I was dreading the brotherly talk.

Facebook message from Jennifer: "Party at my house tonight. 2 Kegs. 31 Roadway C."

No explanation for not writing back. No sorrowful apology. Just an invitation.

"Eli."

He said it with solidity, as if answering the question "Which slovenly sibling needs a cane to the membrane?"

Benjy was checking my alarm clock against his ultrasonic Hamas-approved underwater watch, or whatever it was.

"Dude," I said.

"You're three minutes slow."

"Times they are a-changing."

I thought: nothing's changed. But Benjy slackened his stiff-backed stance, smiled, sat, eyed the nonexistent décor.

"Time is relative."

The funniest joke he'd ever made.

"Like Uncle Sal?"

"Like Cousin Charlie."

"You're losing it," I said.

Benjy laughed, palmed my shoulder with a sweat-wet hand. Hair on top was beginning to thin, like Dad's. Looked huskier: eating pizza, packing pounds for winter. We Schwartzes were hibernators. We Schwartzes were hungry.

"This." Benjy held up his arms, gestured toward the walls.

"This is it, big bro. Not what you expected?"

"Pretty shitty."

"My thoughts exactly," I said, shut my laptop, fell backward onto the bed. Still had the cars, trucks, and buses blanket nostalgically spread atop my one-thousand-plus thread-count Egyptian cotton sheets. Blanket was soft, stained, emblematic of my nonexistent romantic prospects.

"You're twelve," Benjy said, stood. "Thirteen at the oldest."

"Oh, and you're so mature?"

Thought he might tickle me or fart in my face. A regression to the old sibling roles. Instead he faked a shin-kick, sat back on the floor, opened my laptop, navigated, raised eyebrows at the screen, frowned, closed the laptop.

It always amazed me: the brevity of online interaction, the speed at which a mood could shift.

"Fuck," Benjy said.

"What?"

"Just fuck, celibate boy."

"I have a date tonight," I said. "Might try to fuck, actually."

"Didn't know you had a social life."

"And I didn't know you had a penis. Funny how the world works."

But Benjy didn't laugh. Not because he was offended—I'd accused him of genital deficiency enough times that the words had lost all effect—but because whatever he'd seen on the screen had made him suddenly subdued.

"Mom's shitty, huh?" he said.

"What makes you say that?"

"Just get the sense."

"No more miserable than she was before."

"I might stay at Dad's."

"Really?"

"I don't even have a room here, or a bed."

"Well, the couch is pretty comfortable," I said in consolation. "I sleep on it a lot. I might sleep out tonight, anyway, if my date goes well."

Worth it to lose my bed for a night if it meant my brother might think I had a life. He stroked the carpet with his fingers, absently pocketed a piece of lint.

"Okay, Romeo," Benjy said.

three

Facts About My Brother:

- Had a perfect score on a standardized math test at the age of eleven. People expected big things. He tried really hard to live up to these expectations, only got into a state school.

- Before college, girls did not, historically, want his bod.

- So when one does (see: Erin Kahn), it's a big deal.

- As a kid, people thought I was the happy one. Probably because he wore glasses, orthodontic headgear.

- The headgear worked. My teeth are crooked; his aren't.

- Once told me that "America is made up of innocent vectors of immaturity mashed up in a blender with dead frogs and dead babies."

- Told me this the one time we smoked pot together. My brother's only drug experience. For a while I tried to get some deeper meaning out of this idea—vectors et al.—but eventually accepted it was nothing more than stoned nonsense.

- I wanted everything to mean something.

- Or at least for something to mean something.

four

Dan's car smelled like cheap cologne. He drove a black SUV, bumped Jay-Z, repeated lines under his breath, out of time.

"You know, Jay writes all his raps in his head," I said. I'd seen a thing on TV. "Doesn't write them down at all."

I liked that a brain could be so filled with words, all else pushed to the margins, made irrelevant.

"No doubt," Dan said, "H to the Izzo . . ."

Turned my seat warmer full blast, watched the suburbs unfold out my window like a flip-book, houses getting incrementally larger, then smaller again once we got close to Jennifer's.

Crowd was comprised of high school's leftovers— dropouts, Head-First kids, CC students—all domed-out on plastic-handle vodka, Busch Light. Wasn't friends with the Head-First kids during high school, wasn't *not* friends with them, either. Somewhere in between: too fucked up for the rich kids, too rich for the fucked-up kids. I always thought they were cool, not giving a shit that girls like Sherri Sacks wouldn't give them the time of day.

Henry Villeva and Jamal Green giggled in a corner,

traded pulls on a nitrous canister. Tried to picture their faces when they'd found Jeremy. Did they go blue like in movies, say, "Oh, shit," touch his body? If I were hanging, who would find me? Benjy, probably. All scientific, checking for a pulse, methodically dialing 911 on his cell.

Jennifer Estes approached us.

"You made it."

Not an excited "You made it"—no implied "I'm so glad," no hello hug. Immediately obvious: she'd invited me purely out of pity, had sent a mass Evite to everyone on her friend list, had zero interest in setting sweet fricticious fires with our prematurely winter-worn bodies. My suspicion was confirmed when a muscled blond bro in a shirt unbuttoned to reveal a recently shaven chest put his arm around Jennifer.

"Stef," he said, held out a hand in an offer of false solidarity, an offer betrayed by a tooth-sharpening tongue click that said "I'm not worried about you Jew boys, as you have no chance with my señorita. But you better stay away from her just in case, because I'm old-school and wouldn't blink at kicking the shit out of you."

"Short for Stephanie?" I said, which was the wrong thing to say.

Stef instinctively flexed.

"Stefan," he said.

"Keg's over there," Jennifer said. Situation defused.

Never has a finger pointed to free alcohol been the cause of such sadness. As if she'd decreed, "Drink away your pathetic sorrows, round man; mourn the speedy decline of your sexual peak."

Guy next to me in line was a short, slug-like white dude with a wispy attempt at facial hair.

"Yo, yo," he said. "Big Schwartz! May the Schwartz be with you!"

"Good one," I said, because it wasn't a good one. I looked over his shoulder, scoped the par-tay, watched my lost love dance lowdown, lusty butt-to-floor-back-into-big hands (shaven-chest), tickled senseless by her own displayed sexuality, smiling, head-shaking, diva-snapping, spinning like a spiffy globe on the axis of her red-heeled shoes.

"No chance," the comedian said.

"In sleep perchance to dream?"

"2Pac, right? Or is that Fiddy?"

"I'm too sober for this party."

"Dude? Bro, you used to be in my gym class! After-school gym. Mr. Zibikis, remember?"

I remembered. Failed gym freshman year because Sammel's brother let me ride with him during his lunch break. We'd loop the school's surrounding streets, bumping eighties hip-hop I pretended to like ironically, but secretly envied for its uncomplicated exuberance. Rap's pre-pubescence: before peeps got gats, got grillz, got serious. Thus, after-school gym.

"Oh, yeah."

"That shit sucked!"

Only memory of the class was that after school they'd let geese shit on the field as a method of fertilizing the grass. One time Mr. Zibikis, an aging alcoholic who'd been demoted from football coach to after-school gym teacher, let us throw javelins at the geese, told us whoever hit one could go home. No one did, but I remember chasing geese around the girls' softball field, chucking spears like we were Roman soldiers in the heart of Caesar's army (*Rome*, HBO, 2005–2007).

"Remember that time he let us throw javelins at the geese?" I said.

"Yeah. Yeah, that was ill. So what you up to these days?"

Not sure why I was so afraid of this question. Maybe because I was supposed to have gone to college, and we were supposed to have a conversation where I said I was in college, he said he wasn't, we were both proud of our positions, and though we each looked down slightly on the other's, our hearts still could be united by drugs, booze, girls, and one beautiful memory of attempted winged-animal assassination.

"Not much. Living at home with my mom."

"You didn't go to school?"

"No."

"Why not?"

"I don't know. Just didn't work out."

"Why not?"

"Smoked too much weed . . . fucked up in high school."

"Your family pissed?"

"Yeah."

"So what you doing now, working?"

"No."

"So what the fuck you doing with yourself, kid?"

"Nothing, really. TV, Internet . . ."

"Must be sweet, man."

"It's not that sweet. Actually, it's pretty boring."

"I'll take boring over working any day."

"I'm not really rich anymore. We moved over by the highway."

"Where at?"

"Elm Condos."

"Elm Condos? Damn. Those shits ain't bad. Compared to this neighborhood, anyway."

True. Our apartment was small, antiseptic, but double the price of a duplex like this one. I was still a bourgeois stoner with a rich daddy. No personal allowance, but he put food on the table, high thread-count sheets on my pillow-top Tempur-Pedic. A common and confusing situation for fuckups like me: cash poor, well insured, unmotivated.

"What about you?"

"Pepsi factory."

"How's that?"

"It's a Pepsi factory."

"What do people do in Pepsi factories?"

I'd seen TV docs about labor laws, sweatshops, the factory strike of 1909. Understood labor as concept, couldn't picture the specifics. Was the Pepsi mixed in giant tubs by elves? Was there a guy whose only job was to add the sugar? I entertained a romantic notion that I too could bottle Pepsi. But it wasn't feasible. Unlike Dad, I was all thumbs, no knack for mechanical contraptions outside the kitchen. Nothing manly about me.

"We just bottle it. It's pretty easy, actually. Boring, but easy. It's union, though, so the money's okay."

Felt like I was in a John Hughes movie, only I was playing the wrong role, not the trodden romantic lead but the rich ass-hole or the comic-relief stoner. Filled the guy's beer in consolation for the fact that his life was probably shittier than mine.

Dan was talking to Nikki, the Whole Foods cashier with green eyes, chemical-red hair. I'd brought Dan a beer, but he already had one. Chugged his beer, took the one I'd brought, chugged it too. Nikki looked on impressed, the way younger girls sometimes look at older guys who were cool in high school, regardless of their current status.

"This is Nikki."

Never formally met, but I'd seen her name tag, watched her scan bell peppers with amorously unloving slacker imprecision.

"You work at Whole Foods."

"I know where I work."

"I go there a lot."

"I know," she said, raised an eyebrow. "A lot."

"I find it peaceful."

"I don't. All those privileged assholes. You should hear how people talk to me. So what are you, a cook or something?"

Nose ring exaggerated the movement of her nostrils. It sparkled, spelled trouble in a good way.

"I just like cooking."

"Haven't seen you in there in a while."

"Yeah. I moved. I don't have a car, so I can't really get there. And my new kitchen sucks."

"I hate cooking," she said.

"Me too," Dan said.

Smiled at each other. Apparently Dan liked girls. The most unlikely soul could find a counterpart. Who was mine? Across the room Beth Cahill pretended to fellate a beer bottle. She'd been anonymous in high school. Now she craved attention, no matter how she got it. Considered making a move, but it wasn't a good match. I was a lethargic non-Lothario; she worked in the sex industry. Besides, I didn't have weed or a basement. Only pickup line I'd ever successfully used: "Want to come back to my basement and smoke weed?"

If I'd had any money, might have paid her to sit by my side, whisper vulgarities to distract me from the pain of losing the illusion of Jennifer.

Instead went to the back porch. Empty. All the smokers were out front. Window in the adjacent house lit up blue with TV light. Could barely make out the people inside, but thought it was a young couple, radiant in the blue light, laughing together as another comedian fed them one-liners to soothe their frozen souls.

Lit my cigarette. Screen door opened. Alison Ghee walked out, proving our lives weren't perpendicular lines, but curved, crooked, moving jaggedly. Eyes bulged out of her face, blue like the TV light, endearingly dilated, incongruous with her pale cheeks, which hadn't developed that healthy, rosy winter sheen.

Alison wobbled toward me wearing ten-inch boots and the expression of no expression I'd seen on myself in Kahn's mirror, numbed out on the feeling of no feeling. A good expression to have, a scary one to see on someone else. Smile looked pinned to her face: unintentional, uncomfortable. Her walk an inglorious attempt to glide, like a vintage Italian bicycle (*Breaking Away*, Twentieth Century Fox, 1979), grace of its thin frame betrayed by airless tires. Hips were there in theory—wide bony waist for one day when . . . —but not substantiated by meat-stuffed skin. Alison's factory-faded jeans had nothing to cling to. They scrunched of their own accord, stayed put with the help of a white nylon belt.

She sat by my side, pulled up her jacket in an attempt to protect her exposed neck from the wind. I offered a cigarette. She accepted. Clearly fucked up. I envied her position, wanted to join her internal city, walk its honey-sweet streets.

"You got any more of whatever you got?"

"Dude," she said slowly, pouty "D," enunciated "uuuude."

"Dude."

"Schwartzy. I been looking for you."

Inched her chair closer to mine, then back, as if she wanted to cozy up, let me warm her in the pudgy flab of my gut, but was suddenly overcome by a deep fear of physical intimacy. As if, upon closer inspection, she understood the neediness in my stare. Alison scooched back in the other direction, eyes now pointed at the stick of moon, a skinny slit among the atmosphere's other objects of mocking magnificence.

"I was going to call you."

"Call me?" she said, emphasis on the "?" "How could you call me?"

"On the telephone."

Waited for her to tell me I was funny. Fucked-up people always thought I was funny.

"I didn't give you my number. So how could you have called me?"

Good point. Chair seemed to be floating further away, like her hallucinatory imaginings were manifesting in the physical world. Wanted to tell Alison everything about my life: mother, brother, Kahn; about the dream I'd had a few nights ago where I was sitting in a velvet throne while Sheila Glent-Kahn poured olive oil on my back, rubbed it in as I watched Dad and Benjy wrestle in French-cut lingerie in a giant cage on my flatscreen. Wanted her to understand. I was ready to confess, purge, await comfort.

"Kahn is living in my house."

Alison nodded. Cigarette was already lipstick-stained, sentimental red, reminiscent of perfume ads, the kind that lets you peel back, sniff, feel a phantom female presence.

"I love my mother but I don't know how to express it," I said.

More nodding.

"My mother doesn't know how to express it, either, or maybe she doesn't love me," I continued. "My father definitely doesn't love me. My brother slipped away into the real world and I'm alone. I've got Kahn, but I'm afraid of Kahn. I'm afraid of becoming Kahn, but part of me knows I'm already Kahn, that he's just the part of me I want to keep away from the world. I think Kahn might be in love with me."

"Kahn?" she said, laughing.

The kind of laugh that goes with smudged lipstick: lungy, part-laugh, part-cough, part-face-first-flop-onto-cast-iron-deck-table. Looked like it hurt. She pulled herself up from the table, face now imprisoned by table-made crisscross pink marks. Alison tried to look at me with a straight face, then laughed again, holding the chair's frozen arms for support.

"In love with you? That's silly. Kahn, in love with . . . *you*?"

"What's so funny? You don't even know who Kahn is."

"Kahn, of course. That guy who works at CVS. The guy who develops one-hour photo. With the funny mustache. He's not in love with you."

The word "you" was accompanied by a patronizing poke to my nose.

"Well, yeah, you're right. That particular Kahn is not in love with me. I'm talking about a different Kahn. That's Indian Kahn. One-Hour Photo Kahn. I'm talking about wheelchair actor Kahn. Jewish Kahn."

"You fucking Jews," she said, in a way that was joking, but not really. Maybe her bone was on behalf of Jeremy, residual anger at the synagogue for housing his sadness.

"Fucking Jews? We're not so bad. Don't say fucking Jews."

"You liked it when I fucked *you*."

Another nose poke.

"That's true. I did like it. There were a lot of things I

liked about it. Some things I didn't like. But I liked the idea of it. I certainly appreciated the gesture."

"Appreciated the gesture?" Alison contemplated that one by blowing smoke in my face.

"Oh, I see," she said, laughing again, the way movie gangsters laugh before brass knuckles to your dome. "I see. You want me to fuck you again? You want me to slide my wet pussy over your Jew cock? Would that make you feel better, make your sadness go away? Is that it? Mommy doesn't love you so little old Alison comes to the rescue? Hahaha. Eli Schwartz. Hahahaha."

Heaved an ankle onto my thigh, licked her lips, puckered.

"C'mon, big boy," she said. "Show me what you got."

"Jesus," I said, cried.

Hadn't cried since childhood. I'd been trying to cry for years, force it out by leaning over raw onion, eating extra wasabi. I wanted catharsis. Now the tears came: unmitigated, embarrassingly.

Alison removed her leg. Unpuckered, unstiffened, unslutted.

"I'm such a pussy," I said. Sounded like "Fufufufu pussy."

"I'm being mean," Alison said. "I don't mean to be mean. Not to Eli Schwartz. I don't want to be mean."

"Such a fucking pussy."

"A pussy in a good way," she said, which didn't help.

Blubbering now, wiping my face on the arm of Alison's jacket. Wiping off her jacket with my hand. Wiping off my hand on my own jacket.

"Eliii. You're a nice guy. You're too nice. I'm not nice. I'm not a happy person for you. I'm not the girl who's the girl you like."

"What girl?"

"Schwartz, you're so sad. I'm just feeling good tonight, you know? Feeling good, feeling tall. You're a sad fucking dude. Sometimes I'm a sad fucking chick. But tonight I'm flying. I don't need all this, you know, crying and shit."

This made me cry more.

"It's not your fault," Alison said.

"I thought I was funny?" I said, still snotting, still wiping, still spilling salty tears.

"We're not what we need," she said, like it made perfect sense. Then gave me a look that maybe said, "It's possible I don't actually believe what I just said, but I'm being strong and cruel because it's easier than facing up to the more complicated feelings buried deep beneath my veneer of fucked-up-ness."

Seen that look in movies. The part of the movie when everything gets bad. Wanted that part of the movie to be over. Trying to write my own movie: unclichéd, less sad, more surprising. The other actors weren't reciting the right lines.

Watched her walk away. Same hunched walk. Same pigeon-toed stuttering steps, slow, barely balanced, trying not to slip on the iced-over stoop. Where was the soundtrack? Some old-school American standard, singer's musty, smoke-muted refrain calling Alison back into my arms, back into the pathetic cradle of my confusion.

Couldn't find Dan. Must have gone with Nikki, off to an upstairs room to unzip winter wear, search drawers for a condom, give up, Dan promising to pull out, secretly excited to explode on her stomach.

Jennifer and Stef stood in a circle of people laughing, smiling, drinking, Jennifer blushing. Guests revolved around her at an incalculably slow pace; they were her moons.

"Ben," I said into the phone. Never called him Ben. Hoped it would make me sound serious, situation appropriately dire.

"I thought you had a date."

"Didn't go so well."

"Have you been crying?"

"I'm not a pussy. Just sensitive. I'm a sensitive man, okay?"

"I'm coming," he said, because he was a martyr.

Benjy drove, Erin rode shotgun. I hopped in back, slouched, stretched.

"What were you doing out here?" Benjy said, like his spine was crawling with ghetto-lice.

"I don't know," I said. "Looking for something, I guess."

"A mugging?"

Erin hit him on the arm, said, "Apologize." Something of her mother in her: she wanted to take care of people.

"Sorry," Benjy said, which surprised me. He rarely conceded. Drove with both hands on the wheel, radio off. Sensed that I'd intruded on a non-me-related tension, given the duo excuse to focus on a problem not their own.

"Was it a good party?" Erin said.

"Not really."

"How'd you get here?" Benjy said. Unclear whether he was asking about the party or my state of existence.

"Dan," I said. An accurate, if incomprehensive answer to both questions.

"We're going to get ice cream," Erin said. Benjy's silence made it clear this unnecessary endeavor was neither his idea nor a good one. "Do you want to come?"

Too cold for ice cream. Store empty; counter kid flipped through Cliff's Notes for *Othello*. Steel soft-serve machines mumbled their own mourner's Kaddish. We ate with hands tucked into sleeves, plastic spoons poking out like cheap prostheses.

Benjy drove the back route, off the highway, on the road with the speed bumps. Hopped speed bumps like hurdles.

Erin said, "Slow down."

Benjy eased off the gas.

"That's the house I grew up in," she said, pointing.

"But you didn't go to our high school."

"Private school. Country Day. I was one of those horse-riding girls."

Erin was still looking out the window even though we'd passed the house.

"She has different parents than I had."

"Who?" I said.

"My sister. They split when she was six. They were together my whole childhood. We went to Nantucket in the summer."

"Mary seems nice, though."

"She is," Erin said. "But it's different. It's different now. Maybe it's better. It's probably better. I'm sure my mother's happier. He drove her nuts. But she still takes care of him; he still drives her nuts. I know she tries. She tries too hard. He doesn't try at all."

"He does," I said.

"What the fuck do you know?" Benjy said.

"It's just different now," Erin said.

I wanted to say, "He loves you," but wasn't the type of guy who said things like that, and wasn't even sure it was true. Lit a cigarette.

"You can't smoke in here," Benjy said.

Threw it out the window. Dropped Erin at our old house, watched the automatic security light go on, hold her like a spotlight as she punched the garage code. Garage opened, swallowed Erin. Still looked like our house.

Mom asleep in front of the TV. Empty wine bottle on the floor, Argentine, average-priced. White noise of an infomercial. Mom's shallow breath. Lifted her gently—he at the feet, me at the head—carried her to bed. She woke for a moment.

"What's going on?"

"Bedtime, Mom," Benjy said. "You stole my bed."

When we came out of Mom's room, Benjy put clean sheets on the couch, then lay down in all his clothes, including shoes, stared up at the ceiling.

five

Wounded Women:

- TV too has wounded women. They wear leather, wear their anger on their full-sleeve tattoos. Angry at fathers, other abusing menemies: mustached uncle, sado/slutty ex, handsy priest. This anger is transferred to all men, even the plaid-shirted, soft-eyed virgin who wants to hold her tenderly, whisper sweet street-vernacular into her sleeping ear. She pushes plaid-shirt away, afraid of letting herself love, letting herself be vulnerable again. Episode continues after a short commercial break. Somehow plaid-shirt proves himself. He is there for her. Breaks down her barrier. She opens herself. Fucking ensues, etc. Maybe they cry in front of each other. Maybe they learn to see the world as something less than aggressive.

- TV never told me how to break down the barrier, and the truth is TV doesn't know. Truth is those barriers stand. Barriers like grief, which sticks to Mom, sticks to Alison, sticks to them like gum in hair. Only option is to cut until you're ugly, keep cutting, feel the ridges of your skull-scars as physical incarnations of your loss. Those barriers stand, and maybe they age. Age and become nostalgia. Age and become their own separate deaths: death of the sadness, death of the original feeling.

- Wanted to bring Alison to the birth of new feeling. Sad too. Birth of new feeling meant the death of old feeling. Alison already thought everything was dead.

six

Couldn't sleep. Condo heat nonadjustable, no settings but on and off. It was on. Radiator rattling, ready to burst from the wall with the force of a freewheeling subway car, nuts and bolts airborne, machinery burning. I smacked it a couple times to no avail. Contemplated finding a hammer, fucking shit up, dueling to death. Smelled like death: sautéed mouse corpse. Plus the heat. Not even an all-encompassing heat that kills chill. This heat was menopausal: hot flashes upsetting my delicate balance. Hot air aimed straight at me in intermittent bursts. Then the quick return of cold. Sweating and shivering, I was up. Nothing to be done.

Wrapped myself in a flannel robe. Worn, holey. Soft, semi-holy. My housecoat. My smoking jacket. My uniform. Tiptoed toward the kitchenette. Benjy deep in unconscious unrest on the foldout. No relief from dreams. Face down, legs spread, biting hard into pillow. One shoe still on. Other sideways on the floor.

"Please stop," his dream-self said.

Stop what? Excess of familial responsibility? Butt-spanking bogeyman? Nocturnal ball gag and ass-banditry (*Pulp Fiction*, Miramax, 1994)?

We were different that way. I woke sweaty and foul-smelling. He slept shittily. Even in dreams he bore the brunt with bit lip. Like a grunt on the front lines of some hellish nothing war. He took pride in his ability to survive without complaint.

Behind Benjy the sun strode from clouds, tentatively, out of annoyed necessity, like some dude emerging from fuck-bed, late for work, still admiring his conquest's sleeping body, awaiting toaster waffles. Clouds went pink, then cleared. Boston skyline into view, temporarily inflamed by sun-love, twisted with diminishing beauty. In a matter of minutes it would all be gone, gray. Reminded me of coming down from mushrooms, lamenting my dwindling visions, but comforted by the coming concreteness. We were out of coffee.

Also out of cereal, bagels, waffles, bananas, grapefruit, oatmeal, all forms of prenoon nourishment. Couldn't turn on the TV; didn't want to wake Benjy, incite sleep-deprived wrath. No newspaper anymore—Mom had canceled our subscription. Nothing to do but watch daylight emerge, urge myself into daylight. Strapped on a pair of beaten boots. Needed to walk and think, escape condo confinement.

Walked the breakdown lane, slowly, smoking, freezing. Took off my headphones to hear the world: light purr of engines, fragments of music coming out the partially open windows of wind-bearing smokers, wind. Thought it would be funny if Dad saw me on his way to work, took me for a derelict. Considered hitchhiking, catching a ride up the coast, down the coast, west—anywhere. What was the use? Had no money, was wearing a bathrobe. No one picked up hitchhikers these days. Maybe some cannibal molester passing through (*Seat Belt Meat Belt*, Universal, 1984).

Sat at Dunkin' with coffee and the *Globe*, taking in the familiar smells of by-the-dozen doughnuts, coffee en mass, chemically diluted urine, and stale gas that filtered up through the heating vents into the mostly empty dining area.

Read about the war, football. Skimmed the obits, looking for worthwhile lives: people who'd traveled, broken the restraints this town invisibly slid over our cold-sick selves. Other news: Quinosset Cinema West showing a retrospective—a dead Frenchie auteur whose films took on the legitimacy of history, whose own history hissed with black, pedophilic asterisks. Metro police blotter: A woman had stolen five hundies worth of housewares from Bloomingdale's. Claimed temporary insanity; her Amex was overdrawn. She wanted to serve with shining silverware. Opened the classifieds, quickly closed them.

A woman sobbed at the next table. Mrs. Sacks, my old Whole Foods friend. Small town, etc.

"Eli," she managed.

Gave a slight wave, stood as if to walk over. She held out her hand to stop me.

"I'm okay," she said, blew her nose.

Went to the bathroom instead.

When I came out, Mrs. Sacks was sitting at my table, fixing smudged eye shadow in a hand mirror. Still crying a bit, so she wasn't having much success. Black Lycra shirt bore the word "Superstar," embossed in sequins across her well-proportioned chest. Sequins mocked her tears and dark eyes with their luster.

"Eli."

"Mrs. Sacks. Hi."

"You doing okay?" she said, as if I had been the one crying, as if she sensed I was still drying my own damp face.

A maternal voice—at once forgiving and resolute, like the safety net beneath a tightrope walker—a voice I'd never heard her use. This was how she'd spoken to Sherri as a child, how she'd bred the confidence Sherri expelled with every ass-wiggly step.

"I guess," I said, wanting to please her, to not let her down.

"That's good. Everything will work out fine."

"I hope so."

Tears were gone and she smiled, amused by the absurdity of her own public outburst. Some trauma had sent her here. More cheating from Mark? Problems with Chef Barash? Bad luck breast exam or Pap smear? Her face said: "The world comes down on all of us. Money and healthy sex lives can't save us. But we persevere; we are from Quinosset, home of the QHS She-Devils, second-ranked women's tennis team east of the Mississippi."

I nodded in agreement. Mrs. Sacks looked around the empty Dunkin'.

"It's silly, really," she said, sipped her coffee, checked out her own gigantic, sparkling chest, then met my eyes, as if to accuse *me* of staring at her breasts, which I was. "This town."

"I know what you mean," I said, because I did, if not specifically.

"Do you like it here, Eli? It's not a bad place, is it?"

"Not so bad."

"There are worse places in the world."

"Certainly."

"A lot worse," she said, motioning to my newspaper. Then, looking again at the empty tables, "I guess it doesn't fill up for a couple hours. That's when people go to work."

She took a stick of lip gloss, applied it without looking in the mirror. Mirror rested like a paperweight on my newspaper. Radio wasn't on, but you could hear the morning patter—Spanglish—from the two cashiers.

"Now they're all asleep. It's like we're the only people in the world."

"There are other people," I said, nodded toward the cashiers.

Mrs. Sacks smiled.

"You're funny."

"Why does everyone think I'm funny?"

"There's something Dutch about your face."

"What does that even mean?"

"Holland," she said. "My kinda town," winked.

Her car was shiny, stiff with factory smell. ZLX played the acoustic adult-contemp version of Eric Clapton's "Layla." Mrs. Sacks sang along. Never occurred to me that women like her listened to music.

"What are you doing today?" she said.

"No plans."

"Want some breakfast? I'll make you eggs."

"Okay."

Kitchen was like the others, like my old kitchen. Fridge stocked with fresh produce from Whole Foods. Walls covered in prom pics, bar mitzvah pics. One poster-sized glamour shot of Sherri wearing a bikini, holding a lollipop in her mouth. She'd done a Club Med ad when we were seniors; this was the winning shot. Everyone acted like she'd won a Pulitzer, when all she'd done was be herself: large breasted, well moisturized and exfoliated, seventeen years old.

"I'm a terrible cook," Mrs. Sacks said. "Eddie used to cook for me, amazing things."

Used to?

"I'll make the eggs," I said.

Found smoked salmon in the fridge, made lox scramble. Felt good cooking in her cast-iron skillet. Ate next to each other on stools at her center counter.

"This is delicious," Mrs. Sacks said, leaned over, touched my shoulder.

"You're a sweet kid." She sounded drunk.

"You're not so bad yourself."

Mrs. Sacks brushed my cheek with her hair. I put a hand on her waist, rubbed the soft velour of her pastel-pink yoga pants. Kissed, closed-mouthed, divots in chapped lips interlocking.

"Come to the bedroom."

Followed her up the stairs. No one mentioned *The Graduate*. May-December bone-jobs were common these days. All those female teachers sucking face with prematurely mustached son-surrogates.

The house smelled like potpourri. Reminded me of my other grandmother, who was dead.

Mrs. Sacks stripped naked, sat on the bed, stared out the window. Great shape for her age. Wondered how much work she'd had done. Tan but no tanline. Pictured her in the tanning salon, in that space-pod-like tube: naked, blindfolded, basting in artificial sun.

I was still wearing a bathrobe. She tugged it.

"Hefner," she said, grown-up-giggling.

Removed the robe. Lifted my shirt, unzipped my pants. Pulled them down, hovered over her, looked in her narrow, bloodshot eyes. Put a finger on her nipple, watched it harden.

"Feels nice," she said, rubbed the down on my shoulders. "I want to feel you inside me."

"Really?" I said. "Me?"

Kissed me again, warmly, open-mouthed. Didn't use my tongue. Didn't seem the thing to do with an older woman. She smelled like my mother's perfume. Bit my earlobe, guided me inside with her hand. Sheets were soft. I estimated the thread count, ejaculated immediately.

"Sorry."

Mrs. Sacks recoiled.

"I thought you were supposed to be good at this. Young and strong."

"I thought so too," I said. "Guess not."

She looked out the window again, away from me. Tried to hide the fact that she was crying.

"This is all wrong."

Reached for my boxers.

"I'm sorry," I repeated.

Mrs. Sacks turned back to me, wrapped her hand around my ankle.

"It's not your fault. It's my fault."

"It's nobody's fault."

She let go. I stood, dressed. Mrs. Sacks watched, really looked at me.

"Don't worry," she said. Not sure if she meant I shouldn't worry about her, or about myself.

"I should go," I said.

As I was walking out the door, Sherri walked in with two other girls. Surprised to see me. So surprised she screamed. Must have thought I was robbing her house.

"Relax," I said. "I was just helping your mother fix her TV. I'm leaving now."

Mrs. Sacks came running down the stairs. Also in a bathrobe. We didn't look like lovers.

"Mom?"

"Eli was just looking at the leaky faucet."

Moved out the door.

seven

American Dream:

- Maybe my American dream is sex that isn't sad.

- Sex that isn't sad is R-rated, culled from rom-coms (no nipples).

- She removes her shirt in slow motion, revealing her pale stomach one inch at a time.

- Twirl her hair between my fingers.

- She holds my hand over her beating heart; her face as we quietly hump like barbiturated gorillas, her eyes staring into mine, hair falling across my face, brushed back, falling again.

- My perfectly complacent face at the moment of climax. Hers too.

- "Oh," she says, and I say, "Mmmm."

- Afterward, in bed, she stares out the window. Watch her profile as reflected in the bureau mirror.

- She wears one of my shirts, sleeps peacefully.

- In the morning I make eggs. Smell wakes her. Saunters in, yawning. Hand her a cup of coffee. Smiles.

eight

For Mrs. Sacks, Hard Body, Soft Heart:

- 3 organic cage-free eggs
- Salt and pepper
- Capers
- Olives
- Fresh herbs
- 4 oz. Nova Scotia lox
- Wasabi powder (or paste)
- 1 bottle Tabasco
- Arugula
- Aged balsamic vinegar
- Magnum condoms
- Sexually competent man-child
- Big empty house, some Sunday in fall, wind blowing, auburn leaves falling like fiery sparks, Clapton on the radio singing about his dead son
- Maybe a second man-child just for fun

To Cook:

First make the eggs. Beat well. Salt and pepper the shit out of them. Add capers, olives, fresh herbs. Cook on medium/low heat. Add slices of salmon right before the eggs de-liquefy. Flip. Plate. Add wasabi and Tabasco until your nose runs, mouth waters, eyes well up. Purge your demons. Purge the salty pains of your life. Listen to Clapton sing about his lost child. Understand that at least you have your health, family, wealth. Eat arugula salad on the side. Head upstairs. Take a bubble bath. Shampoo yourself. Dream of a better life. A lusty, perfumed life. Get out of bath. Dry yourself. Move to bed. Better life will arrive in the form of two tongues jostling for position between your legs. Don't forget to remember to forget about everything else. One man will eventually stand, embrace your body, stare into your silky, tired eyes. The other will lick you in the place that birthed a thousand ships.

nine

Wife Three let me in, confident in workout clothes. Everyone wore workout clothes. Maybe in case of al-Qaeda: ready to run.

"Your friend is having a party."

"Isn't it a bit early?"

"You wasted no time getting here, you're still in your pj's."

"They're comfortable."

"Go."

Pointed to the basement, smiled sluttily. Wondered if Wife Three would become Mrs. Sacks one day; if Dan's dad would cheat, and she would have an affair but stay with Dan's dad because of the house, screw some twentysomething while tears smudged her eyeliner. Doubted it. Things were different these days with these third wives. They knew what they were getting into. Divorced in five years, what did she care? Get a nice payoff, marry another rich guy.

Walked down the stairs. Lights dim. Dan in boxers cutting huge lines of coke on the coffee table. Nikki next to him in her Whole Foods getup, hair-drying with a towel.

"Nice bathrobe," she said.

"It's L.L. Bean," I said, then felt stupid for saying it, and for wearing it.

"Chanukah?" Dan said.

"Twelfth birthday."

"Taste?" Dan said.

Stuck a finger in.

Nikki lit a cig, took two drags, put it out.

"I gotta go to work."

"One for the road?"

Passed her the hollowed pen. She sucked one up the non-nose-ringed side.

"I'll call you later," she said, left.

"You two seem to have hit it off."

"Love them redheads."

"She's not a true redhead."

"She's a hip, hip lady."

"Can't you say something that's not from *Dazed and Confused*?"

"Relax," Dan said. "Chill."

Potheads were always telling other people to relax.

"Stepmom's in a good mood today."

"She joined the party."

"You're kidding me."

"She likes the yips. The whites. The coke-ay-eenay. The snow. The blow. The blizzle. The izzle."

"What's the izzle?"

"The kizzoke."

"Oh."

Handed me the pen, cut me one.

"Cool."

"Fifty."

"For a gram?"

"One fifty an eighth."

"I'm broke. My father cut me off."

"Good for him. It's about time he taught you some responsibility. Drugs don't come cheap, you know."

"Wait. Can you give me a ride somewhere? I think I can get money."

"Word."

Benjy was helping Mom zip an overstuffed suitcase. I'd forgotten she was leaving for Florida.

"Oh, good. You boys can help me carry stuff to the cab."

Four suitcases laid out.

"You're bringing a lot of stuff?"

"You never know what the weather will be like there."

She was preoccupied with packing, didn't notice how out of it I was. I was sleep-needy, mildly coked, didn't notice quite how excessively she'd packed.

"I thought you were still asleep in your room. I was just going to wake you up to say goodbye."

Mom looked distinguished in a beige pantsuit, like an ex-newscaster, not an ex-wife.

"You okay?" Benjy said, gave Dan the once-over. They'd been in the same grade.

"Schwartz," Dan said, nodded at Benjy. Never friends. Benjy was in AP classes. Dan wasn't in any classes.

"Everyone's okay," Mom said. "We're all okay."

"I'm not okay," I said, real soft, so no one could hear.

Carried the bags down in the elevator, wheeled them to the waiting cab. Mom hugged us goodbye. Tried to pull her close, instigate maternal embrace. She was in a rush, pecked my cheek, escaped my grip.

"Don't forget to bring the apple cake to your father's."

Back upstairs, fished through the boxes in my room I'd never unpacked. Dan watched *The Surreal Life* in the living room. Benjy knocked on my door, came in without waiting for my response.

"What are you looking for?"

"Nothing."

Continued digging.

"You're totally fucked."

"I'm fine."

"You realize it's eleven in the morning?"

"I thought it was earlier."

"What you got, hidden stash in there?"

"I'm not looking for drugs."

He didn't believe me.

"I don't believe you."

"Here it is."

Pulled out the '61 Maris I'd stolen from Mark Sacks years before I'd had sex with his wife.

"Baseball cards?"

"This is a '61 Maris."

Kept digging, pulling out other cards I thought might be worth something. No time for sentiment.

"You're broke."

"It's business. Baseball cards are kid stuff. I'm just trying to grow up, make responsible financial decisions."

"Dad cut you off."

"You knew about it?"

"He mentioned it."

"Since when do you talk to Dad?"

"I talk to Dad all the time."

"Well, next time, tell him to give me some fucking money."

Walked out of the room with my cards.

"Let's go," I said to Dan, who was wholly engrossed in the goings on of the *Surreal Life* house.

Dan said, "I always thought Vanilla Ice was a total loser, but he actually seems like a pretty cool guy."

Did a couple key bumps, set off for the card shop.

ten

Facts About My Mother:

- Mom hasn't worked since I've been alive.

- Before marriage she was a secretary. Picture her
  in an old seventies skirt-suit, sun orange, gingko
  green. Sprightly in a conical bra, heels. Bends
  down to pick up a dropped pen. Men pretend
  not to notice. But they notice. Mom raises an
  eyebrow. Cute guy raises both eyebrows. Mom
  laughs, shakes her head, touches her hair. Sits
  back at her desk, types in sweet staccato, falling
  into rhythm, toe-tapping, punctuated by imagined
  hand-clapping.

- Then she lived a life of quasi-luxury that was
  luxurious enough for a poor girl from Lynn. Saw
  herself in mirrors, liked what she saw. Arranged
  the photos to reflect the family she wanted to
  have, pretended to have. Slept well.

- Dad fucked it all up.

- Our lives aren't so different.

eleven

Money:

- Safe to say I wasn't instilled with respect for the dollar. Let's not play the blame game.

twelve

Amy's Baseball Card Heaven was still standing, tucked between the Verizon store and Starbucks on the Grande Street drag. Back in the day, Grande Street was mom-and-pop central, center of Q-town social life, semi-quaint, filled with indie shops run by locals, mostly South American and Middle Eastern men who spent their days chatting up stay-at-home stroller moms and watching staticky soccer on bunny-eared portables.

Delightfully uncorporate: Five Alive Pizza, Tom's Deli, I Scream (for Ice Cream and Soy-Based Ice Cream Alternatives), Espresso Express, Hair and Nails by Patricia, Video-rama, Magazine Bistro, Grande Street Hardware, Homer's Oddities.

Mothers sat on benches pushing strollers, comparing dye jobs, complaining about au pairs. Little League went down in the park: kids in oversized caps, eager dads looking on in collarless linen shirts, mandals.

Teenagers smoked butts by the T stop. Set off stink bombs, cherry bombs, assessed each other with scrupulous eyes, imagining hidden treasures under folds of fat; got stoned, wore homemade tee shirts emblazoned with declarative ironed-on statements like "I Brake for Retards," "Jesus Hates Me!" and "Jesus Breaks Retards."

Kids hung at Amy's. She sold Italian ice, cards, comics. A local girl with blond bangs, stonewashed jeans. Liked the Dead and Zeppelin, still dropped acid once or twice a year. Seemed like someone who could have been a schoolteacher, but was too distracted by shapes in the lava lamp. Amy liked me because I stood alone, away from the other kids, examining the *Beckett Baseball Card Monthly* price guide with academic rigor. Same rigor, applied to my schoolwork, would have made me a B student at least, might have saved me from the very journey I was about to make.

I eventually transitioned from the card store to the teen smoking area. Amy wasn't doing much business anymore. Baseball cards were over. Rest of Grande Street was changing too. Same guy owned all the lots, increased rents in conjunction with rising property values in the area. Shops were pushed out by high-end restaurants, spas, boutiques, etc. Blockbuster underpriced and outstocked Video-rama. Espresso Express couldn't compete with Starbucks. Little League took a loss; soccer was the new sport.

Amy's survived because Amy, surprisingly, had good economic sense. Cards were over, true, but video games were a whole new market, as yet untapped in Quinosset. Nostalgic Amy still sold a few cards and comics, but rent money came from the first-person shooters, the high-megabit outlets for adolescent aggression.

Dan and I pulled up.

"I can't go in," I said. "You have to do it for me."

Suddenly overwhelmed by the prospect of facing Amy. Didn't want to let her down. She'd watched me all those years. How could I explain the bathrobe, unshaven face, bloodshot eyes? How can one apologize for not living up to expectations you might have only imagined they'd had for you?

"What?"

"I can't see Amy."

"Don't be a pussy."

"She'll know I'm all fucked up."

"Who cares?"

"Can't you just go in and sell the cards?"

"Fuck that. I won't even know what they're worth, if she's ripping me off or not."

"She's a fair woman."

"She likes you. She'll give you a better deal."

"I used to be in love with her."

"Don't be a fag."

"I just said I was in love with a woman. How can I be a fag?"

"You said you *used* to be in love with her. Now you're a fag because you won't go in."

His logic was sound.

"Fine. I'll do it."

Walked in, stood to the side while Amy scraped fluorescent ice. Mothers took me for a potential pedophile, stared me down. I grinned, flicked a comic book.

Store was different. Not just the display, but the store itself: depth of counters, length of walls, brightness of overhead lights. She'd expanded, taken over the lot next door. Extra space was filled by beanbag chairs and gaming consoles, eyes-wide preteens hooked in, headphoned.

Could have been a TV studio set—a space remade to resemble a rich kid's basement, but out of context—no accompanying hallways leading to kitchens where maids mope before ovens, mothers lean in—hand-over-receiver—listen to fathers sugar-croon to future wife twos, threes. Here everything sounded like bam, tweet, bing. Kid heaven.

But the kids didn't look happy. More like overworked employees: angry, beyond focus, dreaming digital fires, flames flaring up on their flatscreens. Trade the consoles for laptops, Italian ice for espresso, you got a de-stubbled version of the Wi-Fi Starbucks, where out-of-work office dads spent afternoons rewording resumes, cruising job sites.

"Can I get watermelon, sour apple, honey vanilla, green tea, banana, and black cherry," one of the kids said.

"I can't fit all those flavors in one cup," Amy said. "I can only do two at a time."

"Better give me a bigger cup."

His mother—black-clad, booty-less, attractive—texted on her cell phone and talked to another kid's mom at the same time.

"That's soooo Marni."

"Can you believe it? I mean, O-M-G."

Wondered how old they were, if they'd gone to QHS, class of '89, married twin varsity wrestlers who were now accountants, never left. Did they IM bored from home each day:

HoTMom713: I'm bored

KSpade4Eva: Let's get Brazilian waxes!

HoTMom713: But I have to drop the kids at karate

HotMom713: and then go to Spoga class!

Were they into bisexual furry porn? Did they write Martha Stewart in jail? Take pole-dancing classes? Watch

The Hills? Like to have sex during their periods with the lights on so they could watch the blood cover their husbands' bodies, imagine it was his, warm and dark, a sign of both life and impending death?

"I want them all," the kid said. "The healthy ones and the good ones. I need a balanced diet."

At "balanced diet" his mother snapped into action.

"What's going on?"

Gave Amy a look similar to the one she'd given me so I wouldn't molest her son.

"Your kid wants like ten flavors in his ice. Some are flavors I don't have."

"She doesn't have all the flavors," mom said to the kid.

"I want them," the kid said.

"Remember, we talked about this," mom said. "Sometimes you can't get everything you want." Then, to Amy, "Just give him the flavors you do have."

"I can only fit two in a cup," Amy said. "How about sour apple and watermelon?"

"That's it?" mom said.

"That's not a lot of flavors," the other mother added.

"What about green tea?" the kid said.

"Green tea is a type of tea," Amy said. "It's not an ice flavor."

"He needs his antioxidants," mom said.

"How about I add half a scoop of banana?"

Kid started crying.

"Fine," mom said, produced an Amex. "Whatev."

The new superheroes all had six-pack abs, no nipples. Evil bioterrorist was bearded, turbaned. I was shaking from the coke. Pages of the comic were glossy, felt nice. Tried to spin the comic on my finger. It fell.

"You bend it you gotta pay for it."

Picked up the comic. The mothers had ushered their sons back into the world, ready to crush it.

"It's me."

Amy gave me the once-over.

"Who's you?"

"Amy, it's me." Walked toward her.

"Eli?"

"Yeah."

"My God, you look like shit. What's with the bathrobe?"

"I don't know. It's comfortable."

Noticed the console kids noticing me, avoiding eye contact. Dug through my pockets, pulled out the cards.

"I'm sorry, I didn't mean . . ."

"I need to sell these." Laid them on the table.

"I don't really buy cards anymore."

"Please."

"You're broke."

"I know."

"I mean, you're not really broke, I guess."

"I'm rich-people broke."

"What happened?"

"We moved."

"Most people move eventually."

"I prefer to stay still."

"You're shaking like a leaf now."

"I could use the money."

Amy picked up the cards, gave them her attention. The players looked aged: uniforms out of fashion, of another era with their high stirrups, skin-tight pajama pants. Clemens was skinny, idealistic. Griffey Jr. sat smiley with stiff-brimmed cap and laundered jersey, an exemplar of Clintonian economic security. Neither knew about the future—steroid scandals, back injuries, etc.; they stood frozen in early '90s early season optimism.

"How's your mom?"

"Same old," I said, as there was no way to explain it.

Amy looked at me like she understood. I remembered something about a mother of her own, Alzheimered, eating Amy's savings in a rest home off Route 16.

"Those mothers," I said. "It wasn't like that when I was a kid."

"It was. You just don't remember."

She looked at the cards more closely. Knew she didn't need them, but she was like an older, enabling sister—part of her loved part of me. She loved the part of me I worried was gone.

"The Maris is the only one that's worth anything."

"Not the Shaq rookies?"

"The card market's gone down a lot in the past few years."

"I'll take anything."

"I still know some people at the conventions. I can give you seventy-five for the Maris, another seventy-five for all the rest?"

"People always said these things would be a *good investment.*"

"I'm being generous," Amy said, handed me the cash.

Felt like there was more to be said between us: loss of innocence, evil swiftness of time, unbeautiful demands of late capitalism. But mostly I wanted to get the fuck out of there, pretend it never happened, purchase cocaine.

"I have to go."

"You better come back. None of you guys visit anymore."

"Okay," I said, knowing I wouldn't.

• • •

Spent the afternoon into evening snorting, watching *The Surreal Life*. Dan liked Vanilla, but I was partial to the surprisingly sweet relationship between MC Hammer, now a reverend, and Emmanuel Lewis, still, physically, an eight-year-old. In the midst of all the cameras, superficiality, and surface-level grotesquerie, they'd managed something close to love.

Nikki showed up at ten p.m., done with work, shivering.

"Let's take a Jacuzzi."

Invitation wasn't meant for me. I left. Something about Nikki made me uncomfortable, anyway, the way she looked at me, secretly hated me. I'd always be a customer.

thirteen

Flashback:

V.O.:

I watched girls mostly, bodies partially illuminated by the dancing fire like dancers themselves upon a darkly lit stage.

Cut to: We're out by a bonfire, deep as we can get in the shallow suburban woods. Keg on the tail of a pickup, cops coming soon, kids all drunk, disorderly, everything in slow-mo. Me, John, and Matt sit stoned, simultaneously part of the performance and spectators, mumbling clichés halfheartedly—"This town sucks," "As soon as I graduate I'm out of here," "In college we'll get plenty of ass." Matt zones out with headphones. John flicks an issue of *High Times*. I watch the party, finger my forearm hairs, unconsciously clutch my gut, attempt to lick the chappedness from my lips.

V.O.:

There was something urgent in the way they stood, offered themselves to the few acceptable takers. It was as if now, with the moon obscured by trees, details of faces muted, body temperatures polarized— left side warmed by the fire, right side chilled by night—they could do nothing but cling to those larger bodies, football and basketball bodies; with their backs laid out across backseats, they could let themselves be smothered.

fourteen

Streetlamps on, lighting the icy sleet that fell in clusters like Cupid-antidote arrows on my weak helmet of hair. Thought about tomorrow's Thanksgiving football game I wouldn't be attending. Hadn't even gone while I was in high school, or the first year after grad, when everyone goes wearing sweatshirts of their colleges. They hug each other with rosy cheeks, as if there's nothing so great as to be outside in November and have that feeling you're really in New England, a feeling they have even though it's the suburbs and the team never wins.

When I was a kid, remember thinking it would be me one day, on the field, absorbing cheers. Maybe that's why I never went to the games during high school: because it wasn't me with dirt in my cleats, sweaty, perfect locks hanging out the back of my helmet. Would never be me on the field, or hugging long-lost friends in the stands, or as an old man with a faded letter jacket.

Too cold to walk home. No reason to go there anyway. Found myself moving toward Kahn's house.

The weather had killed all the plants, and the yard was flooded with dead leaves like in the years after Dad left, when Mom stopped hiring the landscapers. I could see the dining room through the window. Walls were bare. Wasn't expecting the same old decorations, but figured Kahn would have replaced them with mementos from his own life. Nothing. Just white walls. Felt like a statement, like Kahn's whole life amounted to an empty, tableless dining room; nothing led to anything else, even our objects were impermanent.

Our mezuzah was still in the doorway. A relic, not just from my old family, but from an old world where God existed. Rang the bell. No one came. Waited a minute, jiggled the handle. Door open. Walked in, began taking off my shoes before remembering it wasn't the rule anymore. Kahn didn't even have a doormat.

Music from the living room, jazz again. Expected a scene like last time: Kahn lounging, drinking scotch, watching porn. Kahn was in the same chair, but his body was obscured by a gyrating, thonged ass. Beth Cahill turned so I could see her right nipple in profile.

"You're just in time," Kahn said, enunciating like always, as if onstage, spotlit, spilling soul-juice on a thirsty audience.

"The darkness falls, and Dionysus emerges in all his ragged glory. In your case, my friend, that glory is particularly ragged on this chilly eve."

"He means the robe," Beth said. "He always talks like this when he's fucked up. He's my little fucked-up old man."

Then, turning to Kahn, "Aren't you?" in a baby voice. Thought she might pinch his cheeks. Maybe that's what he paid for.

"I may be in a chair, but I'm not in diapers yet."

"Weren't you at that party last night?" Beth said.

"Yeah, I was, wait . . . how do you two . . ."

"Know each other?"

"Internet, kid. Wave of the future."

"I advertise on the web."

"I know. I've seen your ad."

"Give the kid a dance, will you. He needs some loosening up."

"I've had an eventful day," I said. "Can we do some drugs first? Not sure I'm up for a dance right this moment."

"Fine with me," Beth said. Kahn stared at me, played air drums against his knees, winked. Beth was nothing like her FB pic. Thin trail of dark hair led from top of black thong to bellybutton.

Took out the eight ball I'd bought from Dan.

"So he comes equipped. That's why I like this guy, never empty-handed."

Cut lines on the coffee table that was actually our old glass coffee table we'd decided not to take because it was chipped.

"This is my house," I said to Beth, by way of explaining my presence. "My mother's coffee table."

"Man does not possess property," Kahn said. "But we screwed that up when we killed all the Indians."

"I used to live here."

"You used to jerk off here."

"That too."

"You guys," Beth said.

"No use thinking about what we used to do," Kahn said.

"That's all I think about," I said. "I can't even imagine the future."

"Flying cars," Beth said. "Nuclear war."

"Maybe I'll become a dancer," Kahn said. "In the hazy orange light of postapocalyptic dawn, I will dance across the earth."

Didn't smile when he said it. Instead punched himself in the kneecap. He was thinking about the past even though he'd said not to. The only places he'd ever walk: the past and the imagined, impossible future.

"In the postapocalypse, we'll all be dead," I said.

"Unless we build a society underground," Beth said.

"You two are young," Kahn said. "You'll never die. Don't let anyone tell you different. Only old people and cripples die."

"Let's get high," I said. Kahn nodded.

Coke, then Oxy. Lifted a framed photo that had been turned facedown on the side table. Erin and Natasha. An old pic because Erin has braces. Natasha is very young, but her face still looks like an adult's. Arms wrapped around Erin in protection.

"It's a nice picture."

"Put that away," Kahn said. "I don't want them to see this."

Beth stuck out her tongue, closed her eyes. Kahn turned up the music.

"Be a doll and shake around a bit."

Beth looked at the stereo, gave a sour face.

"You don't have to," I said.

"You could at least put on something I could dance to."

"This is dance music. You just got to feel that swing, baby."

Beth had no rhythm, but she tried. Stood on my mom's coffee table, shook her hips, tossed her hair, shoved her breasts in our faces. Kahn handed me a couple pills I could tell weren't Oxy.

"Pop these."

Done.

"What were those?"

"The big V."

"Valium?"

"Viagra. We've got a long night ahead of us."

He said, "Give the kid a dance, would ya?" and Beth straddled me so my face was level with her crotch.

Kahn watched. Got the sense from the way he met my eyes that Beth was a proxy for Kahn. That this was acting. That Kahn would have humped me himself, if I'd let him. I didn't mind. Part of me wanted to embrace his broken body, lick his wounds, let his roaming hands handle my maiden skin, touch me in the tender places, the sections serially ignored. I wanted to feel loved like that, and for him to feel loved. Like an older tainted lover you only want to fuck metaphorically, out of respect, partly out of pity.

Beth leaned over, brushed her chin against my shoulder. Big round nipples, pink, dry. Vintage-porn-style heavy knockers, the nipples like weights on some ticktock pendulum making me dizzy with rhythmic sway. Beth cupped her D cups, cooed, aimed them at my open mouth. Nipple rubbed against my stubble.

"Are you, like, his son or something?"

Ran a hand up my shirt, fingered my chest hair.

"Just a friend."

"So are you friends with Jennifer or something?"

"Not really."

"She's a cool girl."

"Yeah."

"This guy pays me more than anyone."

Kahn rubbed the top of his exposed cock with his palm, hard and fast, like he was sanding some wood (*Wood and Nail*, Klauset Films, 1991).

"I don't even always have to fuck him," Beth whispered. "I think he's just lonely. Gives me free drugs too."

"I thought you were a stripper?"

"Whatever gets me high."

"Me too."

Beth stuck a hand down my pants.

"You don't . . ."

"I don't mind."

"I'm sorry," I said, removed her hand. "Maybe we can just be friends."

"I don't need saving, if that's what you're into."

"Maybe I'm the one who needs saving."

"I'm certified in CPR. I used to be a lifeguard."

"I'm a good cook."

"I don't date clients."

"Good girl," Kahn said. "Now would you be so kind as to make your way toward me, darling."

"Yes, indeed."

Sucked up the last line of Oxy, said, "I'll trade you some coke for Oxy?"

"Just take a few," Kahn said, handed me the bottle.

Beth got on her knees, etc. Kahn closed his eyes.

"I should go."

Beth tried to say something, but her mouth was full.

"What?"

Removed Kahn's penis from her mouth.

"Don't stop," Kahn said.

"I'll tell Jennifer you say hi," Beth said, absentmind-edly rolled Kahn's foreskin up over the head.

"You're not circumcised?"

"Barbaric ritual."

"But you're a Jew."

"When it's convenient."

"I keep telling him to get it snipped. It would look so much nicer."

"There's only one rabbi I let touch my dick, and he died in '78."

"They're called mohels, guys who do the circumcision."

"That's Hebrew for sadist."

Beth played with his foreskin, folding it back and forth as his penis became flaccid.

"My hot dog's getting soggy."

"That's because it's not kosher," I said. No laughs. Beth resumed the BJ.

When I got outside, it was snowing.

fifteen

Hearing:

- When I was ten, my parents took me to a special-
  ist to get my hearing tested. Worried I was going
  deaf because I never paid attention to anything
  anyone said. Doctor took me into a dark room,
  gave me headphones. I listened to a series of
  beeps, raised one finger each time I heard one.
  Other tests too. Results were suspiciously conclu-
  sive. Nothing wrong with my hearing whatsoever.

sixteen

Things get blurry. Remember leaving Kahn's, hobbling out
the door into the flurry like an old hobo looking for a shelter he knows is just around the corner, if only he can find
it (*The Last DeMille of New Haven,* Sunshine Entertainment, 1961). Pictured Dad flicking on his fireplace with a
remote control. Mom on a plane, sitting next to some fatty,
scrunched low in her seat to become invisible, buying ten
magazines, not reading any. Benjy's eyes that studied me in
a way I was afraid to study myself: pale skin, pubey head-
curls, inflated gut, brown stains on my teeth. Alison Ghee,
somewhere in this town, head spinning like mine, body
tilting, reaching. Jeremy Shaw wasn't trying to hurt anyone,
just make it stop. His dad in that basement, smelling the
body long after it's gone, long after he's left the basement.

Stumbled through the street, still bathrobed, trying to
contain the Viagra-induced erection that had begun to emerge
in my pants. Thought about high school, how I stood off to
the side, watched the others dance that particular American
dance, steps learned from TV, eighties movies. Bad boys,
good girls, wrong side of tracks, part-time job, hand up shirt,
beneath bleachers, pierced ear, kissing in rain. Played my own
role beautifully. So beautifully I forgot it was a role. Got high

in the corner, woods, car. Showed up to class with bloodshot eyes, not caring who knew. They all knew, didn't care. Not even my parents. Not even myself. I had headphones on. Always wore headphones.

Walked to the high school, just to see what it looked like as the first snow fell. Field was mine if I wanted it. Fans cheered, clock ticked down. Dad waved from the stands. Stepped back in the pocket, couldn't find an open receiver, took to the open field, twisting and tumbling past the opposing defense. Danced beneath goalposts.

I lay down in the end zone, watched the snow hover and slowly fall, particles clinging to my body like dust accumulating on a flatscreen. Shut my eyes.

There was a woman—Beth Cahill's body, my mother's face—removing a bathrobe, kneeling beside me, gently kissing my neck. You are a stripper but you are also my mother. I cannot have sex with you. I am not your mother, she said. Face morphed into Mrs. Sacks's. Took off the robe, stuck her hand down my pants. You are not my mother, but you are still *a* mother. Actually, I *am your* mother, she said, and I realized it was Sheila Glent-Kahn. I was sucking milk from her nipple. Then she got on top, slowly rode me. I thought you were a lesbian, and she said, I am nothing but a figment of your thoughts. Alison was sucking my toe, singing a nursery rhyme about blackbirds. I was her mother. Then I heard Jennifer Estes speak softly. Not just thought I heard, knew I heard. "I know him," she said. "My mother said she'd take him," and I thought, I have so many mothers, I was inside them all, heart beating slower than theirs, in counterpoint, steady, until they cut that cord, we became separate songs. Felt myself lifted in the air, Sheila still on top of me, her sweat dripping, soaking my chest, football crowd cheering us on. When I woke up, I was on a strange couch.

seventeen

Places My Father Might Have Gone During Those Missing
Months from 1975 to 1976:

- Florida orange grove where he worked the fields,
  ripe as the oranges themselves, smiling, making
  nighttime love to young Cubana girl, Linda, large-
  eyed, soft-spoken, dressed in thin calico cotton,
  perfumed by the same fruit she diligently picks.

- Hitchhiking across America, soundtracked by
  Paul Simon, slim as a vegan hippie, sexually prowl-
  ing, perhaps contemplating an adventure in
  homosexuality.

- Los Angeles with his almost movie-star looks. He
  was an extra in four films, once got a speaking
  role. "Loaf of bread," his only line, no agent, no
  bleach-toothed Tennessee transplant waitress to
  give him the time of day, no talent for speaking,
  just staring into the distance with angry eyebrows.

eighteen

The couch was old; duct tape covered a couple holes. Recognized the room, couldn't place it. Wooden yellow bookshelf, some children's books, Bible, *The Poetry of Pablo Neruda*, two medical texts. On the floor: Sony PlayStation, games, DVDs. TV also Sony, not a flatscreen, but a nice one, LCD, high-def compatible, built-in DVD, VCR, couple years old at most. Above it hung a wooden cross.

Spanish came from the next room. Roused myself and entered. Jennifer Estes and Dan's maid drank coffee at a kitchen table. Jennifer in an EMT jumpsuit. Dan's maid in a maid outfit, not the sexy French kind, but what actual maids wear: oversized tee shirt, undersized spandex, sneakers. Felt like someone was sticking kabob skewers through one ear, pulling them out the other.

"What am I doing here?"

"You're an idiot," Jennifer said.

"I know."

Dan's maid poured coffee. Smell made me nauseous. Last thing I remembered was Jennifer's soft touch against my body.

"Did you and me?"

Jennifer smacked me.

"Do you remember anything?"

"No. Was I good?"

"What? No, we didn't . . . we didn't do that. Far from it. You were on the field when the game started. Passed out in the end zone."

"What?"

"I work the games as an EMT. You're lucky my mom was there. They were going to arrest you. They let her take you into her custody after I made sure you weren't going to die."

"What the fuck?"

Dan's maid was leaning against the stove, shoulders hunched, checking me out.

"Ropa vieja," the woman—who was also Jennifer's mother—said.

Jennifer looked puzzled.

"Inside joke," I said, lifted my coffee off the table, put it back down. Hands shaky—afraid I might spill. But I liked the feeling of steam in my face. Instead of lifting, thought it would be easier to lean my head over the coffee. When I tried I lost my balance, fell off the chair, onto the floor. Throat hurt. Overcome by an overwhelming desire to brush my teeth.

"Easy there," Jennifer said, too late.

"What was I doing on the field?"

"You tell us, Casanova. It looked like you were making sweet love to the air."

"Oh, no. I didn't have a . . ."

"Yeah, you did."

"The Viagra."

"What Viagra?"

"Kahn's Viagra."

"Who's Kahn?"

"The guy who gave me the Viagra."

"You're too young for Viagra," Mrs. Estes said.

"I know. I thought it was Valium."

"That's not good for you, either," Mrs. Estes said.

"From the way you slept, I wouldn't be surprised if you'd taken some of that as well. The marching band didn't even wake you up," Jennifer said.

"I don't know," I said, still on the floor. Wanted to lay my head down, leave it there for years, drift into dreams, listen to the two of them speak Spanish, understanding nothing but rhythm of mother/daughter patter. Jennifer would come home pregnant one day. They'd be happy, not sad; freaked out, but happy. House would fill with cribs, toys, slight smells of vomit, urine. Jennifer's body would grow round; she'd look good; she'd be a nurse, a mother. These things would come to define her. When she came home at night she'd be tired, but would feel that definition, same way we feel our arms and legs, same way she would have felt that baby growing inside her. Maybe she had a guy there. TV would suck them in. Fall asleep on the couch. In the morning an alarm would go off. I'd still be there, a fixture on the kitchen floor, never leaving, just listening.

"I have to go to work," Mrs. Estes said.

"Isn't it Thanksgiving?"

"Someone has to make the turkey. You think that woman knows how to use an oven?"

Mrs. Estes put on her coat.

"Goodbye," I said. "You are my savior."

"Get up off the floor. I'll show you a savior," she said, exited.

"What time is it anyway?" I asked Jennifer.

"Little after one."

"How am I going to get home?"

"Bus?"

"Can't afford it."

Opened my wallet to prove the point. All manner of things fell out, none of them money. Picked ripped receipts and old concert tickets from the floor.

"Guess I'll drive you. You live by the Orchard, right?"

"We moved."

Hoping that would explain everything, how I ended up at this station—bathrobed, strung out, Viagra-fied.

"I hope that explains my current behavior."

"Why would it?"

"I don't know."

"You seemed pretty fucked up before you moved."

"That's true."

"That was a weird message you sent me."

"I know."

"I felt bad for you."

"Do you still? I'm trying to get my shit together."

Rolled her eyes.

"Looks that way."

"Yeah."

Drove home. Snow had dissolved, dampened the left-over leaves. Everything almost brown.

"What's the deal with Alison Ghee?" I said.

"She's a ghost."

"I know. She told me."

"That's because you're a ghost too," Jennifer said.

"Don't be so dramatic," I said.

When we got to my condo, I said, "Thank you."

She didn't say anything, not "Don't mention it," or "No sweat," or "You're welcome," or "Call me when you clean up your act and we can culminate our twenties together, tangled in the dainty web of adult romance."

"Happy Thanksgiving," I said.

"Please take care of yourself," she said.

Decided to show my gratitude by baking Jennifer a pie. All we had were frozen blueberries, but I made do, thawing in the sink, working my hands through the dough, kneading out a nuanced, lightly sugared crust that would soften at her bite, spread gooey love to her taste buds.

Benjy showed up, asked why I wasn't dressed, went to wait downstairs. Clicked his cell shut when I got in the car. Wore the same agitated, nose-scrunched expression I'd seen a couple nights ago when we'd gone to get ice cream.

"Erin?"

"Yeah."

"Where's she?"

"Thanksgiving."

"I got that. I mean, literally, where?"

"Our old house."

"You invite her to Dad's?"

Wondered if Benjy needed Dad to approve of his life even though he didn't approve of Dad's.

No answer from Benjy.

"Can we drop off this pie?"

"No. We're late."

Looked out the window, tapped my feet. Benjy groaned. Pie in the backseat cooled while another man sidled up to Jennifer at home, warmed her. But Benjy was in worse shape than I was. He too needed pie.

"Dude," I said. "Big brother."

Tried to hang an arm around his slim shoulders, comfort him. Or at least to share misery, be companions in the drama of our fucked fam. But all I did was knock his hand from the wheel, causing the car to briefly swerve into on-coming traffic before Benjy instinctively fixed the situation, reeled us back from the precipice of death as he always did: with hard-won accuracy, ill humor, and lingering anger at his little bro.

"I was just . . ." I said.

Benjy said, "You were what?"

Must have been how he'd felt all these years when I'd rejected his futile affections, turned a deaf ear on the warmth beneath his cold concerns. Because truth is he could understand my predicament about as much as I understood his. We'd grown jaded in the same house, un-der the same rules, betrayed by the same slutty dad. But our insides were opposites, DNA mysteriously unmatched, problems unexplainable. Our discordant fraternity got to the root of the real human problem: the inability to express headspace content to one another, emerge empathetic, al-leviated.

Not sure what upset him so—the fact of our immigra-tion into Elm Condos? It was deeper than that. Maybe re-lated to some Erin experience I didn't understand, some force within the nature of relationships, and particularly his, that I would never understand, even if Benjy explained it in detail, shed public tears, recounted with stunning veri-similitude the exact words, gestures, and feelings they'd exchanged.

Then Benjy surprised me.

"You got any pot?"

"Since when do you smoke pot?"

"I don't. But these things can be pretty unbearable so-ber."

"I've been trying to tell you that for years."

"You were right," he said, like an admission of lifelong failure to attack the problem correctly. As if now he suddenly saw that we were the same, hopeless. That the only solution was to get high, giggle. Only solution: give up. Wanted to shout no, beg him to take it back, to restore confidence to the one person in my life who'd ever done anything right, the one person who gave me hope about myself, gave me someone to aspire to in my own way— less dickish than Benjy, but equally amour-skilled, equally esteemed in society's eyes (our mother's eyes, our father's eyes). Felt like pleading, "I'm the one that's wrong, I'm the fuckup in this family, no room for you, no space for two sniffling whiners—you keep rocking, let your momentum carry you over this spiky hurdle clear to the other side!"

Benjy looked at the clock, back at the road.

"We're late."

Stopped at Exxon to pee. Stood in line five minutes, got impatient, trekked back to the car with coffee.

"Not quite weed," I said. "But caffeine is still a drug."

A few minutes later, out of nowhere, Benjy asked if I'd ever fucked a woman.

"Yes. Just yesterday, in fact."

Benjy scratched an imaginary goatee, adjusted the rearview, the heat, scratched his arm, touched his turn signal.

"You've never fucked a woman," he said. "I can tell."

He and Kahn sensed things about my sexual history that even I wasn't aware of. They called me out, understood my pitiful past, my current wants.

"I've actually fucked two pretty recently. You'll never believe who the last one was . . ."

"I'm not talking about making love," Benjy said. "Not that weak sauce."

"Weak sauce?"

"Everyone and their mother's made love."

"Even our mother?"

"Our mother makes love all the time."

"Really?"

"It's so obvious. We've seen it in movies. Imitated. That doesn't count. Love is easy. Love is the default position."

"Not that easy . . ."

"I mean really fucked a woman. Capital F."

"As opposed to the other kind of fucking?"

Benjy couldn't hear. Like Kahn, he was in monologue mode, intent only on getting the words in line and out his mouth.

"Really slammed her. Violently. Bitten her. Sucked her blood."

"Brother, are you trying to tell me you're a vampire? Because that would be too much."

"What I mean is sex in which all your anger comes out, and after, you feel calm. But not during. You feel like a teapot that's been sweating on low heat for hours and now, suddenly, you've come to boil."

"Good metaphor, English major."

"Smoke is coming out of you. You're screaming. She's just taking it, taking it. Taking it and screaming too. Not your name. Not out of pleasure. Just screaming for the goddamn hell of it. Because she can. Because human beings have bodies and are able to scream and can make these incredible noises if they really want to. Maybe because it hurts, too, hurts but also feels good, hurts because it's life, and real, and you can feel it."

"I guess not," I said. "Definitely haven't fucked."

"Then you don't know what I'm talking about."

"Shit, dude," I said. "Fuckin' A, man," I added, meaning, "I'm alone, you're alone."

Passed pastures that weren't golf courses: real America. Trees bare, leaves everywhere.

"You brought the apple cake?" Benjy said.

"Forgot."

Turned up the radio. Benjy turned it down, off, back on again.

"Erin's room's my old room," he said.

nineteen

Note About Architecture:

- When he got remarried they bought property out in Sudbury. Dad designed the new house himself, like the old one. Something in the architecture gave the impression that the two had been sprung from the same DNA, siblings.

- First house was a first child—possibly a mistake, but born from tremendous passion.

- Second house was a second child. More money pumped in, less undivided affection.

- One is a ranch home backdropped by Jewish suburbia, the other a five-level villa nouveau in the heart of goyish, pastoral New England.

- Look closely, you'll see they hold themselves the same: layout, location of bathrooms, height of sinks, etc.

- First time I went it was like being in one of those
  dreams where you're in your house, but it's not
  your house.

twenty

Men in the living room, though the area so spacious, the crowd so mesmerized by football on the 58-inch Panasonic HD plasma, that neither "living" nor "room" accurately described the situation. Women in the kitchen. Benjy and I sat with the men, even though I wanted to check out the food.

The men: Dad, Uncle Sal, Pam's two brothers, Steve and Doug. Steve and Doug were jocks with firm handshakes, knuckles like large marbles. Co-owned a store that sold men's big and tall suits, had one of those stupid local TV spots where they'd get an ex-Celtic to say the suits are a "real score!" The jingle: "Steve and Doug, big and tall, come see them in the Natick Mall . . . You'll have a ball!"

Steve and Doug thought they were hot shit, decked out in matching gray double-breasted suits that accentuated the width of their shoulders and the fact that they didn't have necks. First thing Steve did upon shaking my hand was pat me on the stomach, tell me I was ready for a big and tall. Come in for a measuring.

Dad asked if we wanted anything from the kitchen.

"I'll take a beer," I said.

Steve smacked me on the stomach again. Doug laughed. Pam came back with apps, beers, said, "Hi, Eli."

Put the tray down, kissed my cheek, winked, tried for my affection, which I somehow couldn't give, though I wanted to, knew she was kind, innocent, a real person who also happened to be married to my father.

Watched the game. Sal sat silent. He'd been a commie, lone employee of *Journal Rouge*. Then his daughter Julie was killed on 9/11. She'd become a stockbroker to rebel against her hippie parents, taken a job at the World Trade: the ultimate fuck-you to Uncle Sal. Aunt Erica left Sal shortly after Julie was killed, because a marriage can rarely survive the life of a child, let alone the death of one. Sal retired the newsletter. He now approved of Bush's war on terror.

These days Sal didn't do much of anything. My father supported him financially. He sat with his head in the newspaper; couldn't look at the house's interior, a paean to materialism, paid for by the same capitalist blood money he now accepted and I had been severed from.

My uncle Ned had been the star of earlier Thanksgivings. My coconspirator, telling me stories about taking peyote with Indians in Arizona, smoking hash with Indians in India. Sometimes brought lady friends, called them "lady friends." Gave me a *Playboy* for my bar mitzvah. Then he got diagnosed, started dying. I biked to his house every Thursday to watch Discovery Channel.

Didn't go to the funeral. Too much of a pussy—afraid of coffins, crying, not crying, bodies buried under dirt for eternity. Everyone said it was so nice, Ned would have liked it, etc. Dad came back to the house for the first time since he'd left. Hung around for a bit eating lox, looking at Mom, nothing he could do, though he could have held her, kissed her, made coffee, made love (*The Sharp Points of a Flower*, Dreamworks, 2002), and maybe he did when no one else was around.

Did go to Julie's funeral, though I hadn't really known her, and she'd locked me in a closet when I was five. Drove out to Albany a week after the towers came down. When a plane flew overhead thought I could see all the cars veer a tiny bit, drivers' eyes following the flight pattern.

At the funeral Benjy whispered she'd flashed him a tit once at Passover. Couldn't help imagining her tits even though she was my cousin, dead. Crowd was filled with old lefties who knew less of what to make of 9/11 than I did, but one thing was clear: death is the same in all forms. Cancer, terrorists, suicide, etc.—dead remain dead, grieving remain grieving.

Doorbell rang.

"Who else is . . ." I started to whisper to Benjy, stopped short when I heard that voice, ringing like a siren.

"Pamela Weiss-Schwartz," Mrs. Sacks said. "Look at you."

Pam led the Sackses into the living room, all three. Had no idea they'd been invited. But Dad and Mark were poker buds, old pals, the kind of new-money Jews who posed on sailboats and coughed cigar smoke just to prove that in post-ethnic America, everyone had the right to act like a WASP. Plus Pam and Mrs. S. were pals, shared a personal trainer with titty-pecs and garish tats that they could gawk over together on girls' night.

Mark more imposing than ever in an adroitly tailored Steve and Doug big and tall. Grinned like a guy who'd spent a summer at sex camp, called my father "big guy," ruffled his hair. In a swift motion, he scooped a pig in a blanket with one hand, held out the other for high-fives.

"Score?"

"Pats up twenty-one seven," Doug said.

"Shit," Mark said. "I got fifty bucks on Dallas to cover."

"You bet against the Pats?" Dad said.

"Gotta go where the money is, my friend. No way the Cowboys aren't coming within ten in Dallas on Thanksgiving Day."

"Smart man," Steve said, high-fiving Mark for the second time in a minute.

"Beer me," Mark said to Dad, who looked at Pam, who went to get Mark a beer.

Table could have accommodated twice as many. Dad sat at the head. Mark at the other end between Doug's wife Kathleen and Steve's wife Judy.

The twins, Paul and Cole (named after Pam's favorite singer, Paula Cole), were alone at the kids' table, no doubt preparing to crawl under the grown-ups' table, tie everyone's shoelaces together. Beautiful children in a way Benjy and I had never been. We'd been handsome, adorable even: dark curls, pudgy cheeks. But they were gentile beautiful: blond, confident. As if the stork—confused by Dad's Sudbury palace—had screwed up, dropped Aryan babies on the doorstep.

Went into the kitchen to check on the food. Pam poured wine from a bottle into a crystal chalice.

"Hi, Eli."

"Anything I can do?"

"If you could take the sweet potatoes out of the oven and put them in a serving bowl that would be great."

"No prob."

Opened the oven. Sweet potatoes weren't done. Secretly bumped the temp to 475, so they'd char on the outside how I liked them. Pam walked back with the wine.

I hit booze gold. Literally: full bottle of Goldschläger. Swigged.

Pam tapped her wineglass.

"I just wanted to say a few words about how nice it is to have everyone here, under one roof, in this house. All the people who are so important to us."

"Cheers to Pam," Steve said, raising his glass. "Now let's get to the noshing."

"Noshing means snacking," Benjy said. "We already did that with the pigs in blankets."

"Whatever," Steve said.

"Let Pam talk," Dad said.

"The food will come in a minute," Pam said. "But I just thought since it is, after all, Thanksgiving, that we could all go around and say one thing that we're thankful for."

"But we're Jews," Mark said. "We don't do this sort of thing."

"It does seem a bit goyish," Judy added.

"I'll start," Dad said. "I'm thankful for my sweet wife and our two wonderful sons."

"You have four sons," Mark reminded him.

"The other two I'm not so thankful for," Dad said, laughed, so everyone would know he was joking.

"He's joking," Pam said, concerned.

"I'm joking," Dad said, insincere.

"I'll joke you," Steve said, idiotically.

Doug picked his nose.

"Well, I'm thankful for the fifty bucks I'm about to win on this football game," Mark said.

"And I'm thankful for the fifty bucks you're about to lose when the Pats win," Steve said.

"Boys," Pam said, like she would say it to the twins.

"Doug and I are thankful for having such wonderful relatives to invite us over for Thanksgiving," Kathleen said.

"And I'm just thankful for everything," Judy said. "With all that's going on in the world these days, in the Middle East, and Iraq."

Everyone got somber. Or at least, with the exception of Uncle Sal, who was already somber, they pretended to.

"Maybe we should have a moment of silence," Kathleen said.

We did. Figured Mrs. Sacks was thinking about Eddie Barash, Benjy about Erin, Dad about Pam. Already drunk, imagining the body that lay in wait when the guests had dispersed, twins gone to bed. He'd been such a good husband, backing her up on the thank-yous, not letting Steve be an ass. No one was thinking about the dead and dying in Iraq. And what about Israel—our own people—Tay-Sachs carriers the lot of us: killing, dying?

"Now can we eat?" Mark said.

"Yes," Pam said, forgetting we were still supposed to be offering thanks.

"Wait," Sherri interrupted. "I still haven't said what I'm thankful for."

I thought: Oh, fuck.

"Well, go ahead, sweetie," Pam said.

Mrs. S. and I made brief, brow-raised eye contact.

"I'm thankful I have two wonderful parents who love each other so much that they can look past each other's shortcomings, and make their marriage work even after . . ."

"Thanks, sweetie," Mark cut her off.

"The sweet potatoes," I said, got up to go check.

On my way, I said, "Hey, guys," to the twins.

"Hey, pothead," Paul said.

"Hey, stoner," Cole said. "Gotten stoned lately?"

"He's stoned now."

"You guys don't even know what stoned means."

"You're a drug addict."

"Who told you that?"

"Everyone."

"Fuck," I said.

"You said fuck," they said.

"Shh . . ."

"Eli said *fuck*," they screamed. The table turned to look at us.

"Eli!" Pam said.

"Eli's an expert on fucking," Sherri said.

"Sher, please," Mrs. Sacks said.

"Eli, you big dog," Steve said.

"I'm not an expert," I said.

"Got that right," I imagined Mrs. Sacks mumbling.

"Yup," Sherri said. "He'll fuck just about anything. Just like you, Dad."

"Stop saying fuck," Pam said.

"Fuck, fuck, fuck, fuck, fuck," the twins said.

"You fucked my daughter?" Mark said.

Uncle Sal stared out the window.

"Are you kidding?" Sherri said.

"This is awesome," Steve said. Doug nodded.

"He fucked your wife, you schmuck," Sherri said.

"You fucked Eli?" Steve said to Judy.

"I did no such thing," Judy said.

"She didn't," I offered.

"Not her—*Mom*," Sherri said.

Mrs. Sacks clutched her chest the way Jewish women do when they want you to think they're having heart attacks.

"Fuck, fuck, fuck, fuck," the twins said.

"Enough!" Pam yelled.

Too late. Mark had walked over to my side of the table.

"You ruined the sanctity of my marriage," he said, punched me in the face.

Fell backward, taking Sherri along with me, who then knocked over one of the twins. My uncles held Mark back. Twins were still on the ground, wincing in pain or faking it. Sherri on the ground too, sitting, laughing like it was the funniest thing she'd ever seen. Pam crouched above her boys, kissed their boo-boos. Sal sipped water, inspected the chandelier.

"That fucking hurt," I said.

"There's more where that came from, you little shit," Mark said.

Mrs. Sacks was crying. No one made a move to comfort her.

Benjy stood in the corner on his cell, talking to Erin, telling her about his insane family, it wasn't his fault, nothing was his fault, nurture had ruined his nature. A different kind of brother would have had my back, punched Mark's mug until it spurted beet-red blood.

"This is insane," I said, walked away, through the kitchen, out to the yard. Swimming pool tarp covered in leaves like a booby trap. Yard was huge: trees, tree house. Wondered if he'd built the tree house himself, if the twins had handed him tools, worn toy hard hats.

I deserved the black eye.

Dad came outside, looked around at his own property as if he'd never seen it before. Looked at me with the same expression.

"I'm trying not to be angry at you," he said.

"And I'm trying not to be angry at you."

Dad shrugged. Not the confrontational type.

"I told Mark Sacks he had to leave."

"Probably a good idea."

Pause.

"So you . . ." He looked back down at the ground.

"What?"

"So you had sex with his wife?"

"Sort of."

"Sort of?"

"I guess I did."

"She's a beautiful woman."

"I guess."

"A bit old for you maybe."

He almost chuckled. Reminded me of being a kid, when he wanted to punish me but found my act-outs too amusing. Like when I peed on Mom's satin pumps, semi-on-purpose.

"And married," I said.

"And married."

Kicked the dirt, thought about what my character would say if we were in a movie. Tell his father he was so fucking sad. Talk about Mom, the divorce, how these things affected him, insulated him. Plus the drugs, computer screen, hours upon hours of TV that shaped an alternative reality in which he existed. But ready. Ready now to face the real world, with a clear head and empty, open heart. Ready but he needed help. Ready to *decide* to be ready. He wouldn't use those exact words. Good actor could convey that stuff with a nod, flick of the eyes. Audience gets the gist, sympathizes. Father reaches over, pats his shoulder, hugs, cries, kisses the swelling bruise above his eye. In an indie, Dad might not touch him at all. He reaches his hand, lets it linger above the boy's shoulder as the boy faces the horizon (in the film it is sunset, summer), lingers with the intention of consolation, not the ability to provide it.

Dad and I weren't actors. I did want his hand on my back. More so, wanted to ask about money, could I have some. Didn't seem like the right moment.

"Well, you really fucked up Thanksgiving," he said.

"I fuck everything up."

Dad paused, all calculated, trying to act, shimmer in the spotlight, like moonlight, which was actually the automatic security light. Or maybe he didn't. Maybe I just wanted him to—wanted him to have depth, wanted his physical actions to hint at complex interiority, torn-apart insides, longing for a lost family that, in reality, he must have hardly missed with his better life, better wife, Hallmark-quality spawn.

He said, "I don't know. I don't fucking know. I mean I know and I don't, but mostly I don't." Looked at the sky like someone was up there, steering.

"Your eye okay?"

"When you disappeared for those six months, where did you go?"

"What are you talking about?"

"You know, in 1975, when you disappeared."

"Sal is crazy. He doesn't know what he's talking about. I never went anywhere."

I shivered. Dad nodded toward the door. We walked inside. Hand didn't grace my shoulder. Don't know if it lingered over it, as he stood behind me, holding the door open.

Pam gave me frozen peas to put on my eye. Aside from the Sackses, everyone was still there, though the twins had been fed, pushed aside, enough trouble for one night. Turkey on the table, cold. Sweet potatoes—not bad. Nobody ate much. Wine had been put away.

"Pats are looking good this year," Steve said.

"By the second half Belichick figures out their defense," Dad said.

Judy said, "If you guys are gonna talk about football, then we'll talk about *Desperate Housewives*. Who else watches?"

I watched. I was one of them: desperate. Imagined my neighborhood was like the fictional one—filled with sexy, lonely women looking for a little action, venues for their winter tans.

"I can't stand that Lynette," Pam said.

"Eva Longoria's hot," Steve said. Doug nodded. Uncle Sal ate slowly. Four years since I'd seen him. Couldn't remember what he'd been like before, probably because his family never came to Thanksgiving. Do remember Mom saying, "They think they're better than us." Didn't know why: we had a bigger house, nicer cars.

Only been to their house once, age eleven. Dad had taken Benjy and me to the Baseball Hall of Fame. One last bonding experience before the divorce.

On the way home we'd stopped at Uncle Sal's. House was small, no paved driveway. Adults drank tea instead of coffee. Julie put on the TV. Watched *Sesame Street* even though we were much too old for it, because they didn't have cable. Next time I saw them was four years later, year following the divorce, when everyone came for Passover at Dad's new house, and Julie allegedly revealed her sweet pink nip to Benjy. She was older than Benjy, conservative. I think the flashing was inspired by the house—by a foreignness in the architecture—the same foreignness that drew her into the worlds of high finance and eternal silence.

Pam hurried out dessert. Apple pie, my blueberry pie, brownies, ice cream, other stuff. Pies were decent. Dessert was quick. No one took coffee. It was cold, dark. People wanted to get home. Not a cozy house. Automatic fireplace, but I couldn't picture it warming anyone as they cracked chestnuts, sipped mulled cider, book in hand, ready to doze on the couch, awake to light dew on the windows, delicate aroma of embers. The house was like an anorexic mother—sexy but dysfunctional, all ribs and angles, no bosom. Meant for warm seasons. Would have made sense in Florida.

"I think we're gonna get going," Benjy said.

"Okay," Pam said. "So nice having you boys."

"Take care," I said to Uncle Sal.

He leaned over, kissed my cheek. Minty breath, dry lips.

"If you ever feel like making it to Albany, you're more than welcome."

For a moment considered joining Sal in mellow-mourning, a monk's life, cigarette-free, walks in the woods, growing my own tomatoes.

Dad said, "I'll walk you guys out."

Stood in the doorway while Benjy got his coat. Good moment to ask about money. No time for politics. Best shot was to play dumb, ask straight out for cash, not mentioning I only needed it because my last few installments had never arrived.

"Can I have some money?"

"I can't give you any more money."

"Why not? I know you can afford it. You're rich."

"I'm not rich," he said, because rich people never admit to being rich.

"You are," I said.

"That has nothing to do with it."

"So what then?"

"I won't support your drug habits anymore."

"I won't spend it on drugs."

"Eli." He said my name in a way that seemed to explain his entire argument.

"C'mon, Dad, for old time's sake."

"You should be nicer to Pam. She really wants you to like her."

"I know. Look, I won't spend it on drugs, okay?"

"I don't believe you."

"I want to buy my girlfriend a birthday present."

"Mrs. Sacks?"

"Someone else."

"Who is she?"

"Just this girl. Look, I just need some . . . I just . . ."

"Why don't you just get a job?" he said.

Obvious solution. Maybe it was. Simple economic law: work, get paid.

"Who would hire me?"

Benjy came back with his coat. Dad shook Benjy's hand, then mine, slipped something into my palm.

Only a twenty.

"Better then nothing," I said to Benjy. "How much you get?"

"More," he said. "I deserve it more."

"I know."

Road was dark, mostly empty. No lights. All that existed was the car itself, lit orange by the dashboard, clock blinking 12:00, never set, Benjy's eyes on the road, my eyes on Benjy, watching as he steered with just two fingers, making infinitesimal corrections as the road turned and widened like a living being.

twenty-one

Spaghetti Bolognese:

- He made it every Wednesday when Mom was at tennis.

- First he cracked a beer, tuned to ZLX (Boston's only classic rock!), rolled up his sleeves, undid his tie, aproned himself.

- I popped the tab on a root beer.

- Benjy was in his room doing homework.

- "Don't you have homework too?"

- Said I did it already.

- A recipe handed down from his father, who got it abroad in World War II, at least that's what he told me.

- An inauthentic version of an authentic Italian dish.

- But Dad made the sauce carefully, methodically, taking time to evenly chop the onions, tear the basil, simmer low and slow, stirring occasionally, salting to taste.

- Each time it tasted different. Not better or worse. Just different.

- After, we'd watch some seasonal sporting event, rooting silently, horizontal like men who deserved their rest.

- Even in this time-tweaked nostalgic dream, we don't share anything but space, occasional head nods; wind whips at the window; Mom arrives clucking about women we don't care about, whose mother is remarrying a gentile, what the Samuels kid got on his SATs, and wasn't there a game on last night?

twenty-two

Mrs. Estes answered the door.

"Hola," I said, like an idiot.

"Hi, Eli." She looked tired. Hair pulled back, forehead-skin stretched.

"Happy Thanksgiving."

"There's dessert on the table. Apple tart's my best."

Adults in the dining room, slouched in chairs, loosening belts. One guy asleep at the table. *SportsCenter* danced noiseless on the wall-mounted Sony. Athletes mocked us: the slovenly, stomachs drooping like sad eyes; or the women: so skinny, plastic straws bent in all the wrong places.

Wife Three had wine-stained lips. Sat on Dan's dad's lap in purple velvet (low cut, one freckle on the lip of her cleavage) sipping champagne, feeding him chocolate covered strawberries while he stroked her hemline. She fed him without looking at him. Gaze wandered the party, fixing for a moment on the TV, passing to other guests, walls, windows; legs crossed, bouncing slightly, right foot bent down like a ballerina's. Mascara had caked, flaked off her lashes. It stuck in little pieces to her cheek, resembled one of those tear tattoos people in prison get to commemorate their dead homeys. Dan's dad had his eyes closed. Licked his lips, then Wife Three's finger, pretending to bite her wedding ring. When he opened his eyes he saw me.

"Big E. Hit up that dessert cart."

"No thanks. I'm stuffed," I said, rubbed my stomach for emphasis.

"C'mon, buddy, there's still some apple tart left. Wife's specialty."

"Too full."

"More leftovers for me, then."

"Dan around?"

"He's down there with his chica."

"Dan's quite the stud these days."

"A real Adonis."

"Right," Wife Three said. "Like father like son."

"We're all the same. Wild animals in the kingdom of love."

Scratched the air with imaginary bear claws. Wife Three pretended not to notice.

"What happened to your eye?" she said.

"I was fighting for my kingdom."

"Thatta boy," Dan's dad said.

"I'm gonna go find Dan," I said, walked toward the basement. Passed people I'd known once, former friends of my parents, members of the temple. They kept talking. Didn't interrupt. Offered silent condemnation: "You were all at my bar mitzvah. You told me I was a man. You were lying."

Lights off downstairs. European techno pulsed steady like a robot heartbeat. Two figures merged in the center of the bed. Hardly resembled the way people fuck in movies. Facing each other, backs straight, legs bent like squatting baseball catchers, together a multi-limbed Hindu god

(*Buddha of Pittsburgh*, Enscott LLC, 1995). Movement so slow it felt like I was watching through a strobe light. Large tattoo in black ink covered Nikki's back. Not meant to be anything specific, just curving lines, dipping and bending with her body. Resembled a page of sheet music rippled by a fan from across the room. Dan's eyes closed, face void. Like Buddha beneath the tree, body light, unweighted by thought, almost floating on her rippling body, not like a boat, more like buoy: bobbing, forgiving.

Faces inched toward each other like they were leaning in to whisper. Muscles in Nikki's back tightened; tattoo changed form. Dan's eyelids fluttered like a butterfly's wings. He yelled, "YOWZA!"

Stepped back onto the stairs, waited five minutes (timed on my cell), knocked on the wall.

"We'll be up in a minute."

"Dan. It's Eli."

"Hold on."

Waited in the stairway, scratched the skin on my hand until I drew blood, rubbed the blood on Dan's wall.

"Okay, come in."

He wore a white terry-cloth bathrobe, the kind you get in hotels, only his had "Daniel" in gold stitching. Loading a bong. Nikki sat next to him on the bed in an oversized basketball jersey that functioned as a nightgown.

"Nice robe."

"That means a lot coming from a robe expert like yourself."

"I know a thing or two."

"What happened to you?" Nikki said.

"I don't know. Maybe I was conceived by a weak sperm" (*Bill Hicks: Sane Man*, Sacred Cow Productions, 1989).

"I meant what happened to your eye?"

"Oh. Got punched in the face."

Dan lit the bong, coughed.

"You need one of these."

"Was thinking of something a little stronger."

"No doubt."

"Heard about your football game mishap," Nikki said. "What were you doing on the field, anyway?"

"Reliving old glories?" Dan said.

"Something like that."

"I heard they were going to arrest you for indecent exposure," Nikki said.

"Didn't I have all my clothes on?"

"It was still indecent."

"Call of the wild," Dan said, beat his chest, howled. Bong hit made me hyperaware of my black eye. Thought I could feel the color changing, turning blue, swelling fast.

"I'm feeling light-headed."

"Good shit, huh?"

"I guess."

"So who all's gonna be at this party?" Nikki said.

"'Dem hos," Dan said.

"You're retarded," Nikki said.

"You know you love it," Dan said. He was cutting up coke on the coffee table. She scratched his back. Dan sucked up a line.

"Take two," he said. "For your eye."

"So generous," Nikki said.

"I have twenty bucks."

"Keep it," Dan said. "It's the holidays."

"Look at old Santa over here," Nikki said.

"It's Thanksgiving," I said. "Not Christmas."

"I'm Jewish, anyway," Dan said.

"All you Jews," Nikki said as I did my snorting. "And

what are you thankful for?"

"Less than I should be," I said.

"You should be thanking me," Dan said.

"Thanks."

"Give me some of that," Nikki said, sat up.

"Let's get out of here," Dan said.

"I don't want to see all those people," I said.

"I have more coke, too," Dan said. "And booze. Let's take some tequila shots."

"Okay," I said, rolled off the bed, onto the floor, spread my limbs like I was making a snow angel.

twenty-three

Uncle Ned:

- Uncle Ned's TV was an old Panasonic with wood-colored plastic frame. The color green came out blue.

- TV was so old it didn't have a place to plug in a cable cord. He'd had a guy come, attach a device.

- "Why don't you just get a new TV?"

- He said, "What's the point?"

- He in his bed, me on a living room armchair I'd dragged into the bedroom, left there because Ned said it wasn't like he hung out in the living room anymore.

- By the end, they had him hooked up to morphine. Wanted to die at home, not in a hospital, but in his own bed, between the sheets where he'd lain with a hundred women (so he said), some beautiful, some less so; each markedly singular. He'd watched them scream, cry, dig nails into his flesh, whisper demons in his ear, sleep across his chest.

- Ned would tell me about these women, speech between poetry and gibberish. Sometimes he'd turn down the morphine. Words took on the clarity of a ringing bell: precise, mournful.

- Usually he'd pump up the drugs, become less coherent, quoting Lennon, Lenin, Lenny Bruce. Sometimes whispering, often veering into the incomprehensible, where the words lost meaning, simply became sounds, sounds of a failing body, still alive, pushing forward, even so.

- Watched the hawk tear its claws into the field mouse, blood squirting, eyeball crushed by its beak.

twenty-four

Things I Remember:

1. Tequila tastes like urine mixed with fire.

2. Dan's basement is a merry-go-round, complete with childhood pictures of Dad running through his own backyard naked, mammoth dick between his legs, slapping against his inner thighs.

3. Upstairs. Standing of my own accord, poor posture.

"Wife Three," I say, "you know Mary was getting some on the side when God knocked her up."

"Get him out of here," Dan's dad says.

"His brother was such a good kid," someone else says, about me.

Touch Wife Three's arm, but it isn't soft.

"I thought you were Jacob, but you are Esau," I say.

4. Traffic lights are the same colors as Christmas.
   Need to bend my legs in order to lie down in the
   backseat. Nikki has her hand down Dan's pants.
   Not helping his driving.

5. The music is inside my colon but I am constipated.
   Recognize some faces. Mostly look the same
   as they did at graduation. "I am constipated," I
   say. Lucky. Otherwise I'd shit my pants.

6. I am on TV. On TV on the football field with an
   erection and a cop is shaking me, laughing. On
   TV and also at a party. In two places at once. I
   am being hoisted in the air. Am I God?

7. "Schwartz, Schwartz, Schwartz!"

8. "Shelly Peters," I say, because I see her in the
   kitchen smoking a cigarette, black tights clinging to her thighs. "You gave me love once when I
   needed it, when the world spun, and it's spinning
   now, let me suck your nipple like a pacifier?"

9. Outside on the ground. Cold. Other eye hurts.

10. Where are you, Jeremy Shaw? What has
    happened to your body? Have you been eaten,
    crapped out, used to fertilize dying grass? Am I
    lying in your liver, swimming through your
    bowels, crying in your eyes?

11. In a car, smoking crack.

12. Home. Home is where the heart is but I can't get in so I climb through the window.

13. Bloody, covered in glass. A pain in my leg like no pain I have ever experienced.

twenty-five

So I guess we drank tequila, took more bong hits, blew lines of coke, Oxy. Dan said, "You sure you want to come to this party?" I said something incoherent, either "Fuck me up the ass, my balls are hungry for maiden fair and bleached blond hair," or "Fuck you, fat ass, I'm still hungry from Thanksgiving and I want to eat pussy," depending on if you're listening to Dan or Nikki. Either way, they both agree I wanted an eligible female to accept my touch in an abandoned bedroom or locked bathroom.

Went upstairs where the Thanksgiving party was winding down. Wife Three sat on the couch with her girlfriends. They drank cognac, watched the Thanksgiving episode of *Grey's Anatomy*. I grabbed Wife Three's arm, screamed unintelligible theological musings. Dan's dad saw me harassing his wife, instructed Dan to assist me in vacating the premises. Dan dragged me out to the car.

In the car, passed out then woke up because Nikki was giving Dan road-head while he smoked a joint, and he was swerving all over the road. Cop pulled us over, but the cop was Jason Newmark, who'd graduated a few years ahead of Dan. Used to sell thirty packs of Miller High Life to underclassmen for thirty bucks, insisting it really was "the champagne of beers," he wasn't ripping them off. He was going to arrest us, but Dan slipped him a fifty. Newmark said, "Have fun, you fuckups."

Dan found a parking spot in the middle of a neighbor's driveway. When he slammed the car into park I woke up, said, "Now I am a nomad. I used to be a first baseman. It was Little League but it still counts for something."

"This guy's fucking crazy," Dan said, meaning it as a compliment. Got out of the car. I fell on the ground. Dan helped me up. Nikki's makeup was messed. She looked in a hand mirror, as if she was going to fix it, didn't bother.

"Your rich friends better not give me shit."

"It's not high school anymore," Dan said. "We're all the same now."

"You're wrong," Nikki said. "We used to be the same. Now we're different."

"She's right," I said. "We don't belong."

"We haven't even gone in yet," Dan said. Went in.

Party was bumpin'. Dan said, "Shit is off the heezy." Nikki said, "You know you're white, right?"

Stood leaning against a wall trying to keep my balance.

"Holy shit," John said. "It's Schwartz."

"I'm the Ghost of Christmas Past."

"Good to see you're raging."

"What choice do I have?"

Two high school girls walked by wearing black halters, speaking into cell phones, strutting.

"I know them like I know myself."

"You've been hanging out with high school girls?" John said.

"Niiiice," Matt said.

"I get older, they stay . . ." Dan started to say, but Nikki nudged him, said, "Just shut up."

Bobby Feld walked by trailing the girls, turned to us, said, "Whassuuup."

"Schwartz," John said, "why the fuck haven't you visited us?"

"Visitation is for model prisoners only," I said.

"You've been in jail?" Matt said.

"Not jail, Yale. He goes to Yale."

"It's true. I'm an econ major," I said.

"You're a major pain in my ass," Dan said.

"Let's get high," John said.

"I'm already at Pluto," I said. That's what we used to say in high school when we were so stoned that getting more stoned would be a waste of pot.

"Pluto's not a planet anymore," Matt said. "I saw it on the news."

"Then I'm already at Neptune."

"Pluto's still there," John said. "It didn't disappear. They just changed what it was called."

"Shit changes," I said.

Walked into the main room. "Here's the celebrity," someone said, with regard to me. On the plasma: home video from that morning's football game. I lay on my back in my bathrobe.

"At least your dick looks big," Dan whispered.

Two cops and two refs stood over me, deciding, chuckling, pretending to be serious. Jennifer Estes walked over, knelt, held my hand, felt for a pulse, stroked my hair, looked up at the cops. Not laughing. She said something, then they said something, then the cops helped her put me on a stretcher, carried me away. Crowd cheered.

adam wilson

Crowd at the party cheered too, chanted my name. QHS had won, and two former players said I should be the new mascot (Boner Man?), hoisted me on their shoulders. Raised my arms, gave the "V." Then wobbled and the players put me down.

Stumbled into the kitchen. Saw Shelly Peters, my first vagina. She introduced her boyfriend. I mentioned the night of pure adolescent delight we'd shared, bodies ripe, unsullied, emanating delicate aromas like baby chimpanzees or scented liquid hand soap. Her boyfriend didn't punch me until I asked if I could suck her nipple. Tossed me into the backyard. Passed out. John and Matt left me there while they tried and failed to convince girls they were different than they were in high school: mature now, practiced lovers, deserving of ear nibbles, power-thrusts from gym-toned calf muscles.

Some people came outside, drew on my face in magic marker: a penis on my cheek pointing toward my mouth. Cops came. Woke up when I heard the sirens. John dragged me to his Wrangler.

Rolled up the window, lit a small pipe of what was apparently red rock opium, the synthetic stuff we used to smoke in high school that might have just been incense. Mistook the fake opium for crack, smoked it anyway. Listened to classic rock radio, drove in circles. Matt said, "It's always the same. You think you're a different person until you come back and everyone's the same and you're the same too. The girls still treat you the same."

Conscious enough to get out of the car. Stumbled beneath streetlamp, edged my way to the driveway, punched the garage code. Didn't work. (I kind of remember this.) Walked up the steps. Didn't want to wake Mom, so I didn't knock. Picked up one of the rocks from the rock garden,

202

heaved it through the kitchen window. Window broke but didn't shatter. Hoisted myself up on the ledge, climbed on through, cutting my arms and face in the process. Dripping blood, lay on the floor. Alarm went off. Stood, turned toward the basement stairs to get some sleep. Something hit me from behind, knocked me over. Felt like a team of baby sharks was biting through the flesh of my leg.

twenty-six

Flatscreen:

- Some nights—high, eyes closed, music off, focused on functional hum: dryer, dishwasher, bathroom pipes—my skull expands, shape-shifts to a massive plasma-flat, wide as a football field, Mc-Mansion tall, super-high-def, high-res, wireless, static-free, angel-winged for when the weather's right, planets aligned, time to rise, kite-like, above the clouds, into the atmosphere, into orbit, out of orbit, into space, sun-aimed, body still attached, legs trailing like a tagalong electrical cable, unplugged.

- On-screen: line after line of LED-lit brain code, nonverbal thoughts translated to conversational English, Courier fourteen-point font, each distinct thought lettered, numbered, Roman-numeraled; synapses visible, connections color-coded, sensibly arranged, mapped for maximum comprehension, all clear to anyone outside looking at my flatscreen head, but not to me, internally trapped, no view but wiring, only a tiny window to the outside.

- Floating through space, looking for a single mirror, a moon would do, anything to reflect skull-screen for my personal perusal.

- Then just when I'm about to find my moon-mirror, achieve some kind of clarity, I fall, without warning. Down to earth, back in bed, FS off, screen blank, head back to being a head.

- Remaining: weak glow coming from the nexus of my skull like a shitty single-watt headlamp, no help through the black, so I open my eyes.

twenty-seven

Kahn sat in front of me holding a smoking rifle.

"He comes like an apparition through my window, but it turns out he is made of flesh and blood like the rest of us."

"You shot me."

"An arrow not unlike Cupid's."

"Except there's a bullet in me."

"I guess I fucked up. I'm an old man and I fucked up."

"It's not your fault. You thought I was breaking in."

"You *were* breaking in."

"Right."

Alarm still going off. Footsteps came from the hallway. Kahn lifted my leg, looked at it.

"I'm not a doctor. But I once played one on TV. Season two, episode four, *Blacks and White Coats*. A gritty urban medical drama. I was a special guest: widower brain surgeon with a heart of gold."

"Not sure that helps our situation."

"It was a crappy show but they paid union."

Benjy and Erin ran in. Benjy in his boxers holding a baseball bat. Blood all over my old kitchen.

"Get a towel," Kahn said, "and some rubbing alcohol"—

he paused—"stat." Then to me, "You'll be all right, just a flesh wound."

"Do you really know that, or are you just pretending to be a doctor?"

"I'm just trying to help."

Benjy came back with the materials.

"What the hell happened?"

Benjy still held the baseball bat.

Kahn doused my leg with rubbing alcohol, wiped it with the towel. He had to lean from his wheelchair. Awkwardly bandaged me with his left hand alone, while he steadied the chair with his right. Gauze held in his teeth. Reminded me of *Wood and Nail*: Kahn's labored craftsmanship, his intensity of concentration. Moles and burn scars spotted his outstretched arms. Bare feet atrophied, askance, hardened by white mold. Feet heavy with white warts, spiky black warts, like perma-cleats. Overgrown toenails curled stiffly upward.

"The garage code didn't work. So I climbed in through the window. Forgot I don't live here anymore."

Benjy shook his head.

"Honest mistake," Kahn said. "Once Robert Redford shot at me for the same reason, only I *knew* it wasn't my own house."

"Is that why . . ." Benjy started to say, looked at Kahn's wheelchair, stopped himself.

"No. Bob could never have hit me. He's a terrible shot. That's why all Hollywood votes Republican: they don't think we need gun control laws because none of them could hit a fat man from across a kitchen anyway. Unfortunately for old E., I am one of the rare thespians who also happens to be a formidable marksman."

"I was unlucky before that."

"No kidding, fat boy," Natasha said. She'd come into the room. "You're bleeding out your head, you've got two black eyes, and you got a dick on your face."

"What?"

"Someone drew a penis on your face," Benjy said.

"It looks like it's pissing blood into your mouth," Erin said.

"Great. Fantastic."

Waited for the ambulance.

"White people are crazy," Natasha said.

"I've neutralized the wound," Kahn said.

"What does that mean?" Benjy said.

"I have no idea," Kahn said.

Kitchen floor looked like a slaughterhouse (*Fast Food Nation*, RPC, 2006). Red and blue flashed in the window.

"Prop up the head," Kahn said. Benjy got a pillow from the living room, put it under my head.

I am at home. I am at home and this is my fucked-up family.

Jennifer Estes entered in white.

"My guardian angel."

Knelt, examined my wound.

"Twice in one day," I said. "It really must be fate."

She and some dude put me on a stretcher, carried me out to the ambulance. Benjy rode with us. Didn't hold my hand, but I could see him when I tried to lift my head. Jennifer let me squeeze her forearm.

"I baked you a pie," I said.

She leaned in close to my face.

"Stay with us," she said, and I did.

Part III

one

Possible Ending #1 (Daytime Soap):

I'm written out, etched into sweet relief. Benjy knuckles dirt, discards tempered tears like wiper fluid. Someone speaks; they all speak. No one has anything to say. Never really knew me. Homeys pour forties. Otherwise, I go un-missed. Even if I'm missed, I don't know it because I'm dead.

two

"Florida," my mother said.

Pacing the room, scrutinizing machines like a government inspector—reading serial numbers, fingering an IV tube—even though she had no idea what the machines did, let alone if they were doing it successfully. One machine was a balloon attached to the underside of my calf that alternately inflated or deflated every couple minutes, elevating my leg half a foot in the air, like a yoga-robot posing me (*Hatha3000*, MouthEar Films, 2006).

Mom must have flown back, come straight to the hospital. Dressed all wrong, still in Thanksgiving stilettos, black tights, spaghetti strap dress that showed off her eight-minute biceps.

"Florida's a nice place."

Walked to the window, opened the curtains, looked out the window. Like a TV soap: Thanksgiving, fuckup son in hospital bed, Mom staring into sunlight, makeup smudged, reapplied in hand mirror while son sleeps. Heart monitor thumps electric blips. Hospitals are designed to feel like sets, what with well-lit bare rooms; generic, prop furniture, all grays, muted blues; machines that look archaic, two-tone, low-pixel screens providing retro eighties vibe. Or maybe it seemed that way because I'd been watching too many prime-time medical dramas, uneagerly anticipating my own encounters with the life machines, taking comfort in their theoretically altruistic attendants. TV in my actual hospital room, muted. Bosomy woman in a low-cut shirt hid a knife in a drawer, blew kisses at a bearded man. Averted my eyes, watched Mom, the way she pushed with her legs to open the window, the tightening of her veined, muscled thighs.

No idea how long she'd been in the room, if she'd stared at me while I'd slept; sipped coffee; thought of my body, the way my pale face blended with the white sheets; imagined the blood that covered the floor of the old house, seeped through the carpet, dripped through the cracks in the floorboard, thickened, blackened.

Sunshine highlighted her highlights; she pulled the strands into a low ponytail, the kind she wore for tennis.

"I could see myself there. I was there and I could see myself there. No winter, outdoor tennis year round. Maybe I could start playing golf, too. Lot of women play golf these days. Wear a bit of plaid; I think that would be cute. Not really my game, too slow. But I could get into it. Jeff's a big golfer. Jeff Goldblum, not the actor. He spells it differently. He's an insurance salesman. A nice man, Eli, and I think you'll like him when you meet him."

The balloon was meant to help circulation. Could feel the blood moving. Thought again of the blood that poured from my body when I was shot. Even that puddle, not enough to stop the flow of oxygen to my brain. I, who always felt so fragile, melodramatically straddling the borderline between here and the eternal, I had been shot, lived to tell the tale. Wounded. Soldiers get wounded. Mom was a soldier too, wounded by Dad's unshaven face, and now she was in love, it seemed, from the way she looked out the window as if she were staring at an ocean, index finger tracing rings around the inside of her palm. In love with a man who wouldn't hurt her, a man she'd chosen for that exact reason. Imagined a child's face on an adult body; a child wearing an unstylish but respectable suit, his hairless cheek rubbing against my mother's. An insurance salesman, practically his job to be reliable. Goldblum-Spelled-Differently was reliable; I wasn't. Things had started to go well for her, and I was like a baby crying on a monitor, demanding attention just as a gentle man has poured the wine, begun to rub her shoulders, slipped the straps down, whistled half a bar of some familiar melody, one she hasn't heard in years. Not sure if it was her or me, or both, but somewhere there was the sense that one of us had to quit on the other, drift out of cell phone range. Or we'd be pulled back like heavy magnets, ceaselessly weakened by the force it takes to pry ourselves apart.

"I think you'll like Jeff. Jeff Goldblum. It's a ridiculous name, I know. But he spells it differently, and he has a nice face. Blue eyes even though he's Jewish. Obviously Jewish with a name like Goldblum, living in Boca. About as Jewish as you can get."

Didn't want to hear about her new boyfriend, but maybe that's all she could talk about. Easier than discussing the trauma that had occurred while she'd abandoned me. Because even though Thanksgiving was my dad's holiday—we went to Mom's for Passover and night one of Chanukah, Dad's for secular holidays: Thanksgiving, Fourth of July, etc.—her absence was still a reminder that our family had become a slump-shouldered Diaspora, that regardless of actual physical proximity, we lived in separate, isolated communities. Not that I blamed her for my being shot, but didn't she, at least a little bit, blame herself?

"Jeff's not rich like your father, though. He has a good job, but he's not rich. Drives a Honda. Not that your father was rich when we first met, either, but you could tell he was hungry for it. He didn't like to wear a shirt and tie, but he was hungry. So was I, really. You are when you're poor. When you're poor and pregnant like I was. Sleeping on a cheap mattress. You've never slept on a cheap mattress. Maybe at summer camp, but not every night for years, or with a pregnant stomach. My parents were never rich. They did okay, but money was different then. People weren't rich like they are now. Jews, I mean. Your father grew up with nothing. We wanted you boys to have it good, nice toys, good schools. Guess it didn't matter in the end, did it?"

Thought she might jump out the window, let her body fall to the pavement. What then? They'd drag her back in here. In the bed next to mine, hooked to more complicated machines, ones that would help her breathe, pump her heart. Maybe Spelled-Differently would visit, maybe he wouldn't. Wanted to tell her it wasn't the end, we were still alive, my leg would heal, we would all heal, salt in your wounds hurts but also cleanses. Didn't she watch television? Didn't she know that in America everyone gets a second chance?

Instead shut my eyes, imagined her stare on my body like a tractor beam, lifting me out of bed, into the air. Abducting me.

"Your father, your father, your father," she said.

Because she still thought about Dad, took each Goldblum-Spelled-Differently limb, measured it against the memory of Dad's; bushified Jeff's eyebrows; pictured new children, prettier versions of Benjy and I, happier;

admired his small, unsunken pectoral muscles, visible because he hardly had any chest hair. Or maybe he had chest hair, had Dad's square jaw, winter-red nose, unemotive eyes. The same, or opposites. Either way, a reaction. Whoever this Goldblum-Spelled-Differently was—tender or brute lover, workaholic or Euro-fied American who lived for scented, aged items: wine, cheese, my mother—he was that way because of my father, because Dad needed a replacement, and Florida is where you replace one life with another.

"I'm tired," she said.

Not just me who'd made her tired—it was Dad, Benjy, the weather, time which sank her cheeks and breasts, made lines on her forehead—but right now it was me, my broken body, the sight of which made her want to lie flat on the floor, feel the tiles form sharp triangles with the bones of her upper back, watch the ceiling light until she saw blue dots, nothing but blue dots covering the world, covering me, her injured son, her never-prodigal son because I'd never left. Instead forced her to become a prodigal mother, returning not to feasts and joy-tears, but to blinking machines that said, "Our beating hearts are only gears, our bones will never truly heal."

"I don't know what we'll do about the condo. I just put down six months. I guess you can stay there for a while. It'll give you time to get something together. Your leg will heal. The doctor said you'll be good as new in a month. You got lucky and you'll heal. You don't want me around, anyway, taking care of you. Your father will come by and check in. You can go live with him if you want. He said that, you know, that you can if you want. I'll make him if he doesn't. It's his turn, now. I don't know if you want to, though. It might be good for you to be on your own. You'll have to get a job, get your own place eventually. You're over eighteen and it's just not my job anymore. Maybe that makes me a horrible mother, I don't know."

She paused, considered the question. I didn't know the answer, either.

"Do you even know how to do laundry? You put the detergent in first. Not a whole cup. About a half or three quarters depending on the load. Do the lights and the darks separate, but you probably already know that. Washing on warm is always a good bet. You can use hot if something's really dirty, dab a little detergent on the stain before you put it in. Just don't overload the machine. It breaks if you overload it. And do the towels separately. I bought you a bunch of new towels. Soft ones, the kind you like. I know your skin's sensitive, it always was, even when you were a baby. You used to get rashes on your skin, and your lips were always so chapped. I bought you new towels and underwear and some thick socks because it's getting cold out. If you run out of socks and underwear you can always go to Filene's and get some more. You know the kind you like. I don't know how you'll get there, but Benjy will be home for break soon and he can drive you places. There's the bus too. I left a bus schedule attached to the fridge. I'm a bad mother, I know. A terrible mother with my son in the hospital, but the doctor said you'd be okay, and the timing, it's just the timing, E."

Thought for a second she might suffocate me with a pillow, free herself, deny, disappear. Not out of hate, but the way grizzly bears eat their young when the salmon aren't running—for their own survival, a last resort (*Grizzly Man*, Lions Gate Films, 2005).

"I have to go," she said. "Benjy will be by here soon."

Looked like she was about to say something, one last thing. But her cell rang, she said, "I have to take," answered the phone, whispered "Jeff," walked out of the room.

three

Facts About My Mother:

- Her name is Susan.

four

Possible Ending #2 (Pay Cable):

Recover, clean up my act, get a job, something I'm qualified for: late-night convenience store clerk, sheltered behind bulletproof glass. College classes during the day.
Dad pays for it. Start at the CC, work my way up to the
state school in Amherst, same as Benjy. Struggle at first,
then excel. Too old for the other kids, but a couple cute
townie chicks look at me from across the bar. They like
my dumb smile after my third bourbon. Mom magnets my
report card to the fridge. Graduate. Attend a stuffy cer-
emony draped inelegantly in ugly-colored cap and gown.
Dad greets me with solid handshake. Get an entry-level
job, hate it but enjoy the camaraderie of hating it along
with other people my age. Get my own apartment with the
money I'm making plus a bit of Dad's money. A nice apartment, but I get lonely at night, still prowl the net trying to
find some semblance of affection to tether myself to. Buy
ties, maybe a tie rack. Visits to Mom with flowers, midnight
phone calls to Benjy. He lets it ring. Move up from entry-
level. Go back to school, get an MBA. Dad loans me money

to start a business. Use that money to make more money. Or lose that money, but nobly. Return to Quinosset one Thanksgiving to find Jennifer Estes in love with the idea of what I've become, considering what I'd been before. Marry, march down the aisle twinkle-toed to Christ-y gospel, stuff our faces with Whole Foods catering, honeymoon on a French-dialect island. I slip one past the goalie, promise I'll stop making stupid sports metaphors. Our children look like her, are beautiful: bubble-cheeked with Latino skin-glow. Nevertheless I'm sad roughly half the time, not so bad considering life is etc.

five

Young, bashful, about my age, cute but wearing too much mascara to complement her purple scrubs. I'd been in and out of sleep, morphine-drip peaceful. Now I was awake, conscious, miserable.

"Do you want to see?"

"Not really."

Liked watching her instead, top of her head when she leaned over, blond highlights, combined smell of perfume and disinfectant that came from her body and clothes. Smelled like the possibility of sex, distracted me from my pain, also alerted me to my own tube-dicked impotence. The nurse hovered, flaunting her gratuitous health in the face of my paper-gown-as-metaphor-for-all-humiliation.

"Does it hurt?"

"My leg?"

"That is where you got shot, isn't it?"

"I'm pretty tough," I managed, mid-wince.

She smiled. From my angle it looked as if she might lean forward, rest her forehead on my pulsating man-tit. Could fall in love with this one, or the next. All these women with stethoscopes, ample teat. But too soon, and no chance, though my interest was probably a good sign of recovery. Vowed to wait before launching a new campaign. At least until I had pants on.

"Everybody hurts," she said. "Even tough guys. On a scale of one to ten?"

"Does nine and a half make me sound like a wuss?"

"It's because you were on so many drugs. Your body has a tolerance to opiates, so the morphine doesn't help as much as it should. I think you even had some opium in your system when you got here."

"I thought it was crack."

"I don't know, man. You might have more problems than a bullet hole in your leg."

"She left me."

"So it's all about a girl, then." The nurse winked. "You're a cutie, honey, no need to get crazy over one chick. There's plenty of fish out there."

"Not any girl. My mother."

"Like I said before, you've got a lot more problems than just this bullet."

"She's moving to Florida to be with Jeff Goldblum."

"I loved him in *The Big Lebowski*."

"That was Jeff Bridges."

"What was Jeff Goldblum in, then?"

"*The Big Chill, Independence Day* . . ."

"That's right. He was that Jewish guy who saves the planet."

"That's the one."

"Well, no wonder she left you for him."

"He sells insurance."

"I think I saw that one, too."

Lights off, local news: civilians dead in Iraq, Brady hopeful for the playoffs. Fell asleep, dreamed Kahn had giant teeth, gnawed my fingers to bone.

• • •

Woke to Benjy in the chair reading *Us Weekly*, sipping hospital OJ with a straw as if he were the sick one, wearing glasses instead of contacts. Hadn't seen him in glasses in years. The pair was cheap, outdated: ovular silver frames more suited to librarians, mustached dentists, and child-nerds than to someone sort-of-normal like Benjy.

"Didn't know you liked celebrity gossip?"

"Mom left this here. There was nothing else to read. How's your leg?"

"Just call me 2pac."

"Not Mr. Shakur?"

"Funny. What's up with you? How's school, Erin? Tell me something to distract from the pain."

"Honestly, I'm kind of fucking everything up for the first time, and I don't know why or what to do about it."

"Story of my life," I said, tried to laugh, but when I laughed my leg hurt and instead of a normal laugh it came out high-pitched, a half-laugh, half-girlish squeal.

"He breaks just like a little girl," Benjy said.

"Okay, Bob Dylan."

"If you're 2pac, then I get to be Dylan, definitely."

"I see you as more of a Jewish Rivers Cuomo."

"I don't know who that is."

"You wouldn't."

"Erin thinks I'm too controlling."

"You are."

"She thinks I put too much pressure on myself to be perfect."

"You do."

"My grades are slipping. I seem to have stopped caring."

"You sound like a robot."

"I think maybe I want to be something easier than a lawyer."

"A doctor?"

"Maybe a rock star."

"You don't have the lifestyle."

"What about an accountant? That's more my pace. Or an actuary? Sit there and do math all day. Comfy office chair. Bit of Internet porn. Home by five. Sounds kind of good."

"Want to open a restaurant with me?"

"The restaurant business is a risky proposition."

"You're a risky proposition."

"Actually, my portfolio is rather risk-free."

"So you're gonna get married?"

"Is it possible that relationships are bullshit?"

"Is it possible you're a giant asshat?"

"At least I didn't get shot."

"Good one, bro."

"Sorry," he said, looked back at the magazine, squeezed my bare, extended foot. Toes tickled, itched.

"Angelina's baby is ridiculous. That kid will be so fucked up."

"I don't know," I said. "She takes him everywhere she goes. It's like he's taped to her tit."

Benjy shook his head. Couldn't tell if he was shaking it at me or at something in the mag.

Later the nurse came back to measure my blood, change my IV, temporarily un-tube me from my urine.

"It's shrinkage," I said, my red-marked love-stick puny, dripping.

"Yeah, yeah, that's what they all say. I've seen that episode" (*Seinfeld*, NBC, 1990–1998).

"You don't know anything about me," I mumbled as she ticked my chart, flipped her hair, adjusted her stethoscope, booty-shuffled back into the unflattering glow of the hospital.

"I mean well."

six

Possible Ending #3 (Miramax):

Attend some superior accredited culinary academy, a training ground for world chef-ery, filled with sweet-drawling
buxom brunettes with sharp palates, soft tongues, long
tongs. Learn from the masters, unlearn my self-taught bad
habits, develop strong calf muscles from all the standing,
dissemble a baby calf in five flat. Shower daily, wear a fresh
new apron, clogs, ironic sideburns. Get a job on the line,
work my way up to sous. I still have a bullet scar, and a
bad-boy limp. Maybe move south—Outer Banks, Virginia
Beach—away from the culinary hubs into the kind of town
that takes in strays, pays them to cook andouille sausage
over an open-flame grill (*Summer on the Banks*, Dimetree
Films, 1995). Waitresses with rip-fringed skirts supported by
unwintered legs supported by nail-painted feet in battered
sneakers. Drink too much, but so does everyone. At least I'm
drinking French wine, sucking oysters, staring at the ocean.
Occasionally Benjy comes down. Walk along the sand, talk
about old times, rivalry we survived, family we survived,
those ridic Thanksgivings like the one after I boned and

deboned Mrs. Sacks, when her hubby punched my eye like Iron Mike. Marry a surfer girl, let her surf my stomach (it ripples!), suspend her infantilism in the comfort of my callused-paw caress. Mom doesn't like that she's not Jewish, but by that point she's remarried to Goldblum-Spelled-Differently, understands everyone just needs someone to make them feel like death isn't a better option.

seven

My doctor's name was Zornstein. When he looked at my chart he chuckled, didn't try to hide it.

"How you holding up, champ?"

"There's still a hole in my leg."

"Should be almost all closed up by now. You'll hardly have a scar."

"Too bad. I wanted a badass one like Fiddy Cent."

"You're lucky. The bullet missed everything. Went right through fat. Didn't hit anything important."

"But I could feel the bullet in me."

"It probably just felt that way. The lump was actually your blood clotting."

"So I'll walk again and everything?"

"You can limp, if you want. For the street cred. But if you want to walk you can do that too."

"When can I leave?"

"Another few days just for observation. You lost a lot of blood. You're lucky that guy who shot you knew how to stop the bleeding."

"He did?"

"Might have saved your life."

"No shit."

"Well, you can thank him yourself. He's waiting for you out in the courtyard. I thought you could use a bit of fresh air today."

"Isn't it freezing out?"

"Five minutes will be good for you. We'll give you a blanket."

The nurse came with a wheelchair, winked in a way I took to be condescending.

"You look in better shape now that all that coke's getting out of your system."

"But what about the morphine?"

"They're trying to wean you off."

"No wonder my leg hurts so much."

She wheeled me across the lobby to the terrace where Kahn sat waiting, watching a small child pick up rocks and throw them while his parents argued at a nearby bench. Father in a hospital gown, hooked to an IV even though he was outside.

"Hey there," I said.

Kahn smiled. Always did when he saw me. Wondered if he smiled when he saw other people too, or if it was just when he saw me, if something about me made life bearable. I didn't usually inspire smiles. Forehead lines, alcoholism, premature aging, balding, whispering, anything but the upward curve of lip Kahn organically produced whenever our eyes met.

Less well-dressed than ever before. Royal-blue sweatpants. Wheelchair gloves with cutoff fingers. Looked handicapped, homeless even.

"Got any smokes?" I said.

"Don't touch the stuff. Stuff'll kill ya."

"So will bullets."

Kahn looked me up and down, both in wheelchairs, warped reflections in a funhouse mirror.

"We are the same now. Cripples in the eyes of the law."

"Doctor said I'd be fine."

"As God created man in his own image, so I have done with you, my son."

"I'm not your son."

"You are Jesus and I am Jehovah."

When I was stoned he seemed smart; when I was sober he sounded like an idiot. Still, he was here.

"You're nuts," I said. "You know that, right?"

"And you're balls. We're two peas in a pod. Twin testes in the sac of life."

"If that bullet had been a few inches higher, I wouldn't have any nuts."

"So you should be thankful I'm such a good shot."

"Or a bad one. For all I know you could have been aiming for them."

"I may be crazy, but I am not cruel. No man deserves that. I wouldn't even trade my balls if it meant I could get my legs back. Not in a million years."

Looked down at his legs. Pants were baggy, hid how skinny his legs were.

"I'm not pressing charges," he said.

"I didn't think you would."

"Your punishment is that I will live out the rest of my days in your old house, with a bullet lodged in the wall. It's my punishment too."

"Punishment for what?"

"For my sins, kid. We're not like the Catholics. Everyone thinks they have it tough, but they're wrong. The Catholics have it easy. They go to confession, whisper the pleasures in hushed tones like they're phone-sex operators while the priest pretends not to stroke his own schmuck behind that screen. For all we know they've got their flies open half the time, eight-year-old boys blowing them silent while the faithful whisper deepest and darkest about how Mommy didn't love them so they stuck their dick in a jar of marshmallow fluff and let the pet rabbit lick it off. Next thing they know, they've said a few Hail Marys and they're absolved. Sins washed away like chlamydia after three days on penicillin."

"Plus they get to eat wafers in church. We have to fast."

"You fast? Didn't take you for the religious type."

"I don't. I'm not."

"You believe in God?"

"Not sure I believe in anything."

"A nihilist, eh? Filthy word. It means you can't pretend. I used to be an actor. I used to be good at pretending. But I don't know anymore."

"So what do you believe in, then?"

"I believe in honor. Like negroes and Samurai swords-men. I believe in good aged scotch and erect nipples when the night gets under white tee shirts. I believe a blow job can touch your soul, which means I believe in the soul, mainly because I've been blown by some of the best, and I once saw Coltrane at the Vanguard blowing that tenor like he was sucking gold dick for crack. Life is absurd, my friend. Don't forget it. Life is absurd. Absurd as a turd."

"They should put that on your gravestone."

Kahn didn't laugh. Instead looked back at the boy throwing rocks. Felt bad bringing up his gravestone even though we'd been talking about death, and it was impos-sible not to think about it when guys were sitting outside hooked to IVs while their wives cried (like an afternoon movie on cable with the sound turned down), while I myself sat in a wheelchair, forty stitches in my leg, detoxing from morphine. The nurse walked over, said we should go back inside.

"Absurd as a turd," Kahn said again.

She grabbed my handles, turned me around, pushed me toward the doors.

"Is he your father?"

"Sort of," I said, because I didn't know how to explain that Kahn had come to visit and my actual father hadn't.

eight

Ways in Which I Am Like a Rapper:

- Absent father
- Bullet hole
- Verbal dexterity
- Limited education
- Love of butts

nine

Possible Ending #4 (Dark but Ultimately Life-Affirming Screwball Dramedy):

Care for Kahn in the autumn of his life. Hilarity ensues. Benjy marries Erin. She erupts with babies, rounds herself into something soft. I cook large meals on the holidays. Everyone chuckles. Late one night Natasha bites my ear in the bathroom, penetrates me with her pinky, professes love. It's possible I end up a schoolteacher for the mentally unhinged. When Kahn dies I cry fountains, realize how much I've learned, how much I still have to learn.

ten

My room filled with cards with rhyming messages from the gift shop. Said things like "Sending a letter in hopes you get better," because there were no cards that said "Sorry you got shot while breaking and entering, you fucking moron."

Actually, only got one rhyming card, from Uncle Sal. Another card came from Dan. He'd crossed out Hallmark's message, replaced it with "Sorry you got shot while breaking and entering, you fucking moron."

Erin showed with bagels. Sat on the corner of my bed, watched the balloon raise and lower my leg. Light from the window caught the side of her face, reflected outward, adding a golden aura to her sweetly chubby cheek. Or maybe it just looked that way because they'd upped my morphine after I'd complained so much. Remembered that I'd seen her first, before Benjy, in what was now Kahn's office but had once been my bedroom.

"It could have been different. It could have been me and you."

If I hadn't been on morphine I wouldn't have said it and it wouldn't have been excusable. But I had; it was. She didn't get angry. Looked at me like she wanted to hug me, cradle me, open her milk ducts, shower me with warm motherhood. Placed her hands over my hands.

"I accept your mothership," I said. "You are the mothership."

"I'm too young to be a mothership."

"I saw that movie on Lifetime."

"How'd it turn out?"

"She grew to love the child like it was her own."

"But it was her own."

"You're pregnant?"

"Far from it," Erin said, laid her head gently and ignorantly on my wounded leg.

"Owowowowowow."

Erin upright, apologizing.

"It's fine," I said. "Just still a little tender."

"You're the soft one, aren't you? Deep down I mean. You feel things strongly."

"I feel strongly the pain in my leg."

"But in your heart, I mean. In your heart you're tender."

"My soul is of no matter."

"Your brother's a shit."

In my morphine sensitive-state I begged to differ.

"He means well. I really think he does. His heart is in a paper bag, I think. The paper bag's stapled shut with really big staples, like the ones in my leg. But the paper is thin. You can rip it right out."

"Like he ripped mine right out?"

"That's not what I meant."

"The problem is I love him anyway."

"That seems like a good problem."

"It's the worst problem I've ever encountered."

"Fuck," I said.

Erin squeezed my hand.

•   •   •

My peeps showed up too: Dan, Nikki, John, Matt.

I sang, "Oh, Danny boy, the lights are shining . . ."

"Aww, shit, you're tripping out, kid. What they got you hooked up to in there?"

"Schwartz is domed to the dome."

"I lost a lot of blood."

"That's 'cause you got capped, son," Dan said.

Nikki bit her lip, shook her head, raised a single eyebrow.

"Hi, Eli," she said.

"Hey, Jude. Don't make it bad. Take a sad song . . ."

"Kid gets shot, thinks he's John Lennon."

"Paul," I said.

"Who's Paul?" Matt said. "I'm Matt."

"McCartney, you idiot."

"Yo, E., you're famous."

"Yeah. Your video's climbed to ten on YouTube."

"What video?"

"Guy Passes Out on Football Field, Gets Aroused, Gets Standing Ovation."

"Shit."

"You should be psyched. Chicks go crazy for famous people."

Later, dreamed Alison Ghee was in the hospital with me. Siamese twins. Doctors wanted to cut us apart, but if they did she would somehow end up with my penis. Neither of us wanted the operation, but everyone was encouraging us to go through with it, saying if we didn't then one of us—the weaker—would die. Couldn't decide if it would be worse to be castrated or to have a dead girl physically attached to my body. Then my own heartbeat sped, the doctor said, "He's crashing." Realized I was the weaker half. "Do the surgery,"

Alison said. The doctor said, "Emergency separation," held up a knife, was about to cut when I woke up.

My real doctor was standing over me.

"Mr. Schwartz."

"I just had the weirdest fucking dream."

"My name is Zornstein, not Freud."

"I'm looking for the guy with that crazy-colored coat or whatever."

"Stay away from that guy."

"But he's not even real. He's a character in a musical."

"Exactly," Zornstein said. "Good news. Your leg is healing nicely. We've decided to discharge you."

"You think I'm ready?"

"As far as your leg goes, yes."

"But am I ready to face the world with a clear head and a heavy heart?"

"That is what we're concerned about. I'm recommending that you see a psychiatrist. Not a Freudian or an Old Testament dream interpreter. Just a good old Quinosset shrink with a nice couch and pills that will make you happy. I've discussed it with your mother and she concurred and said your father would be more than willing to pay for it. I'm going to give you pain medication, but you really have to get some help. I don't like giving pain meds to drug users, but you did get shot. Now, before we can let you go, we need someone to come pick you up."

"Okay."

"Make the arrangements. Someone else needs your bed."

eleven

Possible Ending #5 (Hollywood PG-13, but Its Heart Is Rated R):

After recovering from my injury, play catch with Dad in the backyard. He sees the bud of talent that only needs nurture, manipulation. Soon I'm pitching in Pawtucket, a call away from the bigs. My knuckleball zigs; my unprecedented story of late-age (for baseball) bloom is shown on local cable, complete with family interviews and astonishment at my courage in forgoing a downward drug spiral for a chance at athletic transcendence. Go to schools, talk to kids about the importance of hard work, win awards for community leadership, consider myself part of a community even if that community's in Rhode Island. Dad comes to my games, wears tee shirts with my name on them. Groupies, RI-accented bleached blondes. They throw themselves at me, unattractively. But I take the bait, sink my overgrown nails (for the knuckleball) into their pale rumps. Later, girl in boozy slumber, cry into the echoey high ceilings of my apartment. Tom Petty plays.

twelve

Pam picked me up, brought me back to Sudbury, submerged me out of sight in yet another basement bedroom. Room furnished with mattress-bed and mini-desk from the last time I'd stayed there, ten years prior. Undecorated. I slept.

Didn't see Dad until that night, when he came into my room smelling of Old Spice, still wearing his office clothes, though his tie was loose and his five-o'clock shadow had morphed into an almost-beard. He was backlit by the hallway light. From my low angle in the partial darkness he looked distorted and gigantic, twenty feet tall like a figure on a drive-in screen.

"Hello, son," he said. He never called me son.

"Hello, father," I said, like I was Luke muddafuckin' Skywalker.

"Pam made dinner if you want some."

He meant Julio had made dinner. Pam had put it into serving bowls, set the table. Didn't ask where Julio had been for Thanksgiving, but glad he was here now with a mustache that reminded me of channel 238 OldWest, yellowed film, six-shooters, men on horses across Texas canyons, sun obscured by nothing, señoritas dancing as nighttime falls.

Never eaten in the kitchen before. Only been there for special occasions that took place in the dining room. This was the day-to-day: ceramic plates, ill-matched silverware. Twins were sleeping at a friend's house, so it was just the three of us. A window-peeper would think we were normal, American as *Idol*. Must have been countless meals at this table: mouths full of food, days discussed, glances exchanged, drinks spilled, wiped up. Now we sat close to silent.

"This is nice," Pam said.

First nonhospital grub I'd eaten in days. Took seconds on potatoes, thirds on salad, fourths on steak. Dad watched from across the table, trying to figure out why I was there, how he should feel about it.

Wondered why he hadn't shown at the hospital, if it was spite or if it simply saddened him to see his ignored son, bullet-holed, hooked to machines. He'd always been a coward—leaving us, giving me cash when he didn't want to. Hoped he still was one.

Pam smiled at the other end, watching me eat the way my grandmother did when I was thirteen and everyone kept calling me a growing boy, shoving food down my throat. Dad tucked his chair, walked out of the room, said "Good night" even though it was only nine.

Pam chatted with Julio in the kitchen. Couldn't make out the words, but the rhythm of their banter was comfortable, sprinkled with laughter. Hoped that they were confidants, patrolled the same domain, were familiar with each other's smells and moods; that he knew it was her period from the subtleties of her posture, the speed at which her eyes panned the room. In a different life he might have had a horse; she might have ridden sidesaddle.

Crutched back to the basement stairs, body a pendulum, circulation improving, sensations growing stronger in my toes.

Snow fell onto the glass atrium ceiling, as if the world were an oversized snow globe, only me on the outside—an unlikely God—shaking that shit up. Felt dizzy, almost lost my balance, managed to maintain composure, made my way to the stairs, sat on my ass, stretched my legs, bumped down, step-by-step. Somewhere in the house, up the stairs, then up the stairs again, the unseen au pair watched Conan, or watched the same snow out her window, computer producing ringing bells, IMs from across the world singing, "Good night, sweet child, come home soon—TTYL."

thirteen

Found During a Daytime Search of Father's House While Looking for Clues as to His Missing Months:

- Rogaine.

- Brochures for rehab clinic.

- No old baseball glove.

- No old photos of me.

- Okay, two old photos of me. Newborn in both, fat-faced like now, spit spilling over my lip, down my neck, but pretty cute, must say.

- Hidden stash of black licorice behind dresser.

- Hidden carton of Snickers in his desk drawer.

- Innocuous computer porn.

- Hidden photo album featuring photos of him and Mom in their youth, marginally hip, hanging with the Sackses, ties loosed, drinks pink and frothy, hair hanging free, wet.

- Lots of the pictures are of young Mrs. Sacks, back when her name was ____. Breasts smaller, but her face—in black-and-white, well-shadowed, cigarette dangling, lips curled dangerously—is the same face.

- Mom has beauty too, a different kind. More of a stately, restrained beauty.

- Best kitchen appliances this side of Kitchen Stadium.

- Every kind of catalog imaginable.

- Would be too easy to say he had architecture magazines. He didn't.

fourteen

Possible Ending #6 (Festival Fave):

Ingredients for Spaghetti Bolognese appear on the counter.
Pam's out that night with the girls, gossiping about wallet
size, which parts of which people they know are made of
plastic. Just me and the man. Pats on the radio, color man
calling it as he sees it, Brady in the pocket taking snow-
fudged snaps, snow falling on the atrium ceiling. Dad nods.
I nod. These nods communicate things that words can't.
Soon we're at the counter chopping onions, washing fresh
herbs, sitting as it simmers, licking wooden spoons like sat-
isfied Italians. There's wine, '86, year of my birth. Saved
by Dad for such an occasion. Joke about the Sox never
winning it in our lifetimes but then they did, how great
was that, and your brother's a funny guy, with his stress
and short hair, his holier-than-fuck-all attitude but he's a
good guy and did you see Uncle Sal at Thanksgiving, everything turns to shit someday, but not quite true because
Pam is love. But maybe there's no bottle, no Bolognese,
just Chinese takeout, couple beers, talking Dad's old life,
and where did he go? "Oh, that, son," he says. "I went [   ]
so I could [   ], only to return like a coward. Don't you fol-

low my path. You be free by doing [   ] and you'll succeed."
Eat dumplings straight from containers, fingers sticky with
starch.

fifteen

Dad worked during the day. Pam did errands, had lunch dates. Twins were at school. Afternoons they'd come home. I'd see them in the yard dripping mucus like broken snot-faucets. Thought I should love them the way I wanted Benjy to love me and maybe he did, give them advice, ease their boogers into tissues, heat hot chocolate on the stove. Wanted to do those things, would have if they'd shown any inkling of interest in me, any up-looking fraternal affection. But like the rest, they too rejected my advances, ignored my hot chocolate and offers to toss the ball, eyed me only in passing before disappearing into the backyard jungle.

Dinner convo centered around the twins: soccer, school. They would smile—already had adult teeth, though their mouths were still small, which gave the impression they were all teeth, half-canine, just wide-smiling chompers—say cute things about their days at school that made Pam gush, Julio cackle from the next room. Even Dad would smile, scratch his chin, give me a look that said, "I know they're little shits, but you've got to give them credit."

Hardly saw Dad. Thought he'd eventually come into my room, sit down, put his hand on my shoulder. Wait out a long silence. Then he would speak, slowly, precisely, as if he'd been planning the speech for years. No idea what he would say—couldn't get that far in the fantasy—but thought he'd say something. Or at least sit, stammer, back out. He kept coming home from work, eating dinner, retiring to his bed and personal flatscreen.

One night I left a note that said "November 1975–March 1976???????: _____ (please account for your whereabouts)," but he didn't mention it, probably threw it away before Pam saw and asked about a thing she didn't know about, didn't need to.

Got my stitches out. Zornstein was wrong; the scar was beautiful. Had its own meaning that couldn't be articulated in any way other than raised, dotted flesh. Lying in bed, traced its outline with my finger, memorizing its contours. During the day wished it visible outside my clothes.

My leg got better. Walked, slowly at first, across the foyer. Eventually stopped needing to hold the banister when I went upstairs for meals. One morning, walked into the kitchen, tapped Pam on the shoulder, said, "I'd like to go home now."

While I was packing, Dad took half a step into my room, pulled his foot back, stood framed by the doorway.

"You're going to stop doing drugs now," he said, like he wanted it to be a statement, knew it was a question.

sixteen

Possible Ending #7 (Gritty Art House):

Strung out, selling my ass and mouth in the old Combat Zone out by the Chinatown gates for sips from the glass dick. Dream flaxen-filtered unrealistic escapes, sleep in the Pit with the Pit kids. Parents stage interventions (which means they care!), send me off to clean sheets, over-ample orange juice. Doesn't work—not at twenty-five, twenty-six, twenty-eight, thirty-three, etc.—eventually they give up, occasionally staring at my prom pic, understanding it was all my own doing, still feeling guilt about their roles in my ruin. Meet a girl, older, dirty-blond doll hair, stained white skirt from when she was a '90s hippie, before all those mushrooms made her see ghosts in the streetlights. Sniffly fuck, city-silenced. Retreat and return like moody dogs. Weigh less than the corner dogs, eat dumpster doughnuts, scratch Estes into my chappy, deveined arm. If I don't die or parse the years in prison reading bad poetry, then I end up pleasure-stripped, Anonymous, a reluctant convert. Get the kind of job they give the guys like me, make a meager life, recite aphorisms.

seventeen

Home wasn't really home—it was the condo—but it felt more like home than Dad's place. The doorman recognized me, nodded with the solemn if condescending respect usually reserved for the elderly.

"Hey, brother," to Benjy, who was home for Christmas break.

"Hey," he managed, lethargic, feet on the ottoman, bare. Callused heels from years of nervous pacing.

"My scar looks like Bill Clinton," I said.

"What does that mean?"

"I don't know. Maybe I'll get a few BJs, gain popularity in the African American community."

"Are you high?"

"Actually, I'm off my pain meds. Any food in the house?"

Sliced tomatoes, cheese. He passed me the bread. Working the line, some greasy spoon, graveyard shift, radio mumbling low in the background, customers enjoying the fact that we were brothers—it legitimized us as salt-of-the-earth guys. Maybe our parents had owned the diner before dying in a car crash. Benjy had been on his way to college, had come home to help out, never left. Harbored some bitterness about it, but it all washed away when those pretty girls with blue eyelids sat at the counter drinking milkshakes, watching our bodies move in counterpoint behind the counter, entranced by the rhythmic scrape of metal on griddle, the almost imperceptible wiggle in our ass cheeks when the horns kicked in on the old-school soul station you could hardly hear over the whir of the ceiling fan and the bubbling deep fryer.

"How's Erin?"

But Benjy was on a different wavelength. Put the bread down, held back tears, held himself steady on the granite counter, wiped face, forehead, cringed, sat, blew his nose. All I could do was finish the sandwiches, plate them, pour Benjy a glass of water, put my hand on his shoulder, squeeze like a schmucky sitcom character, say, "It's okay."

"Our DNA is fucked," he said. "Absolutely, uncombatively effed."

"It's okay."

"I fucked up."

"It's okay."

The only thing TV had taught me to say. In this, TV was correct.

"It's okay."

"I cheated on Erin."

"That's not okay."

OMFGWTF, it wasn't. Poor, sweet Erin! The bastard had betrayed my former future sister-in-law, the sensitive cherubic soul who'd held my hand in the hospital bed, healed my wound with her sisterly cuddle-fingers. And what did she get in return for this kindness plus all the kindnesses she'd heaped on my square-headed sibling— warming his cold soul, wetting his cock, welcoming him into her veggie-healthed family? She got Ben's taint in another lover's mouth, some slutty college girl no doubt, Jewish sorority drunk-party-diddler with a decent nose job, a lot of practice, a purveyor of enough attentions to convince my never-popular brother to hurt his one and only for a night with this lip-glossed poli-sci tart.

Benjy withheld tears, trembled, bit his lip so hard it trickled blood.

"It's like I was channeling Dad to see if I really was his son."

"That was the dumbest thing you've ever said and done."

"No shit," Benjy said, rested his head on my shoulder.

"You fucker," I whispered.

Benjy said he might vomit. Watched the news, then the sports news, then three episodes of a syndicated sitcom in which divorced parents make do by living next door, exposing their overly handsome kids to the perils and joys of adult dating, and asking if maybe just maybe even the ugliest of circumstances can be remolded into a series of whimsical, fart-charged episodes, unburdened by the silly sadness of postnuclear parenting, elevated by laugh track, always ending with a lesson learned.

He said he'd told Erin and she'd cried in a way that made him understand for the first time that someone actually cared what he did and didn't do. If I'd been feeling more generous I might have told him I cared.

"I assume she dumped you?"

"We're currently taking a break while she sleeps with other guys for revenge."

Felt like I, too, had been dumped. Like the dream of functional life-sharing had been shattered for us both if not even Benjy could get it together to love correctly, with patience and honesty, unswayed by swinging legs and beckoning, sparkle-glossed lips, the call of new ass blinding his peripheries, simple-titted stimulus enough to dislodge straight-and-narrow progress. There was no way to live right, love fair, make a cake and eat it without putting on ugly pounds around the eyes. We were here, eternal, side by side, in shared shitty solitude, hands shaky, leg lit up like the north side at Christmas, collective eyes glued to the tube that holds us numbly captive, joins us in familial misery as we share, at least, in the beauty of an average sandwich.

Benjy asked me to change the channel and without thinking it over I punched his perfect, brace-straightened teeth.

Later, holding ice to his swelling mouth, I asked, "Have you talked to Mom at all?"

"Mom has a fourteen-point-eight handicap."

"Oh."

"Says the weather stays around seventy."

Couldn't sleep. Lay in bed picturing Jeff Goldblum the actor, since I'd never seen Goldblum-Spelled-Differently. In the morning I kissed Benjy on the ear.

eighteen

Possible Ending #8 (*Casablanca*):

This is the beginning of a beautiful friendship.

nineteen

The Circumstances of Benjy's Cheating as I Learned Later,
Which Certainly Neither Justifies His Actions nor Exoner-
ates Him, but Does Make Him Slightly More Sympathetic,
Considering:

- Before Erin he'd been a virgin.

- Not by choice, but because no one else had ever
  wanted to have sex with him.

- Erin had slept with fifteen guys.

- Benjy felt threatened by that, and had mentioned
  to Erin that at some point he would like to have
  sex with someone else in order to feel as though
  they were on slightly more even ground.

- Erin had thought this was stupid, but agreed that
  at some time in the FAR future, if they decided
  to get married (which was still a long way off),
  it might be a good/okay idea for them to take a

"break" so that Benjy could experience intercourse with another, and, at the very least, see that Erin definitively was the girl for him.

- For Benjy, two months *was* the FAR future.

- Plus his school was forty-five minutes from Erin and they only saw each other every other weekend.

- That day Erin and a six-two guy who wore popped-collar polos had been talking back and forth on their mutual Facebook walls.

- In one of these wall posts, Erin had written, "Hey Sexy ;)"

- Benjy has a very low tolerance for alcohol.

- Erica Greene can be very persuasive.

- She just wanted to show him something in her room. It would only take a second. But maybe they could put some music on. And he was so cute. And a nice guy. Her face was so babyish and sweet that nothing they did together could possibly seem wrong.

- People always cheat in movies.

- People always cheat in real life.

twenty

American Dream:

- Another American dream is the act of moving. It's the part where you're in the car, light the ciga-rette, song comes on, sun sets, breeze blows in off the ocean, all problems left behind.

twenty-one

Driving classes were at the VFW off Route 1, a decent bike
ride. Almost got hit four times trying to cross the highway. A while since I'd ridden. That stuff about not forgetting how to ride a bike turns out to be bullshit. True, you
don't fall over; you remember how to balance, go no hands,
turn corners, brake, change gears, etc., but the important
stuff—avoiding cars, merging into traffic—must be relearned. I'd been practicing on our street, doing circles,
feeling the thump in my ass when I dropped the front
wheel off the curb. Wing over to Pizza Palace, peek in the
window, watch youth B-ball teams forget losses by burning
the roofs of their mouths. Watched couples share booths,
hardly looking at one another, waiting for cheese to cool,
waiting for their lives to grow sideways like overgrown
weeds, each stem a weight out of balance.

Real winter now, almost Christmas. Skin on my hands
was dry, flaking. Perched on my bike as if stopping midway
on a journey to a specific place: maybe a minimum-wage
job with a cute girl across the room who made it all worthwhile, maybe a family gathered around a television.

Then flick my cig, swing down to the gas station minimart, camera following me, director telling me not to smile, never smile. Score would lift—waves of strings like blades of dead grass bowed by a strong wind. At Mobil, I'd pick up smokes, Diet Coke, drop gears, push up the hill back to the condo. Zornstein said this was good for my leg.

But this was my first big trip, traversing main streets, highways. Saw death on the bumper of each passing car. They say you feel immortal once you've been shot and lived, nothing can touch you, God must be watching your back. Bullshit. God was nowhere, certainly not on the highway slowing down speeding cell-phone drivers. Still, I made it to class.

Thought I had the wrong place because the crowd looked more suited for an AA meeting than a driving class. Men and women ranging from early twenties (me) to the gray-haired and -bearded of indeterminate age (guy with gray hair and beard) sat quietly in chairs waiting for the teacher to arrive. First day of school still made everyone nervous, still held that hint of mystery. Who knew what would happen in the new school year? Maybe the girl sitting next to you would gaze into your eyes in a way that meant you had her heart forever.

The girl sitting next to me was an obese bald man with sweat stains. Breath smelled like a jar of toilet mold left out overnight, festering on the counter.

"I'm Bill. Took this class before. Piece of cake."

"Why are you here again?" I said.

"Fifty-three speeding tickets."

"Oh."

"I'm an adrenaline junkie."

"Do you have any gum?"

"Don't chew the stuff. Bad for your jaw."

The teacher was both bald and pony-tailed, wore a

blond tweed blazer that would have been hip on a bearded artist, but on him looked like a remnant from another life when he was doing something other than teaching remedial driving. (Studying physics? Fucking in the back of a Chevy? Tap-dancing?)

"Welcome to Adult Driving," he said. "I'm Mr. Beaver."

Half the class giggled. Other half wasn't paying attention. Beaver made us go around, say names, why we were there.

"Zeke's the name," Zeke said.

"And why are you here, Zeke?"

"I got caught."

Maria only had two drinks, but she hardly weighs anything and the cop was a racist. Then there was Fred, who'd hid the crack rocks in his foreskin, hadn't foreseen that it would hurt like hell and the cops might wonder why he kept scratching his junk during interrogation.

"Maybe a bit too much information," Beaver said.

"I should have just stuck it up my ass like a normal person."

When it was my turn, I said, "My name is Eli Schwartz, and I have never driven in my life."

"You gotta be kidding me," Zeke said. "Aren't you an American?"

"Guess I am now."

"If you never had a car," Fred said, "where'd you get hand jobs when you were in high school?"

"Don't tell me you never got hand jobs," Zeke said.

"Maybe he's gay," Bob said. "Which I got no problem with."

"I'm not gay."

"Never driven, never gotten a hand job. Sounds gay to me."

"Gay guys jerk each other off all the time."

"Good point."

"I've gotten hand jobs."

"Settle down, class," Beaver said.

Shut my eyes, pictured myself behind the wheel of a fire-engine-red '89 LeBaron, top down, west on I-90, highway empty, endless. Took a long breath. We went over basic safety. Beaver put on a video from the eighties called *The Sauce: A Driver's Worst Friend* (???, 198?).

In the video, a succession of actors attempts to debunk drunk-driving myths. The first, a fat man with brown teeth, says, "If I eat enough, it will counteract the alcohol." We see him scarf pies, wash them down with glass after glass of red wine. Watch him stumble to his car. In the next shot he lies bloody by the side of the road.

Second guy wears a comically oversized golf outfit at a table full of empty beers. "It's just a golf cart," he says. "I can get as drunk as I want." Gets in the cart, drives off a small cliff.

"That's why I never play golf," Fred said. "Dangerous game."

In the third skit, it took me a moment to recognize the actor, but when I did it hit me like a bullet—the one that hit me. The man is handsome, with waves of orange hair, thick eyebrows. High cheeks, distant look in his eyes as though he knows he's too good for this after-school bullshit, but it's all his agent could get and he's got mouths to feed (including his own, which is hungry for everything: bodies, powders, engines gunning under lamplit Hollywood highways). Kahn's eyes pan while the camera stays still. Stumbles into a diner. "If I drink enough coffee," young Kahn says to the camera, "I'll be fine to drive."

Watched him walk, striding, as if he just can't help it even though he's supposed to be pretending to be drunk.

Strange that Kahn can walk, that the movement of his legs is preserved, locked up in a VFW off Route 1 in Dedham. A wonderful walk: confident, straight-toed, as though he could burst into dance at any moment if so inclined.

Kahn walks out of the diner, into a sedan. Reverses straight into a cop car. In the next shot, he's arrested by a guy wearing a cop suit that looks leftover from a porn shoot. Kahn smiles at the camera, though he's probably not supposed to.

A few more skits like this, then all the drunk drivers stand with linked arms, say in unison, "Sauce: the driver's *worst* friend."

Beaver turned off the reel. The lights went on, but I was still thinking of Kahn, who was now two people, one of whom was young, good-looking, had no idea he should heed his own cheaply rendered advice about car safety.

twenty-two

Possible Ending #9 (Real Life):

This is what happens to guys like me: We mine the QHS class of 2014 for legs and a slim worldview. Dads hook us up with jobs we're not qualified to do, or jobs that don't require much doing. Buy cars, develop coke habits, shed baby fat. Afternoons at the gym to armor ourselves against those who think we're laughingstocks (plus homoerotic locker room voyeurism). Someday it's time to get serious if we want to make real money. Dad's on Wife Three, considering retirement. Mom still in Florida. Not sure how Benjy figures in, but he's probably off somewhere too, being an actuary, disapproving of my lifestyle, envying my money/work ratio, secretly loving my sorry ass. So I get serious, get off the coke, take over the Schwartz family business, court and charm some JAP-ed out family friend I've known forevs—a lesser Sherri Sacks: less bitchy, less sexy. Doesn't like Godard, Buñuel, Cassavetes, Howard Hawkes, etc., so we sniffle our way through rom-coms, sniffling for different reasons, neither of us actually sniffling. Children are spoiled rich kids, but we love them, at least I do, attempting to provide the

family I myself never had. Kahn is their wacky/sad outra-
geous uncle, but Wife One fears molestation, so he stops
coming around, much to my chagrin, much to his too, because now he has no one. Don't believe in God, but I say a
simple prayer each night before bed: "Dear Other, let these
kids lose their virginity when it's age appropriate." Divorce,
for the better. She gets the kids though I want them more.
I get Wife Two. I like her because she's young, knows the
young people's music, doesn't mind Kahn or occasional cocaine use. Attend concerts, glug wine from plastic cups, are
eternally out of place, but okay even though my kids hate
us, fair enough, small trade-off, until I get old, lonely, ugly,
sleepy, farty, boozy, happy (briefly), shitty. Mostly I wonder about those other endings, all weighty and romantic,
stiff with meaning. Imagine myself on a stage slinging fake,
swarthy smiles to the studio audience, or in an alleyway
losing blood, losing consciousness, losing the null pain of
upper-upper-middle-class middling.

twenty-three

When in Rome, so I ordered a venti caramel-pumpkin-steamed-soy macchiato, booted my laptop, surveyed the scene. At least for this week, unemployed dads had been replaced by syrup-sweetened-coffee-seeking holiday revelers, done up in matching scarf/sweater sets, as if winter still applied indoors even though the heat was stuck at seventy. Everyone had over-the-shoulder eyes. This was their 54 (*54*, Dollface, 1998): you never knew who might walk in next. Maybe they were looking for old lovers in red cashmere, caffeine-high, nostalgic, cold enough to cuddle. Maybe I was one of them.

My drink was sickly sweet, the kind a five-year-old might "invent," given free reign in the kitchen. No one I knew was there, only a small group of college freshmen at the next table, reunited over eight-dollar pastries, laughing too loud at inside jokes about "snarfs," "MBS," "Remember that time . . ."

Happy, slim—no freshman fifteens—comfortable in the knowledge they'd spend the next three years bullshitting before being gently dropped into the real world, complete with internship-padded résumés, alumni connections.

But I was done being bitter. Bitter had got me nowhere but tube-numb. Triumphantly turned away from the freshmen, scanned my screen, searched the web for employment opportunities.

No idea how to search the web for employment opportunities.

Googled "How to search the web for employment opportunities."

Results were impossible to comprehend. Too many options, too many paid advertisements, too many links to sites offering advice for a small monthly fee of . . . I had no direction, prospects, résumé, qualifications, experience. Stumped, I sipped my drink, watched a bird peck at another bird out the window, unfocused my eyes. When I refocused, noticed a sign that said "Now Hiring."

Manager gave me papers to fill out, said they were looking for people to work weekends during the holidays. He had a Sox tattoo on one wrist, Irish clover on the other. Brim down, bloodshot eyes—my kind of guy. A job that could prolong my inertia by making it financially viable. But it was a start.

"I have no life," I told him. "Weekends are fine."

"We'll be in touch," he said.

Distracted by my first job application, walked right into a woman, knocked her over.

"Eli?" Alison Ghee said.

On the ground, my former lover, not in red cashmere, not high? not quite angry, kind of smiley, looking, if not healthy, then at least sexy-downtrodden down there with fishnet tights, signature slanted bangs.

Helped her up, said, "I'm sorry," brushed the floor-dirt from her coat. Then remembered how mean she'd been the last time I'd seen her, at Jennifer's party.

"Thanks," she said.

I grunted something that sounded like "Ummf."

Actually, it wasn't a grunt, and sounded more like "You're welcome," because it's hard to hold a grudge against a grief-stricken girl who gave you her body amid an epic sex-drought, and might be convinced to do it again, this time in slow-mo, wet soul kisses interspersed throughout.

"What was that?"

"You're welcome," I said.

"Aw. So sweet."

"I've heard that before from you," I said, because I still held a bit of a grudge.

"Before?"

"Remember at Jennifer's party, when you broke my heart?"

"Okay, no idea what you're talking about. You're the one who never called me after our thing or whatever."

"You never gave me your number."

"Touché," she said. "Sorry, it was a weird time."

"You really don't remember the conversation we had at Jennifer's right around Thanksgiving?"

"When I said weird time, I meant super blackout, fucked-up, angry, not in my right mind kind of time. I'm sorry if I said anything mean. I honestly don't remember."

"That's okay. I know the feeling. I've never been in my right mind when I've said anything."

"One of your better qualities."

"That and I'm funny."

Alison didn't laugh.

"Are we even now?" she said.

"Not even close," I said, though I was already imagining stuttering ILY on one knee with Grandma's ring in a field of fresh daisies.

"How about I buy you a coffee?" she said.

"Sure," I said, tossed my caramelized cup of bleh into the garbage, ready for a real drink now that luck had turned my way.

Back in the booth, suddenly silent again, watched the freshman reunion like it was some kind of Platonic ideal (*Plato's Pleasure Palace*, Omega Films, 1976), forever unattainable to us two fuckups.

"Why didn't we turn out like that?" Alison said.

"I think we're more interesting at least."

"You're a romantic."

"That's possible."

She grabbed my application, looked it over.

"Wow. Really aiming high, huh?"

I gave her a "You're on thin ice" look.

She countered with a look of "Sorry, but you walked right into that one, and besides, just because I'm supposed to be nice doesn't mean I have to treat you with kid gloves."

Fair enough.

"Guess I'm not *that* romantic."

"Did you really get shot?"

Pulled up my pant leg, exposed the scar.

"Gangsta-ish."

"Totally, right?"

Out the window, leftover rain colored leftover snow shit-colored.

"I hate winter," Alison said. "I fucking hate it. I hate snow."

"Being inside's not so bad."

"I'm sorry. You're right. I'm being dramatic. And I'm sorry you got shot. No one should have shot you. It's hard enough without people shooting you."

"Thanks," I said, almost adding the word "babe" before remembering it wasn't that kind of movie, or any kind of movie.

A baby screamed at the next table, uncalmed by the rain-drums rattling middlebrow, middle-register world rhythms over the house speakers. His mother—constrained by so-cietal values—didn't smack him. She said, "There, there."

"Were you a happy child?" Alison asked.

"I don't know," I said. "I don't really remember."

For some reason thought of this dream I'd been having where the only way to get out of the dream is to kill your-self, but you know it's a dream so it's okay, but what if it's not a dream?

She said, "It wasn't until high school that I realized not everyone hated themselves."

Apartment was a mess. Alison didn't seem embarrassed that I was embarrassed. Swept the clothes from the bed with a sweeping gesture I'd seen in movies.

"Suave," she said, hopped on the bed, removed her shoes, huddled clothed beneath comforter. Put on a Miles Davis CD Kahn had left me while I was in the hospital. Trumpet blew long, unhurried, not like the way people talk around here: Kahn, Benjy, Mom, Dan, all quick-spitters, words like bullets, more like Coltrane than Miles. The trumpet's voice was like Alison's: breathy, meandering, shaky but also sure.

"Do you have a job?" I said.

"Had one."

"What happened?"

She sang, "Then I got high, then I got high, then I got . . ."

"So what do you do now?"

"Fuck strangers. For money, of course. Sometimes for drugs. Sometimes just for fun."

"Really?"

"Just kidding, fat boy. I get money from my dad. I watch TV most of the time. Stupid shows. Soaps and stuff that I watch with my mom. *Days of Our Lives*, she loves it. Sometimes I just go for walks in Kapler Park. After it's rained. I like it after it's rained."

Saw her walking through Kapler Park post-rain, exhaling smoke, enjoying the dampness in the air even though it frizzed her hair, made her sniffle; enjoyed it because the wet pavement smelled like life. For a second her sad-eyed loner lifestyle didn't seem pathetic, but somehow triumphant, because she'd experienced grief, still managed to walk on a dewy morning, take in the scent of dead wet flowers crushed by the storm at the edge of the woods, watch the sun slowly emerge from between two clouds.

"I watch TV too," I said, kissed her.

This time we faced each other. First I pulled off her panties, licked.

"Do you know where the clit is?"

"I've studied a few diagrams."

"Lick that."

Success. She rumbled like a Rumble Pak, vibrated like a broken fridge, said, "Eli," "My feet are tingling," "Right there." I slurped love syrup until she grabbed my shoulders, pulled me up so I was looking in her eyes, kissed me again, touched her tongue to my teeth, then ears, stomach, sides, thighs, everywhere but . . . until, finally, grazing the underside with her chin, little licks, baby kisses into full-on sucking into "Can I sit on you?"

Sex was slow. Mind too fast, analyzing every moan and minuscule movement. Was that an "AH!" or an "uh?" and why was her hand pulling my hand over the straps, under the chin, music too loud? whose leg was . . .

Then Alison did a thing with her hips, kitten-clawed my handles, up-tempo-ed, kissed my neck, squeezed my nipple, bounced in 6/8 time to Tony Williams's tat-ta-ta-tit-

tat-ti. Tried to keep up, keep steady, keep the world outside
because now I was inside, inside her, outside myself, con-
joined like that dream only I didn't want to separate, just
stay this way forever, two-headed eel into infinity, squish-
squash-egad-eel sounds, swapping air and hair, opposite
of numb, fuzzy with feeling, noticing everything: idiosyn-
cratic beauty, proof she was a single unit, not some repre-
sentative F/21—tiny pink dots around her nipples, errant
curly hair sticking awkwardly from her eyebrow, glassy film
on the surface of her eye (contact lens?), fingernails like
stained glass in the rainbow reflection of an upside-down
DVD, belly-button blond hairs, butt shape indescribable,
blinking in fuck-rhythm, hairspray hair loosed by sweat
(mine?), small trickle down forehead, small trail of saliva,
all muscles working at once, factory gears faithfully turning for mass pleasure production, outside body tied to internal city ever onward in our fuck palace.

"I think I'm . . ."

Alison held my hand, said, "You can if you want."

I let loose a load, didn't feel any lighter, flopped heavy
onto Alison. A good heavy, like sinking into earned sleep.

"I like the weight of you on me," she said.

After, in the living room, Alison scraped candle wax off
Mom's old menorah with her fingernail, collected it in the
palm of her other hand.

"Tonight's the first night."

"We should light the candles."

"I don't know if we have candles. I think we just have
the menorah."

"Oh."

"This is the first year we didn't light them."

Wondered if Kahn had lit candles in our old house,
if Erin was there singing prayers like a lullaby, as Kahn,

who'd been drinking scotch all day, closed his eyes on the couch, put his feet on the chipped coffee table, pictured his old sperm swimming through his ex-wife's body—Sheila's body, another aquarium—being swallowed and nourished by her body at the same time, growing into a person, into that voice singing songs from before the sperm, from a different time when people meant the words.

"Me and Jeremy used to," she said. "When he lived at Beth Shalom."

"Used to what?"

"Go in there on the last night—the eighth night, right? We went late at night. Smoked a bowl and went up there, up on the stage. Spooky being in there so late with just those candles. We would lie down right under the candles. There was the big menorah and the little ones, like they were the big one's children. We didn't kiss or anything. He just unzipped and I pulled my skirt up to my waist."

"I'm sorry."

Alison brushed her bangs from her eyes. They fell right back down.

"I don't even believe in God," she said.

"Me neither."

She let her body fall sideways so her head was resting in my lap. I took a strand of her hair, wrapped it around my finger. Wanted us to be tied together, as if I was her mother, her hair the still-uncut umbilical cord. Closed my eyes, felt like I could fall asleep. Maybe I did fall asleep, or she did, but at some point must have both been looking at the Coke clock because she said, "It's late," left.

This time I got her number, told her I'd cook her a gourmet dinner next Friday.

twenty-four

Possible Ending #10 (American-Made Film About French People):

Sex saves us all. Forget the pleasures of work, family. Lick raw egg from each other's nipples, bathe in bloody bathwater, burn our bodies with candle wax, wax our bodies with waxing wax, stick candles in our etc. Otherwise we drink too much, recite poetry, read from crusty stolen books, ash into wine bottles, inhale asbestos, complain of chronic ailments like gout, tennis elbow, fuck each other's friends, fight, break apart, reconcile, eventually die in black night, but not in the morning, which is really the afternoon. In the morning I dangle in morning light, eat grapefruit. She saunters in wearing my shirt, half-unbuttoned, hair hanging, unwashed, champagne in our OJ. The only meal ever is breakfast. Breakfast is birth.

twenty-five

Sat on the couch, flipped through an old *Sports Illustrated*. Kobe on the cover, draining a fade-away, making everyone forget he may or may not have raped a woman in Colorado. Closed my eyes. Ceiling light buzzed. Had a strange desire to ejaculate on everything in the room—firestorm of jizz, dick a goo-spouting garden hose. Watch the doc's expression when she sees her waiting room, every nook of the couch bubbling with lacquered shine.

"Eli?"

"That's me."

"I'm Dr. Hoffman. Marni Hoffman."

"Hi, Marni."

"You can call me Dr. Hoffman. Come in."

A nice office with lots of books, two matching brown leather recliners that faced each other.

"Sit," she said.

"No couch?"

"That's only for analysis."

"Oh. I was hoping to lie down."

She didn't laugh.

"Go on."

"That's it. I'm out of material."

"Do you often feel like you want to lie down?"

"No. Actually, these days I have a lot of energy. More than I used to. I feel totally restless, like I have all this energy that I can't use in any way."

"What does the energy feel like?"

"I don't know. I mean, it's not like a Gatorade commercial or anything. I don't suddenly want to run around the B-ball court with well-built black men, or wear cool goggles and snowboard off cliffs. The feeling is more vague than that, like when you're having a dream and someone's chasing you and you can't scream. That's kind of what it feels like."

"Is this feeling why you came in today?"

"I think it's all related."

"Related to what?"

Not sure what to say. Hoffman was youngish, forties, younger than my parents. Bit on the skinny side, curveless, nice legs, intelligent face—skinny lips, long neck. Or maybe I just thought so because she had so many books.

"I keep having these weird sex dreams. But they're not erotic or anything, they just involve sex. Like sex is just a part of some circle-of-life bullshit where in these dreams I'm born and I die all in one brilliant act that leaves me waking shamed and sweaty with the strange feeling that I have been castrated. And then I have to reach down and check that my dick's still there, only I realize that it's still part of the dream, and the person who's reaching down isn't me but my mother. My mother just moved to Florida."

"In real life or in the dream?"

"Real life."

Hoffman crossed and uncrossed her legs. Noticed her noticing me noticing.

"I didn't want to come here today, actually. I was forced to. Because I got shot and had lots of drugs in my system."

"Do you want to talk about that?"

"It hurt."

"Being forced to come here?"

"No. Getting shot. My leg got all fucked up."

"Why did you bring it up?"

"Full disclosure."

"Do you think you have a problem with drugs?"

"It seems to be the consensus."

"What do *you* think?"

"I think I have a problem without drugs too."

"So even though you were forced to come here, you think it might be a good idea?"

"I didn't say that. I said that I have some problems. I have no idea if talking to you about them will help at all. In fact, I'm rather skeptical about the whole process."

Hoffman didn't say anything. I looked around the room. No pictures of her family, just books, framed degrees. Her entire life lay behind the wall, all her objects: stocked kitchen, couple flatscreens, dog, 2.8 kids, 1.2 husbands. But in here she had to listen to me. Couldn't turn away, flick the tube, answer her cell. Had to listen to my pent-up pain, sexual retardation. Couldn't laugh, spit, tell her friends, "He fucked Mrs. Sacks and ejaculated prematurely! He passed out on the football field with a boner and got a standing ovation and now he thinks he can get his shit together!" She had to sit there, nod, tell me she understood, I wasn't that different, everything would be okay.

"But I am open to it," I said.

"Well, that's an important place to start."

"I want to make some changes in my life."

"Good," she said.

Wanted to talk about Kahn, about yesterday with Alison, about Mom in Florida, and all these movie endings applied to my own life, how they all seemed either shitty or unrealistic or played-out or unfulfilling or all of the above, but were the only futures I could imagine because I didn't know what people actually did once they became legit humans in the real world with successful relationships, jobs, sex, happiness, romance, etc., or if those things even existed or were just endings to different kinds of movies, bad movies that make people feel good then sad again when they leave the theater because their own lives can't live up.

Instead blurted, "Earlier, when I was in your waiting room, for some reason I felt like I wanted to masturbate all over everything in the waiting room."

The doctor nodded.

"I have a date for the first time ever and I don't know what to do," I said.

"Just be yourself."

"That's the worst advice I've ever heard. I just told you all this weird shit about wanting to masturbate on couches, and you tell me to be myself? I can't be myself. Myself is someone who gets all fucked up and passes out on the football field with a boner because I took too much Viagra the night before. Myself is someone who takes too much Oxy and coke and breaks into houses. I mean, I want this girl to like me."

"Yourself can be other things too," she said. "It doesn't just have to be those things."

"She's coming over for dinner and I don't know what to make."

"What's your best dish?"

"Pheasant."

"What's your second-best dish?"

"Elk stew?"

"Didn't your mother teach you to make chicken?"

"Does Slim Fast count as chicken?"

"What are you really trying to say here, Eli?"

"I don't know."

Long pause. Looked at the ground, then at her, then at the window as if I were looking out it, even though the blinds were drawn.

"I don't know," I said again.

Felt like I could keep saying it, over and over, a mantra. Rhythm of the phrase was consistent grime, like the sound of the old Green Line trains. Said it one more time.

"What don't you know?"

"Anything."

twenty-six

Possible Ending #11 (The Kind of Movie Your Mom Likes Because It Gives Her Hope in Regards to You, and Because She Somehow Doesn't See Herself in the Mother Character):

Head-shrunk, happy-pilled, learn the valuable life lesson that all women aren't my mother, won't always abandon me, will occasionally run a finger through my hair, whisper, "I'm so proud," unironically. Understand Mom's/Dad's pain is not my fault, vice versa. Finally a breakthrough, a revelation: this isn't a story about Mom and Dad after all; it's about learning to tell a story that's not about Mom and Dad but about me and the world, etc., which I'm doing now, sitting in my easy chair, after work, telling Alison about my day, state of mind, inner feelings, what's for dinner, funny thing that happened to Benjy, YouTube clip, new Top 40 song that's bad but kind of catchy, what's in the theater, what's on the tube that night—stories people tell each other every day that keep them going, keep them healthy, keep them from harming themselves and others. Accept my parents' divorce, see them for who they are: flawed human beings who, for reasons partly but not entirely their fault, can't provide the kind of love and support I need. That's okay. I get love and support from others, like my therapist (I have transference issues), Alison, Benjy, who actually does care about and need me too, even if we never tell each other because we're men, embarrassed. Accept my lot in life, work at Starbucks, enjoy simple pleasures like braised short ribs, cold beer, the way Alison's teeth chatter when she laughs (weird, but endearing). Alison is also flawed, as am I, often sad, sometimes a liar, possibly a cheater, still fond of drugs. Learn to live with each other, occasionally fighting, dealing with life's difficulties—death, grief, sickness, sadness, frustration, aging, addiction, etc.—not easy, not so bad either. Visit my dad, Pam, Kahn, Sheila, Mary. Become role models for Natasha, do cooking projects, cry in front of each other, also burp, sing, dance, punch, smoke, sockslide across fresh-waxed hardwood floors.

twenty-seven

A loud bang came from the backyard. Dropped my bike on the front lawn, walked around the house, past the gutter pipes. Another bang. Kahn sat in his wheelchair wearing a blue terry-cloth bathrobe, slippers. Shooting empty liquor bottles lined up on top of the fence.

Beth Cahill stood next to him, fully clothed this time in ski jacket, jeans. She held a cardboard box, wore large headphones. Mostly empty vodka bottle at her feet. Other guests too: young woman with plastic-looking hair, shirtless man with pierced nipples, bull-style nose ring, ski goggles. Both smoked cigs, sat in metal chairs (my smoking chair!), not paying attention to the makeshift artillery range directly to their right.

Beth watched Kahn, who sat motionless, staring at the bottle he'd been aiming for, maybe wondering if his bullet had traveled into the Mitchells' home; if their eight-year-old son or their cocker spaniel, Moses, now lay dead on the floor.

She opened the box, handed Kahn a single bullet. With methodical movement, like a young private under observation by his commanding officer (*Daughter of the*

Desert, Focus Features, 2004), Kahn inserted the bullet into the rifle. Slid forward the bolt, squinted through the scope. Face was method-acting-intense, maybe because he wasn't actually acting, or because he was. Beth kept her eyes on him, on his hands that weren't shaky but surprisingly steady. Behind them, the others laughed, sipped from plastic cups.

Kahn shot. Chair rolled backward. Beth reached out a hand to slow the movement, causing Kahn's chair to swivel so that he now faced me head-on. The bullet hit the fence.

"Land of the dead," Kahn said. "How was it?"

"You tell me."

Nip Ring laughed high-pitched, repeated, "Land of the dead," in campy alto. Girl laughed too. Beth removed her headphones to see what was funny. Waved but didn't smile.

"I don't know," Kahn said. "I've never returned. I have nothing to compare it to."

He picked up the vodka bottle, finished it in one long gulp, chucked it end-over-end like a boomerang in front of him, toward me. Aimed his gun at the bottle.

"Bang," Kahn said, drawing more squeals from the toasted peanut gallery. I didn't flinch. Looked at the gun, tried to remember it aimed at me that night, to imagine the trajectory of its bullet that went through my leg, was now lodged in the living room wall for eternity, or at least until the house is demolished, earth reharvested, large trees to cover empty indoor-space, though probably someone will replace the thing with a cloud-scraping McMansion, be done with it.

"Want a turn?" Kahn said.

Walked to where he was standing, took the gun, stroked its wood stock. Kahn stuck his finger in his own chest.

"Right here. Then we'll be even. An eye for an eye."

"You shot me in the leg," I said. "Not the heart."

"I don't have legs," Kahn said.

"Not technically true," I said, pointed the gun at him, said, "Bang," handed Kahn the gun.

Wind blew through the yard, opened Kahn's untied robe. Shirtless beneath it. Chest looked like a piece of stale fiber-bread, nipples and moles for seeds and grains.

"You must be freezing," I said.

"Inside," Kahn shouted. "Bring me inside."

Beth grabbed the back handles of his chair. I grabbed the wheels from the front. Carried him up onto the porch, through the screen door, into the kitchen. I walked backward, face to face with Kahn. He looked intensely at my face as if Alzheimered, attempting to remember someone who seems familiar, but whose specifics can't be accessed by memory.

From the kitchen, Kahn led the way to the living room, to our old chipped coffee table. Lingered for a moment in the kitchen, trying to remember my greatest meals, that feeling of being alone in the world, late night, house asleep, town asleep, backyard darkness through the sliding doors.

They passed a crack pipe, or something that looked like a crack pipe, might have been a meth pipe. Nip Ring crushed pills with a credit card. The girl kissed his neck, rubbed his shoulders. Beth hit the pipe, removed her jacket.

Kahn flipped the pages of a large book.

"Join us," he said, patted the empty couch seat next to him.

Beth put the pipe in Kahn's mouth, lit it. As he inhaled he moved his face toward the open book. Beth's hands moved in conjunction. A cookbook. Photos on the open page were tightly shot so everything was visible, each fleck of salt unique in its shape and tint. Basil greener than real life. Peppers peeling off the page. Kahn leaned into a bowl of sauce-soaked spaghetti, salivated.

Beth took the pipe from Kahn's mouth. Kahn pulled the book right up to his face until it sequestered his entire line of vision. For a moment I thought his head would be swallowed by the book, that his slim body would disappear within the pages.

"Jambalaya," he said. Beth turned the page. "Shrimp ceviche."

Then he dropped the book to the floor, leaned back into the couch, covered his face with his hands, uncovered, smiled, swallowed.

Beth stood behind the girl, rubbed her belly as she danced. Nip Ring was gyrating, spinning an invisible hula hoop.

Without opening his eyes or moving his head from its reclining position, Kahn said, audible only to me, "You're a good son."

Put his left hand on my thigh. I watched him do this, tensed my muscles even though I wanted to relax, embrace his touch. He didn't rub, just squeezed. Lifted his head, rested it on my shoulder. I let him leave it there. We sat like that. Breath tickled the hair on my arms. I was stiff but felt I should stay still, not upset his precarious balance, let him fade peacefully from consciousness, lavish some much-needed, honest affection on the old dude.

"Good boy," Kahn said, or maybe, "Goodbye."

Nibbled at my neck, squeezed my pathetic bicep, ran a hand from hips up to my ribs. Beth licked the other girl's legs. Nip Ring was pantsless now, doing some kind of chicken dance.

"Beautiful," Kahn said, met my eyes.

I'd like to articulate what I saw in his stare: mortality, humanity, love, death, pain, joy, etc. But it was something else. More like fear that's been stripped of anticipation, fear of pain that already exists, but also an understanding that the disappearance of that pain is a disappearance of everything alive—disappearance into death. An unfair look: shitty with honesty, needy for things we both know I can't give. I'd like to say I squeezed his body, felt his bones through his thinning skin, pressed his wildly beating heart against my own, synchronized.

I didn't. Said, "I should go."

Kahn lifted his head from my shoulder. I tried to stand but Kahn had latched onto my arm with both hands, was pulling me toward him.

"Stay."

"I have to go."

Used my own fingers to unclasp his, which wasn't difficult.

twenty-eight

Possible Ending #12 (circa 1946):

THE END

twenty-nine

Benjy in the bathtub. Door half open. No suds. Curl-pubed cock swayed lean and long in steamy water. Even there we weren't the same. Legs over the side, dripping, immobile, like hanging laundry. Hair frosty with leave-in. Star of David pendant floated above concave chest.

Couldn't believe Benjy still wore it. I'd had the same one—gifts from Dad—must have tossed mine in a bout of anti-Dad, anti-religious fervor, or else lost it immediately to the many drawers and containers that kept our objects hidden, consumed our knickknacks for us to find later: dusty, depressingly unused.

Wished I had the necklace still. Not for solidarity with my never-chosen faith or the throngs of liberal-except-Israel sandal-wearers with DNA similar to mine, but for a secret sameness to share with Benjy beneath our clothes. A repeated reminder of our childhood, of the love-imparting father who'd lived for at least that moment.

Benjy cried, sobbed, held a cell phone to his ear, said, "Baby," said, "Erin," said, "I'm sorry," said, "Fuck," said, "Fuck me," said, "Please," said, "I know but," said, "I don't," said, "I mean," said, "Oh, Ere, please, I made a terrible mistake."

Dropped his cell in the water. Sank until it rested in the hollow cave between his puffy pecs. With his heart in my head brought laptop to the bathroom door, put on Kurt C., acoustic, singing, "All alone is all we are." Sat on the shut toilet saying nothing, in acquiescence of the song's bleakness, but also in defiance because I was here, quiet but consoling in my way; we weren't alone. Passed a bottle of house white Mom had left chilling in the fridge for future consumption.

Benjy must have sensed the strangeness of it all: he naked and drinking, while I, for once, the pacifier, rife with good news I couldn't share—Alison, etc.—and also the sad Kahn story I had to keep buried, to hide from fragile Ben who lay in the rapidly cooling water like an underfed goldfish, waiting, without expectation, for food or death, no matter.

"This is pretty gay," Benjy said.

"Don't be a homophobe," I said.

"Sorry," he said. "Thanks."

Glugged, passed, put his head beneath the water. I silently baptized my brother.

thirty

Possible Ending #13 (*Good Will Hunting* as Directed by Woody Allen):

I am a licensed guidance counselor with a master's degree. Seriously. Office smells of leather, leather cleaner. Filled with dusty psycho-texts I read for years in grad school and now display. Proof of my postadolescent growth. Proof of learned-ness, boring-ness (which I treasure). Mustachioed, but not in a creepy way, just in a Jewy dad way. Still in Quinosset. Kids come to me. Fucked-up teens from QHS, arms crossed with math-protractor-made cuts. Threatening suicide. Threatening escape. Threatening to fuck my daughter. Threatening violence on those who let them down. I nod my head, listen. Respond with knowing advice in a grizzled, smoke-toughened voice that tells them I'm one of them. Stay calm. I'm still one of them. I do not hug, though it's all I want to do, to hold their growing bodies in the dim lamplight of that musty room, tell them everything will end up okay, it did for me (though maybe I'm lying, maybe not).

thirty-one

Friday—date night—came slowly. First it hovered, like the blinking light atop a radio tower in the black center of nighttime, seemingly unprovoked, its web of supporting beams invisible. Sat in driver's ed listening to Beaver ramble. Zeke came in with mustache shaved. Next day he wasn't there. Kept the same seat, kept my eyes glued to the tube. Beaver's even voice was like a lullaby. The word "Friday" a one-word monologue on loop in my head. Couldn't imagine conversation, only images, rom-com images: Alison and I seated at my kitchen table, one candle between us, me spooning salad onto her plate, glasses clinking. Benjy would stay away. Had plans to talk things over with Erin, win back her trust with chocolate and his trademark forgive-me tears. Big night for both of us.

Then it was Friday. Cleaned the kitchen, vacuumed the carpet in the TV room, washed my sheets. I'd become an expert at laundry since Mom had left me with instructions on my hospital bed. My duty now to embrace the washing machine, understand its knobs and idiosyncrasies the way an uncle must learn to understand an orphaned and subsequently adopted niece (*Uncle Fun*, Disney, 1997). By this point I'd developed my own system, knew which detergent I preferred, which spin cycle worked best for linens. There had been experiments with dryer sheets, fabric softeners, antiwrinkle sprays. Watching Benjy I'd learned to fold a tee shirt the way they do in stores, sleeves dipped behind the back.

By lunchtime the house smelled like chemicals. I stood, broom in hand, reflecting on my scrubbings, thinking this is what it must feel like to have a job, to finish a day's work, have something to show for it, something somewhat intangible, emitting a light fragrance, an odor of completion that lingers on your body like sex or cheap cologne. Then: how pathetic to equate two hours of simple chores to the quiet triumph of stepping out of the office as the sun hangs just above the trees, standing with loose tie lighting that victory cigarette, forgetting that tomorrow will be the same, because right now there's a barstool surrounded by your coworkers, who want nothing more than to commiserate over two-for-one margaritas, plates of over-cheesed nachos. Work seemed like a wonderful dream: to feel competent or, at least, paralleled in your incompetence. Hate your boss, smell like coffee and cheap sandwiches because we're all defined by smell dating back to those cavemen who got laid based on scent alone, sweating pheromones, chasing deer in the sun before returning to the dwelling oozing fluids like syrup to be licked by bucktoothed cavewomen with dangling breasts, dark brown eyes, so dark the pupil is indecipherable as its own entity, the eye itself a muddy marble surrounded by thin patches of white like stray pieces of dried deodorant.

Out of deodorant, biked to Store 24 to get some, then to Whole Foods. Picked things that looked fresh: arugula—an aphrodisiac?—Swiss chard, Swiss cheese, cherry tomatoes, tahini, Yukon gold potatoes to make Greek style, fresh swordfish to complement, one giant eggplant. Tapas. Figured I'd give her options.

Saw no one I knew, not Mrs. S., Sheila, or some other object of my milfy desires. Aisles empty. Lunchtime; women in Pilates class contorting their bodies asexually, showing off tight abs to fleshy post-childbirth classmates, imagining teenage Spanish boys whistling at their tanned, toned thighs as they walk across a beach in Barcelona. Because if they kept it up, tightened their calf muscles, sharpened their shoulder blades, they would stave off degeneration, the gradual softening of bones and skin, like old cucumbers, dripping, sticky, tucked away in some refrigerated corner unnoticed.

Let my cart swivel through the aisles like a leashed toddler, which I'd seen at Whole Foods once, watched him grope at chocolate-covered strawberries. Felt stoned but wasn't, wondered what Alison would wear.

Nikki was at checkout, smiling, happy to be interrupted from monotony by someone she knew, even if that someone was me.

"Looks like quite the feast."

"It's not."

"Got a big date or something?"

"It's nothing."

"I don't believe you," she said in a shrill singsong with a melody that reminded me of Mom's ringtone.

"What, did Dan tell you? I haven't seen him in ages."

"Dan didn't tell me shit. We don't speak anymore."

"What happened?"

"He's an asshole."

"But I thought . . ."

"We weren't in love," she said, though I hadn't asked, and by the way she looked at her feet, it seemed as though she wasn't sure if it was true or not.

She totaled my bill. I barely had enough, even though Mom had been sending checks; it was her job now that she was in Florida. Wasn't sure if it was her money or Goldblum-Spelled-Differently's.

"I can just put it in my backpack. I'm on bike."

"So who's the date with?"

"Do you know Alison Ghee?"

"That whore-bag?"

Wanted to defend my date. Instead said, "Is she?"

"Total whore-bag. I used to be friends with Jeremy. He was a good kid."

"I was friends with him too."

"A real chill kid. Not like that bitch Dan."

Biked home, backstreets. Cigarette dangling, flowers in hand, half baguette sticking from my backpack. Imagined myself in the French countryside, cobblestone streets, wind carrying hints of wine, cheese, and female perspiration dripping from unshaven armpits.

Back at the hypothetical love shack, bid my time, one eye on the TV, other on the Coke clock, whose inscription offered the unrealistic advice "Enjoy life." At some point I bathed. Washed parts of my body that hadn't seen soap in years: backs of knees, inside of belly button. Shaved, double-brushed, triple-mouthwashed, even considered giving myself a haircut before concluding I would only make my curls look worse. Instead struggled with a comb, plucked nose hairs, deodorized, aftershaved, foot-powdered.

Mirror confirmed I'd been losing weight. Stretch marks above my hips still visible, but shriveled now, more like battle scars than active wounds. Chest hair had been coming in slowly, curly. And though our faces weren't the same, the slump of my body—like a melting popsicle, shoulders falling earthward, head like a forward-thrust ball bearing forcing my spine into a parabolic bend—reminded me of my dad's. My face, on the other hand, was hers. We shared tiny eyes, half-closed, ever squinting. Noses lurched and bent in a way that might have seemed wholly individual—product of a foul ball or errant elbow—if not shared by us both. They would always be joined, my parents, DNA united in my body and Benjy's, in the way our bodies changed and aged, in our first gray hairs (which Benjy had already), the dwindling pace of our metabolisms. Seeing those two in my own reflection I knew it wouldn't work out with Alison.

Instead of giving up, turned away from the mirror (away from the condemning glare of my parents) and walked to my closet, primed to do battle with my wardrobe. As armies, we were unevenly matched. Downside to losing weight was that now all my clothes made me look like a nineties holdover, still rocking the baggy remnants of grunge, still longing for the ex-Seattle of my imagination, where the coffee tastes like coffee cake, and Doc Martens girls scowl in a way that means they want to rip open your Soundgarden tee shirt, make angry, caffeinated love on a futon of discarded flannel (*Singles*, Warner Bros., 1992).

Also hadn't been clothes shopping since eighth grade, when it was cool to check out girls at the mall, a time just before I'd decided it was even cooler to get stoned in the woods without any girls in a two-mile vicinity. I'd persevered by wearing clothes purchased for me by relatives at various holidays and birthdays, free tee shirts I'd gotten at bar mitzvahs and charity softball games, the occasional dress shirt left behind by Dad. I liked to pretend I had my own style, that there was something slob-chic about my mixed and matched accoutrements. Actually had no style. Now my clothes didn't even fit. Considered squeezing into something of Benjy's, or making a quick bike to the mall, but decided against both because even thin I still out-weighed big bro by thirty pounds, and I didn't want to get sweaty after just having primped.

Settled on a green button-down Dad used to wear while doing carpentry at the old old house. He'd looked rugged in it, sleeves rolled up, his then-chiseled pectoral muscles bulging, vine of unbridled chest hair surmounting the top button in an attempt to garrote his neck. Thought maybe some of that masculinity was contained in the ac-tual shirt, would now confer itself upon me, its wearer. And either I was right, the shirt had magical powers, or I myself had grown manlike without noticing—broadened shoul-ders, absence of pudge around my chin revealing a sharply rectangular jaw, effect of being shot creating a tight ripple across my bushy brow, but I looked okay. Maybe my genes weren't so bad. Maybe it was rogue blood that ran through my body, Don Juan DNA. Moved into the kitchen to pre-pare the meal. Chopping onions, leaned over the cutting board to feel myself cry.

thirty-two

Possible Ending #14 (Unsatisfying):

Hover over the kitchen range: stirring, sniffing, salting, singing unself-consciously along with cable channel 567—Reggae-all-day-mon! Table set for two: no chinks in the china, silverware arranged in formal French style, menorah in the middle, nine candles slow-burning, champagne chilling in the ice-filled sink. Camera moves back to me, closes in, first on my face—awash in concentration, brow bent, eyes brown ovals of intensity oddly complemented by whimsical curls, dimple-pimpled cheeks, lips curled in expectation, tongue darting quasi-sexually, quasi-creepily, but more in an "alone and no one's watching, face free to freak as it pleases" way. Camera moves to my hands: knife-nicked, thick-fingered, fluent in the language of stir, shake, salt, sniff; fluid fingers move like ballet feet, rehearsed enough to give the dual impression of chaos and control. Now camera pulls away, away from hands, out of pan, away and behind my body, lights slowly dimming until I'm just silhouette, shadowed by stove-flame, framed by the peaceful dark and inherent self-triumph of the moment regardless of how things turn out on the date or otherwise. Fade out.

thirty-three

It appeared that she was running late—somewhere in the murky district between fashionably and rudely—so I opened the wine, settled into a glass, which became two glasses, which became the bottle. By ten o'clock, two things were certain: (1) Alison wasn't coming and (2) I was drunk.

Did what anyone in my situation would do: tried her cell every five, leaving tongue-loose messages professing undying affection, promising erotic performance on par with Don Juan (*Don Juan DeMarco*, New Line, 1994). When that didn't work, chugged what remained of the bottle, helmeted my spin-cycling dome, saddled my cycle, set off in search of something to make me forget I'd ever tried.

Empty streets were a giant set stuffed with flashing store facades, seemingly undeep with 3-D depth. No people or animals, only parked cars infinitum. Trees were naked, starving West Coast wusses, unhappily displaced into East Coast winter. Wind hit my face like a slap-happy sibling, saying, "Wake up, sleepyhead, so as to suffer like the rest."

Places people went in these situations were comfort, calm voices. Calm voices came from parents. In this case, parents weren't close, or comforting. Imagined Dad grunting "Better off," Mom caught up in sitcom C-plot saying "Sorry E., one minute, Mindy's about to get that sweater she's been wanting . . ." If I'd known them better, might have uphilled to Sheila and Mary, sobbed into velvet handkerchief, whispered Nina Simone lyrics while Sheila held my hand, mended my broken heart with golden thread.

Obviously ended up where I always ended up, the place that felt like home, the man who might understand. Wondered if, yesterday, I'd made Kahn feel like Alison had made me feel tonight.

Went around back, helmet on, semi-seriously braced for another round of gunfire, bullets and clothes flying, Kahn high, lying naked with closed eyes sending squirts of semen into brisk air, watching it fall like sticky rain on his hairy stomach. Maybe Beth in the backyard with him, swilling chardonnay, tied to a tire swing, softly singing the Lord's Prayer. Or something.

Quiet, dark, would have been star-soaked if it weren't so cloudy. Security-light-soaked when I walked by the security light. A dog barked. Apparently Kahn's bullet had missed. Back door open. No B&E this time. House was quiet too. Reminded me of nights with Mom asleep, sneaking around in socked feet, tiptoe-hopping to music in my head, wanting to jump out windows, smash guitars, stick my penis in anything alive. Strange thing was I liked this feeling, though I hated it now, wondered where Kahn was, wanted anything, even sad, as long as it ended in numbness and the feeling that at least one person in this whole fucking world gave a shit.

No music. Living room empty, lights off. No loose bras, blunt roaches. Ran a hand across the coffee table, groping anything solid. Wandered to Mom's old room. Soundless because the carpeting was still there, still covering Dad's hardwood floors. Imagined Dad still mad about it, knew he didn't give a shit anymore. Felt sad about that.

Guess I should have known Alison would be on the bed, asleep. Or, at least, in incoherent half-sleep, half-high. She wore a white gown. Not a nightgown or a wedding gown. More like an antique ball gown complete with lace garters, pink pillbox hat. Hair had been done in an attempted bouffant, but half the strands had fallen from the shoddily inserted clips, fell against her pale neck. Clown-red lips, cheeks. Turquoise circles around her eyes. Like a little girl playing dress-up.

Possible Ending #15 (Life Imitates Art Imitates Life Imitates Art Imitates): I'd seen this movie. Obvious ending: outright betrayal, lesson learned, life is heartbreak, people who mean well still fuck you over, everyone's sad, greedy, looking out for number one, no consideration for the fragile fat boy whose displayed cynicism only masks a deeper hope that everyone's okay, will ultimately end up all right, that love exists, that happiness may not be stable but at least comes in bursts, that everything worthwhile wasn't just a self-created illusion.

I'd expected something more original from these two—Kahn, especially, who had acted in enough movies to understand their tropes, avoid cliché—figured we were above this, weren't in a movie anymore, were joyfully sliding headfirst into untrammeled territory, unpredictable, undictated by the old narratives we'd studied, shucked.

Maybe it was more gut-punch-holy-shitballs than I'm making it sound. Certainly my gut hurt, face hurt, couldn't breath, speak, barely stayed standing, balls receding into pelvis, pelvis into spine, spine shocked into paralysis, neck extended, tongue bitten, legs wobbly, ears unhearing, gasping for breath like an asthmatic smoker, which I was.

Alison looked like a desert mirage I'd always reach for, never have, never even hate out loud because I wanted to keep the dream alive, accept her explanations, concede some betrayal and psychological instability for the promised reward of occasional days like the one where she came over after coffee, came in my mouth, let me hold her as I fell asleep on the couch. But even on the visceral level I felt less betrayed by the act itself—whatever it was—than by the uncreativity of the actors, the all-else-fails reliance on this trodden, deeply depressing, uncomplicated numb-slutty-spaced-out fever dream.

Alison was on the edge of the bed, sliding off. Gown too big. Gravity only loosed it more. One breast revealed. Pink nipple pointed at the ceiling fan.

"Come dance, my dear," Kahn said, like it was a normal thing to say.

Pulled her arms. Top half tuxedoed, bottom half bare. Pretzel stick legs all scarred, unmoving. Stroked Alison's hair, pressed a palm against her cheek, kissed her ear, rubbed her hip, said, "Let us twirl like children on the merry-go-round."

I felt sick, fell forward into the room, reaching out for Alison, landing face-first in Kahn's lap.

"Good evening," Kahn said, stroked my helmet like it was hair.

Lay there, not ready to retreat or acknowledge the various truths of the situation.

He said, "Let's play your body like a harp," possibly to Alison, possibly to me, possibly to himself. Wasn't even a good line, second-rate, regular scriptwriter out with flu, only some robot feeding the obviously drunk Kahn unworthy dialogue.

Regained my balance, stood, backed toward the door still staring at the near-still-life of Alison and Kahn reenacting some sweet moment from Kahn's remembered or imagined previous legged life. A moment with Sheila, maybe, night he won the Golden Globe, or after *Wood and Nail* at Cannes, audience all gone home, only Kahn and Sheila left in the hotel to celebrate his well-deserved triumph, sip bubbly, stare at the Riviera, buttoned for fun in evening wear, touring the room clasped together, arm to hip, hip to groin, everything ecstatic.

Maybe it was only something he'd seen in a movie once.

Took Kahn's Golden Globe, threw it at him. Globe missed entirely, bounced benignly from quilted sheets.

"Eli," Alison said. "You're wearing a bicycle helmet."

I ran.

thirty-four

Possible Ending #16 (American Coming-of-Age):

Done with this town and all who have done me wrong, get in my new used car, drive toward new life as represented by the ever-nearing horizon. Old song on the radio about days and their dawns. Down Grande, past the card store—Amy in the window scooping slushy—past the empty Little League field, Starbucks, Dunkin' Donuts, Blockbuster, QHS, radio tower. Onto the highway, west like a true American. Into motel country, among the strip malls, mega malls, golden arches, cell-phone towers; through waves of wireless signal, satellite beams, these carpets of information that hover in the air like invisible clouds, ropes of data binding everything but our bodies, so as we move apart, we are still hopelessly connected.

thirty-five

Thing I hate about those movies with the highway ending is they never tell you what comes next: profound loneliness. Not to mention complete lack of direction, stuck in the Midwest, no friends, no job, just this fleeting feeling of freedom before the guy realizes what he had wasn't great but at least it was the start of something decent, what with his okay brother, rich father. Still heartbroken over Alison, Jennifer, Mom, Kahn, etc., still longing for something I'll never achieve because the thing I'm longing for is home, family, and maybe this freedom thing's overrated or not freedom at all because America hates a loner, Middle America hates East Coast Jews, etc.

thirty-six

Sat on the bench outside Starbucks, watching high-tech strollers roll, complete with sunroofs for ultimate vitamin D consumption. Kids viewed windy world through designer shades. Nannies shivered. Single frigid hands controlled stroller handles, weaved charges through paths of Kapler Park, eyes forward, unblinking, other hand holding cell phone to ear to listen as lovers spout grocery lists, parents praise persistence, doctors handle prescriptions, cubicled former sorority sisters in the adrenaline thrall of schadenfreude waste the nine-to-five whispering weakly stimulating gossip about which Tiffanies and Ambers have gained a couple pounds.

We'd been in Amy's talking to Amy, checking out cards, sampling games where death was a mere door to another, fresher life. A regressive step, but also comforting after previous night's events. Nothing to look forward to, it seemed, but the card store and its too-smart children whose joystick hands were quicker than my pot-slowed dinosaur thumbs.

Benjy answered his brand new cell phone, said, "I can't talk now . . . no . . . baby . . . no, I know . . . look . . . look, I'm coming later . . . I love you, okay? . . . I know . . . I love . . . I know . . . I'll call you in an hour . . . yes, I'll pick up the . . . yes . . . sourdough . . . right . . . and soy milk . . . look, I'll, I mean, I love you, okay, bye."

"I wish I had your gene for cooking," he said.

"I wish I had yours for bullshitting."

"I wish I had yours for . . . actually, I only want the cooking one."

"If I were her I would hate you," I said. "I see that now. You are an absolutely terrible person."

"She does. But she also doesn't. It's complicated."

"Everything is more complicated than it might appear to be," I said.

As if to prove it, I unfolded a crumpled mini-map of Massachusetts that had mysteriously appeared in my wallet, hidden beneath years of concert tickets and old receipts that raised my bony ass, bent my crooked back. Map was whitened and wilted, impossible to refold. I opened it up, sounded out the names of foreign towns, ones that might hold more promising futures for myself.

"Quincy," I said. "Beverly. Waltham. North Adams. Marblehead. Lenox."

Benjy took it from my hand, briefly scoped Boston's nonsensical public transit system, then ripped it a thousand ways, watched the paper snow fall from his hands, float on the wind.

"We're working things out."

"Yeah?"

"Actions aren't always forever. She knows it was a mistake. Your thing was probably a mistake too."

"My thing was the truth I refused to look at."

"Nothing is fucked here, dude," Benjy said, like he was Dan or something now, quoting from movies, saying things that meant nothing.

"You're awfully optimistic."

"What's meant to be will be."

Benjy looked at his phone, unconvinced. Put the phone in his pocket. I kicked a cigarette butt, lit another. A black-haired chub of a child rolled happily in wet leaves, oblivious to pants stains. His mom or nanny brushed the leaves off without comment, rubbed his little neck, hoisted him, for a moment, into the air. Wondered if things like that had happened in my childhood, if there were times when I'd been cared for without condition, without scorn, when someone had picked me up by choice, held me like a living trophy. Didn't remember any of my babysitters. Apparently Uncle Ned had slept with one, or so my mother had insinuated. Wondered who she was and where she was now. If I could seek her out, call her up, ask her what he'd said so sweet to coo her in, and if, after, he'd fled, had forced her from the nanny job with shame. Maybe I could say I was sorry. Felt like everything anyone ever said could be an apology if phrased and toned in such a way.

"Mom and Dad never got back together," I said.

"Mom and Dad were a shitty couple to begin with."

"How do you know what they were like to begin with?"

"I'm older than you."

"By two years."

"Your memory's been compromised by drugs. Dad was always a cheater. I once heard him on the phone. A woman whispering about a blow job. I was old enough to know what a blow job was."

"Sure your memory hasn't been compromised?"

"I got a six-seventy on the math SAT."

"That was a while ago, and that's not even that good."

"My memory's been strengthened by the indelible events of our childhood."

"So why did you never hate him?"

"I think I sort of understood. He was married to Mom. Maybe I've been recently trying to understand. Maybe it's time you yourself forgive and forget."

"Oh, fuck off, cheater. If I were her I'd cut your balls off," I said, though my anger was misplaced. He'd been a mensch about my troubles, was here for me now when no one else was.

"Besides, no one's asked for my forgiveness."

"Maybe I'm asking."

I flicked his earlobe, pinched his wind-red cheek.

"Maybe I'm offering."

We sat for a while in postcard repose, nannies gone, sun down, Kapler Park an empty field, covered only in patchy grass, dropped bottles of Vitamin Water, withered Band-Aids, wet leaves. Whatever Benjy said, I would still walk home alone, and he would be off to Erin's to win back the love he had tainted, changed. Time passed.

thirty-seven

Possible Ending #17 (*American Chef*, Wednesdays, 10 p.m.):

But is there a chance that I *do* become a TV chef, that I *have* charisma, superlative cooking skills, more so than the other wannabes facing the food-tube, dreaming Rachael Ray's breasts wound around our schlongs like sugar-cured boob-bacon incongruently (if deliciously) tied to all-beef kosher hot dogs? Wouldn't that be ironic, me, on the output end of the same digital network I've sat receiving for years, wasting away in starch-saturated solitude, failing to think myself away from the glow, letting my eyelids flutter and close, sinking irreparably into the couch cushion? The show is called *American Chef*. I have a catchphrase—"Yowza!"—a signature soufflé, multicolored name brand cookware, funny chef's hat with baseball-style brim, legions of middle-aged mom fans tickled by my keen wit, overuse of butter. Soon there's a cookbook empire, barbecue sauce with my face on it, foodie ex-vegetarian groupies sucking marrow bones, among other things. Wash my hands so often they become permanently shriveled, but otherwise I'm okay, soft in the gut, softhearted. Sit in the steam room, soft-boiling, towel off, last night's lover misting me with spray-fan lemon water in the otherwise empty Back Bay mansion. Just a cab ride from Benjy and Erin's (issues resolved) little new-parent pad (because he apologized and vowed his loyalty), and Mom's penthouse highrise I got her and Jeff under the sole condition they stay together, lifelong companions eating real food (no shakes), drinking aged booze (no screw-top wine), fucking into infinity (behind closed doors), loving life enough to love me too. And maybe the thing is, we're all happy with our food, stuffing ourselves with cold pork belly, hot bouillabaisse, chilled half-shell oysters flown directly from the North Pole, sealed in vacuum bags, delivered by my cadre of overworked interns, each of whom gets a take-home prize. We're nourished in this nuclear winter (2012?), still living off the land while the rest of the world is crying over robots killing robots in Asia, everyone sense-stripped, eating protein pills for breakfast, unconsciously ambling across the webs looking for physicality, not finding it, and here's my happy family, bodies big, full of feeling, full of foie gras, full of joy.

thirty-eight

The other thing I should have seen coming—natural post-script to that shitty night, but too bluntly devastating to truly expect; an extreme act more willful than the average action-paralyzed slacker can conceive of, let alone decide upon, force upon himself—was Kahn shooting himself in the head, which happened the next day.

"I'm sorry," I said to Erin on the phone. "I'm so sorry. I'm so, so sorry."

What you say even if it's not the right thing to say, or what you mean.

Was in the apartment alone. No Benjy in sight. Maybe he was already by Erin's side, using this chance to comfort, console, forget the bullshit, focus on what was truly important. Wanted to walk, stare at leafless trees, think clichéd thoughts about life and death, imagine myself in a third-act montage, taking slugs from paper-bag whiskey, watching the sun disappear behind a cloud. The only way I knew how to react, had been taught to deal with the confrontation of mortality: to imitate grief as I'd seen it on television, hope its methods proved cathartic.

Instead got on my bike. Angry more than anything, still angry at Alison, angry at Kahn for this, angry at Benjy, my parents, etc. Angry but also in pain, shit-scared, guilty-feeling, confused.

Assumed Kahn had done it with the gun he'd shot me with. Maybe a catalyst for a seismic shift in his life, just as it had been in mine, though in my case the shift had propelled me forward toward a closer-to-healthy social life, and possible job. Also nearing a driver's license, had learned to do laundry. Didn't Kahn know that the shooting was good for me? Maybe he did know, knew it was his last great act, had nothing for his daughters. I was his child to save. By killing himself he could teach me some vague lesson about the decay of the soul (which he believed in) that comes with being blown by a twenty-year-old stripper.

But I was being narcissistic again. Kahn's death, like most things, had nothing to do with me.

Wanted to call Erin back, find out if he'd left a note, if she was okay, needed a hug, a homemade babka. Not that there was much to explain. One of the more obvious suicides in history: handicapped, lonely, drug addict. But there had been something in the way Kahn spoke, the words he used, the way his eyes popped while ranting, that made him seem very much alive, more alive than the rest of us, because a failing body can't deny the existence of the body itself.

Biking around, realized I was looking for Alison. Knew I wouldn't find her. Hated her, hoped she was okay.

Rode past her house, then onto some back roads, out of Quinosset. Houses were smaller, cheaper probably, touch faux-rustic—forest greens, deep maroons, maybe a shed out back. Away from the suburban metropolis into what the suburbs used to look like on TV: white picket fence type shit. Basketball hoops hung from garages. People rode bicycles in normal clothes: no spandex, no helmets. Saturday morning, light snow in the dying grass. Middle-aged couple wrapped in scarves holding Styrofoam coffee cups. Teenage boy on snowboard atop half-melted snowman. Tried to imagine Kahn's body as it fell, bones crumbling, blood dripping into the grates, into the central heating where it burned, immaterial ashes propelled back into the air.

Stopped at a diner, the kind in a train car. The waitress smiled even though she must have been freezing in her short skirt. Ordered the eighteen-wheeler, trucker's breakfast complete with pancakes, three eggs, OJ, coffee, bacon, sausage, corned-beef hash, home fries.

Imagined the cops questioning me.

"How did you know him?"

"I sold him drugs and he took my woman."

"Were you there that night?"

"I was there in spirit."

"Cuff him, boys . . ."

"What I mean is he bought my mother's house. Our house. It was never really his house."

"Didn't he shoot you?"

"I think he was in love with me."

Got the check. She drew a smiley face on it, wrote, "Thanks, Fran." For some reason it made me feel a bit better.

Rode past Whole Foods, past the high school. Thought the world would be changed, but everything was as I'd left it.

thirty-nine

Possible Ending #18 (Triumphant):

Maybe you've been waiting for the ending where I write a movie based on these experiences. The writing itself is cathartic, helps me get over all the shit. Success of the film helps me with the other stuff, including finding a true calling. Hollywood becomes my home. Make dear friends who are moved by my story. These friends become family. Eat a lot of sushi. This is the ending you're supposed to imagine happening after the get-in-your-car, head-west ending. Head west until you're in Los Angeles, surrounded by the kind of people who can make things like this happen. Become a waiter for a while. Struggle while you try to write. Hold personal vigils for Kahn. Keep him in your heart. Maybe a new mentor helps. Maybe a girlfriend teaches you to believe in yourself. But this ending is really the beginning to a different kind of movie. It's a movie I've seen. Doesn't end well, and it's a stupid movie to boot. The writer lives alone amid a pile of books. Grows reclusive, heads for the hills. Still hung up on the girl who taught him to believe in himself. Too bad he'd left her soon as his first paycheck arrived, soon as that blonde put a hand on his shoulder, shoved slick tongue down his smoke-sore throat. So the writer lives in the hills in solitude, drinking himself to death. He's working on a follow-up, something epic, something he will never finish.

forty

Ate bagels, watched *Law and Order*, made jokes about Kahn that felt good and sad at the same time, looked at photos, did imitations, scanned selected scenes from his filmography. Mary told me how much I'd meant to Kahn. Wasn't sure what to take from that.

Sheila was busy on the phone making arrangements—caterers, florists. Like throwing a party. Erin lay with her leg across Benjy's, then moved to a wicker chair where she sat unstill, reminiscent of Mom, plucking hair from her arm, twitching her sockless toes. Everyone was always almost crying. But I was glad Benjy was back in good enough graces.

When I went to smoke a cigarette in front of the pool house, Erin came, took a few drags.

"He'd been basically dead for a while," she said, looking at the pool house.

Wanted to tell her that you have to be alive to shoot yourself, alive enough to feel pain.

"My brother's confused," I said. "He means well."

"I know that," she said. "But what a fucker."

"Yeah. It's in the genes."

"You mean his dad jeans?"

For a moment we weren't aware of death. I smiled.

"Jesus," Erin said.

"Christ," I said.

Drove to the service with Benjy. He let me drive. Gorgeous day, two days to Christmas. Starbucks still hadn't called. A small storm had blown through, whitened the streets with snow so light it was like pale dust. Thought how stupid it is that people think heaven is up there, that our invisible bodies are carried out of the earth's orbit into some kingdom.

The woman who'd saved my life was there when we pulled into the lot. Not many people knew Kahn; figured they wouldn't need a parking attendant. But she'd shown up, was wearing her orange mesh vest over a puffy down jacket.

"I'll come in a sec," I said to Benjy.

He walked toward the heavy doors. I stayed behind to say a few words to my secret guardian and fleeting (unreciprocating) love. Wearing a suit of my father's. Pam had given it to me while I was staying at their house. Didn't fit right—wide in the shoulders, long in the inseam—but expensive, too big rather than too small. First time I'd been to the synagogue without Mom. Old enough to have dead friends.

"Thought you'd be here," she said.

"Wouldn't miss it."

"He's the one who shot you, right?"

"The one and only."

"I'm sorry."

"Me too. Thanks for saving my life. I've been meaning to thank you."

"It was nothing," Jennifer said coolly, one knee bent, body slightly bouncing as she waved in another car.

"To me, it wasn't nothing."

"Just doing my job."

The delivery guys from Domino's stepped out of a Taurus. They supposedly smoked pot with their clientele. I wasn't special. Probably one in a line of failed protégés, stoned, bitter at the world, amused by this man, his pain. Felt implicated in Kahn's death. Like the pizza guys, egging him on, waiting for his next explosion to rattle my dull existence. And then of course the fact that I hadn't forgiven, hadn't held him in an afternoon hug, hadn't said I'd understood even if I hadn't.

"Actually, I saved your life twice," Jennifer said.

"I think the first time you just saved my ass."

"Same difference."

Small crowd. Beth Cahill in back wearing a chaste blue dress she'd probably worn to graduation, not since. She sat alone, flicking the pages of her prayer book like it was written in another language. (It was.) No Alison in sight. Didn't want to be worried about her but I was. Erin said he'd been alone when they'd found him.

No one big had shown, none of the names Kahn occasionally dropped. Just the pizza guys, some synagogue regulars.

Zarkoff said, "Seymour Kahn was an accomplished man. The 'King of the Crossover,' as he was often called, he holds the record for appearances on the most shows while playing the same character: the lovable Albert Stamn, who first appeared as a police captain on the short-lived NBC series *Guns and Tarts*."

Zarkoff looked to the back of the room as he spoke, the way they teach you to in school, but it just seemed weird because only the front few rows were filled.

"That's very similar to his IMDB page," I whispered to

Erin. Her hair was pulled back, still wet. Goth-black eyeliner, apparently unafraid of tears.

"Seymour, Kahn to his friends, of whom I was lucky enough to call myself one, was famous throughout Hollywood for his outlandish personality and romantic liaisons. He was the life of the party. The life of many parties."

Zarkoff continued, tiptoed, tempo increasing.

"But behind the veil, behind the mask, Kahn was a tender man with a soft heart. He was troubled, certainly, at times ill. But inside him was a shining soul that touched everyone around him on a personal level. I do not exclude myself. Sometimes he would regale me with tales of his days in the spotlight, and as a young man on the streets of Boston. Though my main role is one of teacher, in Seymour's court I was always student."

Mary stroked Natasha's neck. Sheila, in Jackie O. shades and black, played widow, fair enough. Her face looked calm, as though she'd been expecting this for a long time, from the day they'd met, when he'd slipped his arm around her waist, smiled stained teeth. Her whole life had become a reaction to Kahn's death drive. That's what the health food was about, the yoga, the shining varnish of her wood floors. She wanted to ignore death, ignore death's spectator, who lived in her pool house, played along, not willfully, but acceptingly, knowing there was no other option. But she couldn't ignore it with his DNA in one daughter, demeanor in the other, couldn't ignore it with him needing her the way he did, the way maybe she needed him when no one else was around. Sheila crossed her arms over her chest. Must have been glad to get him out of her life.

Natasha picked something out of her teeth. Mary kept rubbing her neck, expressionless. Benjy cried. He hadn't liked Kahn, but it's easy to cry at funerals. Erin took a

Kleenex, ran it across his face without looking, as if she'd been doing it for years.

"Seymour Kahn was a great man: a wonderful actor, a loving husband and father. He will be remembered fondly by all of us. If anyone else wishes to share words or memories, he or she may come to the podium and do so."

Mary volunteered.

"Most of you don't know me," she said. "And the ones who do probably think I'm a home-wrecker. After all, I'm the one who stole his wife. But Seymour never blamed me. He never played the role of jealous ex. When Sheila and I first began to experiment, he was actually pretty encouraging. Some might even say he was too encouraging."

Light laughter from the audience. Mary smiled, showing bleached teeth. Blinked, wiped her brow, found Sheila's face in the crowd. Sheila nodded. Mary continued.

"I remember when I first started seeing Sheila. We were all living in L.A. then. Natasha had just turned six. I still had my own place, but I spent most of my time at their house in Laurel Canyon. Seymour knew what was going on; we weren't trying to hide it. I would sleep with Sheila in their bed, and Seymour slept in one of the guest rooms. It was a tough time for him for a lot of reasons. He was finding out how hard it was to get acting jobs if you were in a chair. The only parts he could get were as homeless beggars, and he didn't want those parts. 'I want to dance,' he would say, 'I want to be Fred Astaire on wheels! The legless torso of Apollo! I want to wear a bowtie, drink martinis, seduce young girls with my eyes!'"

Her imitation was on. She had his cadence, dramatic pauses, slightly increasing pitch as he became excited. Audience wasn't sure whether to laugh or not, but Sheila was smiling. For a moment Mary had channeled Kahn, the Kahn we all liked.

"I remember I'd come out late at night, to go to the bathroom or get a glass of water. The girls were asleep, and Sheila was asleep, but I'd hear John Coltrane or Mingus coming up from the living room, and I knew we were the only ones awake in the house, and that he was down there battling alone, and there was nothing I, or any of us, could do to help. But especially me. I was just making things worse. In the morning we'd see the empty bottles, so we knew, and we knew he was probably doing other stuff too. But he waited until we were asleep, until the girls were asleep. He didn't want them to see. Eventually I moved into the house. My lease was up and it seemed the obvious thing to do. Seymour was actually the one who suggested it, said I basically lived there anyway. I knew it killed him, but he didn't say anything, just sang, 'Mary, Mary, quite contrary,' and watched as I carried my things up the stairs into his bedroom, then carried his things into the guest room. One day I came home from work—it was spring, early spring, but it already felt like summer. That's what it's like in L.A. 'Always too hot,' Seymour would say, 'just like Hades. We live here because we're masochists.'"

Again, when she did the imitation—speaking from her throat to create the Kahn bark—it seemed, for a second, that Kahn was in the room, calming us, claiming us.

"Actually," Mary said, "when he moved into our pool house in Boston, he said the same thing—that we're masochists because we live in the cold. I guess he thought everyone was a masochist deep down. Also sadists, I think, which is the story I'm trying to get to. This one time shortly after I moved in, on this really hot day, I came home from work, really wiped out. I was in the kitchen making myself a cup of tea, and I happened to see through the window Natasha in the backyard, essentially—sorry, Natasha, you're going to hate me for telling this story—essentially she was torturing our golden retriever, Randall. She had managed to leash him to a tree—this is a six-year-old girl, mind you—and she was whacking him with a stick. Just beating him with all the force her little body could muster. Randall was going crazy, crying and barking, which is why I looked out the window in the first place. I didn't know what to do. I mean, this was California. What if the neighbors saw and complained and our PETA membership was revoked? We would be ostracized from our community, forced to attend sensitivity training! Without really thinking I ran out to the yard, picked up Natasha, and carried her inside, all the while trying to come up with something to say to this child who wasn't mine, but whose mother I was in love with, and whose poor dog I was trying to save. As I was carrying her back across the patio I noticed that Seymour had been out there the whole time, just watching, sipping a beer, and not saying a word. Once I got Natasha inside and banished her to her bedroom to screams of 'You're not my mother,' I went back out to the patio to talk to Seymour. I asked him why he'd sat there silent. 'What could I have said?' he said in a pathetic voice, this really soft whisper, different than his usual singsong. This was the first time I'd ever confronted him, and I wondered what he thought about me parenting his daughter, not to mention sleeping with his wife. 'You could have said stop,' I said. I thought he might unleash on me, spit the type of venom I'd heard about—'His tongue is a knife,' Sheila had warned me—but he just said, 'I have no authority,' then looked me up and down for a long time, assessing me, not like he was checking me out, but like he was trying to understand who I was. 'You'll make a good father someday,' he said. At first I was offended by him referring to me as a father, but later

I came to realize it was a compliment. He was essentially saying that I would make a good replacement for him. And I think this story illustrates, well, either that he hated dogs, which I don't think he did, or something more essential to his character. Namely that he understood his limitations. I know a lot of people think Seymour was a selfish man. But he wasn't selfish. He gave his daughters to Sheila and me to raise even though it pained him more than anything else in his life—more than losing the use of his legs, more than the loss of his career. He gave them up because he knew we'd take better care of them, that he was a terrible father, that he was very sick and very troubled, and couldn't raise his children in the way he wanted to, because his own worldview had become so skewed by his health problems and his physical limitations, which had exacerbated his bad habits and fueled his addictions. He understood this, and he accepted it, which takes a brave man. Instead of mourning the loss of his family, he tried to accept us as a new kind of family, one in which he and I could both play a part. He left Sheila and me to raise his daughters, not because he didn't love them, but because it was the right thing to do."

After Mary, other people said words, what you'd expect, what a party that guy could throw, what a crazy character. Neither Erin nor Sheila stepped up. Natasha was the last to speak.

"My father was an asshole," she said. "I loved him."

Zarkoff led the mourner's Kaddish. I remembered the first line, mumbled the rest. A handful made it to the burial. Beth was there, off to the side like a mistress in a movie. A machine lowered the casket. When it dipped below the surface, Sheila, who'd been so composed, fell to her knees, pressed her hands into the earth as though she could reach in and pull him back up, like those mothers who lift cars to save their babies. She made a low sound, somewhere between an "om" and an orgasmic moan. The sound seemed to come from a different part of her body, not even her stomach, but all the way from her calves and bent knees. Mary just let her, didn't touch her. Said the Kaddish again. This time it sounded like a song, slow pulse set to the rhythm of lightly chattering teeth.

forty-one

Possible Ending #19 [ ]:

Chalk it up to failure of imagination, but I'm out of endings. Seen the movies, taken their clumsy morals, outlandish advice, learned whatever I was meant to learn, unlearned it, relearned it with exceptions that prove the rule, exceptions that don't, asterisks, footnotes, side notes, sometimes subtly, sometimes not. Kahn dead, Mom gone, life goes on, etc. Winter coming, ice-fucked, still jobless, Sheila sad but strong, Benjy and Erin back together, maybe forever, maybe not, everyone not ready to move on, doing it anyway, no choice, I'm the same, smoking, staring at the snow, longing for love, life, etc. Looking for work, no resolution, maybe new life a slight improvement on old life with backslide potential, fall asleep again for years, wake to nuclear war, dying sun, earth barely alive, all the women I've ever met now offscreen, returned to invisible, still there in their own lives (just not mine), working, eating, smiling, singing, me in my movie waiting for the next one to walk in the door.

forty-two

Quiet Christmas/New Year's, saw a couple movies, nothing too interesting. Christmas morning Benjy and I went to Sheila's, watched while her family gave each other gifts, gave us dark chocolate imported from Colombia. Felt like family—warm, witty—but also like a family I would never be a part of. Natasha made a joke about herself being "sweet dark chocolate."

Benjy said, "Dark chocolate's not sweet, it's bitter."

When I looked at Natasha I could see Kahn: his mannerisms, the way he waved his hands, rolled his eyes.

New Year's went to Dad's, watched Dick Clark, helped Pam make cocktail meatballs. The twins threw cake at each other. Dad was quiet, gave me a hundred bucks.

"Look at Dick," he said. "Still going. He had a stroke but now he's back."

That Tuesday got a call from a lawyer about Kahn's will. Benjy drove me to the lawyer's office. Sheila, Mary, Erin, and Natasha were there. Thought there would be a video, like in movies. Kahn would sit, explain life's secrets, confess. Instead the lawyer read out what we got. I got the jazz CDs and a photo he'd taken in 1974 of a young woman, sun-bleached blond hair, deeply tanned, seated on a futon, legs crossed, sipping coffee, smiling. On the back in pen: "The Wellspring of Youth, I drink from thee. Ramona, La Jolla, California, July, 1974."

He also left me a Teflon frying pan he'd bought but never used. Sheila and Mary got the money. Not much left. Natasha got his Golden Globe, Erin his movie collection, mostly porn. Ten containers of frozen semen were found in Kahn's freezer. Stipulated they be given to Sheila and Mary for whatever purposes they might desire.

Starbucks called, said they were looking for someone with more coffee experience.

When the RMV opened for the New Year, I took my driving test. Benjy sat in back. We were in Mom's Camry, not Benjy's car. It had been sitting in our condo lot since she'd left for Florida, but she'd called a few days before my test, said I could have it, late Chanukah, early birthday present. A lot I'd wanted to discuss: usual sappy bullshit, reconcile, muffled crying. Instead she talked, quickly, about golf, her new clubs, a movie she'd seen with Kevin Bacon, and made sure I'd bought gifts for the twins. She must have known about Kahn, heard it through the synagogue gossip-line, but she didn't mention him or the house, which had been put up for sale. Instead she talked on, as if she couldn't stop, muttering inanities, asking about dentist appointments.

"Thanks for the car," I said.

"You should really ask your father to buy you one," she said.

Passed the test. They took my pic. Smiled, looked like an idiot. Benjy let me drive back. Dropped him at the library.

When he left the car, I almost said, "Thank you." I thought about the words, but didn't almost say "I love you," which I'd never said to anyone, not since childhood.

I said, "You're such a fucking nerd."

Benjy grinned, told me to eat a dick, leaned back in through the window, rubbed his forehead against my forehead, said, "License."

Realtor's sign was there in the yard. Snow had cleared. Would be back, but for now the sun hung between two clouds. The house looked like an archival photograph: childhood home, early twenty-first century, still standing, unoccupied.

Soon the house will be filled; it will be a home. New family: better made, better prepared, equally fragile. I can see them, version 3.1: young mother, Japanese, beautiful, decorated in batik-print skirts, dangling earrings, a chiropractor, wears banana-cucumber facial masks, masturbates guilt-free; father an African American Buddhist, shaved head, high cheekbones, horn-rimmed glasses, professor of art history, secretly likes NASCAR, pines for a girl he knew in high school; two children, five and six, boy and girl, raised on free-range chicken, organic vegetables, no prizes in their cereal, bathed at night in jasmine water. I watch them plant trees in the yard, many trees, ten maybe, twenty: oak, spruce, apple, pear, lemon, all tangled among each other in a mess of branches and fruit, creating crossbreeds, new species. The trees grow upward, become sturdy. Stand above the house, catching rain, spreading shadow, filtering sunlight, lending tint to the far corners of the neighborhood.

acknowledgments

Thank you to all of my classmates and teachers at the Columbia MFA program, especially Emily Cooke, Dyannah Byington, James Yeh, Lincoln Michel, Dan Bevacqua, Kalpana Narayanan, Binnie Kirshenbaum, and Sam Lipsyte. Sam deserves a special shout for his knowledge of firearms, and also for going above and beyond the call of duty in regards to reading, commenting, and dispensing life advice. Thank you to Paul Rome for early reading, insight, and friendship. Thank you to everyone at Bookcourt for being my Brooklyn family. Chad Bunning, you're a hero. Thank you to Sam Apple and everyone at the *Faster Times* for being my Internet family. Thank you to Darin Strauss for being a mensch. Thank you to Steve Hanselman and Julia Serebrinsky for being the first people to believe in this book—it meant a lot and still does. Thank you to Julie Cohen for being Julie Cohen. Thank you to Jim Strouse and Andew Gorin for encouragement and conversation. Thank you to Prime Meats on Court St. for not making me put away my laptop. Thank you to the Rapp Family for cheering me on. Thank you to Erin Hosier, you fucking rock star,

acknowledgments

I love you. Thank you to everyone at Harper Perennial, and especially Carrie Kania and Cal Morgan for manning up and buying this fucker. Also thanks to Gregory Henry and Erica Barmash for having my back. Thank you to Oliver Munday for designing such a beautiful cover. Thank you to Michael Signorelli for truly being the best editor I could ever hope to have. I consider myself doubly blessed to have not only found a brilliant editor, but a true friend and brother. Thank you to my father, Jonathan Wilson, for a lifetime of books, book talk, and encouragement. Thank you to my mother, Sharon Kaitz, for being the opposite of the mother in this book. Thank you to Sarah Rapp for Everything. I have infinite gratitude.